## Freak

It was like plunging into freezing waters. I couldn't breathe. I choked. My heart was sending rivers of liquid ice through every artery and vein; I had an iceberg for an aorta. It hurt so much, it left tears in my eyes.

I was too terrified to think at all. She started crying and refused to let go, clutching my hands and pressing them against her body with a strength that should have been beyond her.

Between my fingers, I saw streams of crimson oozing out from where my palms had pressed her skin and although my body was ice, these points of contact were fire. I thought it was all her blood, but when I looked down I knew I was wrong.

I was bleeding too.

*About the author*

Mark Burnell, who has lived and worked in London and Brazil, now lives on a farm in Northumberland. *Freak* is his first novel; his second, *Glittering Savages*, will appear in 1995.

# Freak

## Mark Burnell

**NEW ENGLISH LIBRARY**
Hodder and Stoughton

First published in 1994
by Hodder & Stoughton
A division of Hodder Headline PLC

10 9 8 7 6 5 4 3 2 1

A NEL paperback

British Library Cataloguing in Publication Data

Burnell, Mark
Freak
I. Title
823.914 [F]

ISBN 0–340–61760–8

Phototypeset by Intype, London
Printed and bound in Great Britain by
Cox & Wyman Ltd

Hodder and Stoughton Ltd
A Division of Hodder Headline PLC
338 Euston Road,
London NW1 3BH

For Victoria BIRTS

Many of you know who I am. You read about me in newspapers and heard callers on radio phone-in shows arguing about what I did. You saw so-called experts discuss me on the television. They all told you so much about me, but they missed out the only thing that matters: the truth. As interest in me grew, the media seemed more content to ignore the evidence and chase the fantastic. Just about every single fact I ever read or heard about myself was inaccurate or simply false. This account, therefore, is aimed equally at those of you who have heard of me, and those of you who have not. Only one piece of pure information separates you, and that is my name: Christian Floyd. Now you are all equal.

# Chapter One

I tilted back in my chair and rested the soles of my feet on the edge of my desk. The rain drilled against the tinted glass skin of the building. In front of me, the largest of my computer screens spilled luminous green light onto my shoes. It was the same colour as the leaves of the plants in the atrium. They sprayed a special polish onto the foliage to keep it looking unnaturally bright. The leaves glistened in the beams of concealed spotlights.

Danny Peck tugged on his jacket, picked up a copy of the *Evening Standard* and tossed an empty Coke can into a bin. I finished my coffee, from a mug which had "Parke Millen Securities" printed around it, in a deep blue.

"Working late?" he asked, searching for loose change in his jacket pocket.

"Well, that depends," I replied, "on whether Miss Frankfurt has plans for tonight."

Maria Kohler was my opposite number at Commerzbank. She had a voice better suited to pleasure than business, which was ironic in view of the hours she worked. I'd never seen her but when we spoke over the phone, her voice left tantalizing scars on my imagination. I hoped we would never meet, so I could keep the delightful image intact.

"Bad luck," he said, pushing his chair in. "I'll see you in the morning. You'll probably still be waiting."

"It's worse than you think. I'm supposed to be going out tonight and I promised Katy I wouldn't be late."

3

Danny put three knuckles in his mouth and cried, "Ouch!"

In fact, I'd phoned her earlier to warn her. She made no effort to mask her disappointment and gave me the address of the restaurant. "If you're not back by eight-thirty, we'll go on," she told me.

Once Danny had gone, I was the only European trader left. Normally, a few remained late, but not on that Thursday night. Through the glass partitions and across the other side of the building I spied plenty of North American traders. With the edifice's heart hollowed out and with many walls made from glass, it was possible not only to see what was happening on the other side of the building, but also on different floors. On the uppermost level I could see three men in conversation in one of the conference rooms. One smoked a cigar as fat as a salami. They were lawyers for the banking division, which was housed on the floors below mine.

I lit a Marlboro and started humming "Yesterday". The murmur of the central air-conditioning was audible, now that everyone had gone home. Everyone except the cleaners. The night-crew were coming out of the bowels of the block, silent and staring, moving like ghosts. Two or three appeared in the half-light at the far end of the trading room next to mine. They dropped empty Evian bottles into trolley-bins and cleaned ashtrays. Parke Millen had attempted to ban smoking and failed.

I glanced at a photo-copied list of completed and pending trades. We'd had European unity before the politicians even started thinking about it. We bought and sold European securities freely, the cutlass of satellite communication slashing through the bureaucratic red tape that seemed to shackle everyone else. Finnish companies bought Belgian stock with Swiss francs from a Dutch bank in Lisbon.

Every day I spoke to the same people across Europe.

4

My opposite numbers. I knew their voices intimately, but not their faces. Mostly, my imagination was left to compensate. Occasionally, I had a chance to meet one of them and it was always a shock. The familiar voice never matched the physical form. Hence my desire to never meet Maria Kohler. Would I ever recover from learning that behind the smoky purr there was twenty-three stone of disappointment?

Marvin Davis, an American investment banker from the floor below, passed by my desk. "How you doing, Christian? Hear about the Rhine spill?"

Earlier that afternoon, a chemical refinery near Cologne had leaked thousands of gallons of toxic fluid into the Rhine, when an explosion ruptured a storage tank. The share price had plummeted within minutes of the news breaking. By a neat coincidence, I'd dumped all my holdings in the company the previous week, based on a rumour that they were about to post dreadful forecasts.

"Yes," I told Davis. "There was a bit of chaos out there, I understand."

"You all get shafted?"

"No. I took us out last week."

The smile disappeared. He seemed disappointed by my good news and turned away. "I don't believe your luck, Floyd."

Neither, in truth, did I. But so long as it flowed my way, I'd continue to take all I could get.

Maria Kohler called at twenty past eight. Our business took two minutes to conclude and then I was on my way. I collected my overcoat and put it on, as the carpeted lift ferried me silently and smoothly to the ground floor. At the centre of the huge atrium rose a vast bronze statue of a rearing horse with a Greek warrior brandishing a spear. The uppermost tip easily reached the second storey.

I didn't have far to walk. The underground NCP car park was just a couple of minutes from the office block, but I was still soaked by the time I reached the entrance to the stairwell. The bulb had blown behind the yellow sign. The door hissed as it slowly closed behind me and I was relieved to be out of the howling wind and needle rain. I went down the cold concrete steps which always smelled of urine. The car park was nearly empty, being mostly used by businessmen during the day. To leave a car in this garage overnight was criminally expensive. I was thankful that the company paid for my parking, not to mention the car that I parked.

I walked over to the concrete pillar with 1B painted on it. I liked to park next to it because it was almost impossible to get boxed in there. During the day, this car park was often heavily over-used, and although double-parkers were supposed to leave their keys with the attendants, they sometimes forgot. I once got blocked in by a man who parked his Bristol in front of my car and then went to Chicago for a fortnight. The attendant refused to have the car towed and then tried to charge me for three hundred and thirty-six hours' parking. I suggested that the owner of the Bristol pay the bill. He was reluctant at first, but when I suggested running my key down one side of his pride and joy as a prelude to proper damage, he warmed to the idea.

My shoes sounded unreasonably loud as I walked across the scratched concrete floor. The tapping masked another set of sounds which only became noticeable when I neared my car. I stopped and looked around. The car park's harsh echo made pinpointing the source difficult.

I took two steps forward and spied the slightest shiver of movement to my right. There were three vehicles there. I could just pick out the bonnet of the third. It was a light blue Toyota and, as I stared at the small portion which was visible, it rocked again. I looked up and saw my BMW a little further along, by the pillar with 1B on it. The second vehicle between the Toyota and where I stood was a Volkswagen van which blocked out everything behind the few inches of light blue bonnet that I could see.

How serious could it be? I was in a public car park and it wasn't as though it was the middle of the night. I refrained from calling out, for fear of appearing foolish, and reassured myself that it couldn't be anything too sinister. I stepped forward.

The light was poor but I saw more than enough to understand what was happening. The terror filled her with strength. Both men were far larger than she was, but they could barely contain her attempts to escape from the back seat of the light blue Toyota. One of her assailants had planted a chunky hand across her mouth and was driving his entire body weight against her. Her head was forced back, straining her neck. I was sure any additional pressure would snap it. In the extra gloom of the back of the car it was impossible to accurately separate bodies and movement, but somebody was hitting her.

This was my nightmare too. I wanted to run away and pretend I never saw it, that it never happened. But I didn't. I found I couldn't.

There was a third man, standing by the driver's door. When he spotted me, his eyes widened with surprise. He pointed at me.

"Get lost!" he hissed.

I ignored him. The two men in the car froze for a moment and then looked up from their vile task. The woman twisted her head free from the heavy hand and cried, frantically, "Help me! Oh God, please help me!"

The man tried to put his hand back across her mouth but she shook her head wildly, denying him, until he slapped her so hard that her head hit part of the car's metallic frame and stunned her. I could see blood.

The standing man raised his voice. "You!" he cried. "Do yourself a favour and fuck off!"

I couldn't think. My mouth was dry and my breathing

shallow. The rain hammered the top of the concrete ramp. It echoed in the underground car park. From the street above, I could hear the painful squeal of a bus's brakes over the din of the downpour.

They watched me in disgust and amazement, as I lurched uneasily towards the back of the light blue Toyota. When I was close enough to see the blood on her ripped clothing and on her bruised skin, I thrust my outstretched hands into the back of the car with a reckless force. The man nearest me was fat, the other one slim and short, and it was he who screamed, "Start the car, you bastard!" to the third, who was still standing round the other side. A finger from my left hand poked the fat one in the eye. It was entirely accidental. He rocked backwards and howled in pain. The driver scrambled into the front seat and fumbled with his keys. "Throw the bitch out!" he yelled.

"No," replied the slim one. "She might recognize us!"

While the fat one nursed his eye, and blocked his lesser colleague, I hooked my hands underneath the victim's armpits and began to drag her limp body from the back seat. The car engine coughed once and died.

"Jesus!" yelled the driver, as he turned the key again.

I still hadn't hauled her clear and knew that if the car started I wouldn't be able to hold on to her. The top half of her body would be dragged along the concrete floor of the car park. She was lodged beneath the howling brute. The second ignition attempt failed. I leaned forward, tightening my grasp around her chest and, with an almighty heave, pulled her free. Her feet flopped out of the Toyota and clattered to the ground. The driver started the engine at the third go. But before I could adjust my balance and pull her further away from the vehicle, the slim one manoeuvred his way past his injured colleague and lunged forward. The driver was revving the engine.

"You got her?" he bellowed, his eyes set forward, looking towards the ramp leading up to ground level. Rivulets of rain were meandering down it.

The attacker was leaning out of the car and, to my horror, grabbed both her ankles before I could tow her clear.

"Yes!" he screamed. "Go! Go! Go!"

Letting go of her shoulders, so that her head slumped against the filthy floor, I jumped forward as the driver raised his shoe from the clutch. With my right foot, I kicked the back door as hard as I could. It slammed against the attacker's wrists. The stereo crack of breaking bones filled the car park. His shocked fingers splayed, letting go of her ankles. As the Toyota powered up the slick ramp, an ungodly screech rose from the back seat, in tune with the car's screaming tyres.

Her body was twisted and still. I knelt in the oily dirt at her side and looked down. The adrenalin continued to burn through my body, propping me up when I expected to fall. Her breathing was frail. The skirt was badly torn up one side. High on her thigh there was a vicious laceration which was similar in appearance to one I could see on her stomach. I gently tugged at her shirt and saw another. That was enough. Stab wounds. If there were more, I didn't want to know. I had to get help quickly, but before I left her, what should I do?

I stroked her grubby forehead, wiping away hair matted by blood. She slowly opened her eyes.

"It's okay," I said, not knowing whether it would be.

I looked around for help. Her breathing began to quicken and it scared me. I felt frozen. Was I in shock? Wasn't intense cold one of the symptoms? When I attempted to remove my hands from her, she wouldn't let me.

"Don't," she moaned.

"I have to get help for you," I explained.

"Please," she said again, refusing to relax. "Don't let go."

Those sounded like parting words. As she said this, she clamped my hands to her body, one just below the ribs and one on her left shoulder. I expected her to die at any instant. I looked around in vain for assistance and tried to gather my scattered thoughts. And that was when it happened.

It was like plunging into freezing waters. I couldn't breathe. I choked. My heart was sending rivers of liquid ice through every artery and vein; I had an iceberg for an aorta. It hurt so much, it left tears in my eyes.

I was too terrified to think at all. She started crying and refused to let go, clutching my hands and pressing them against her body with a strength that should have been beyond her. Between my fingers, I saw streams of crimson oozing out from where my palms pressed her skin and although my body was ice, these points of contact were fire. I thought it was all her blood, but when I looked down I knew I was wrong. There was a scarlet stain on my shirt and it was spreading.

I was bleeding too.

# Chapter Two

I don't know how long it lasted. The freezing storm isolated me from my surroundings, from rational thought, from notions of time. All I remember is the biting cold cutting to the bone, leaving me fragile and dazed.

It was only when the icy tide receded that reality returned to focus. I was kneeling in the dirt, clutching her body to mine. Her head was slumped against my shoulder. I felt her breathing on my neck. My arms ached and my heart stung. I lowered her gently back to the ground and pressed a palm over the centre of my chest where it hurt the most. My head was spinning and I felt nauseous.

She was still holding one of my hands but her grip had relaxed. Her eyelids flickered. The overhead lighting was poor but I saw the fluorescent tubes reflected in the scarlet pools around us. We were soaked in blood. I ran a finger through an oval puddle and it was warm and viscous.

I was stunned. Fear and bewilderment jostled for control while I shivered in shock. She opened her eyes and whispered, "Go!"

Her voice anchored me and I tried to pull myself together. "An ambulance," I mumbled, nodding slowly, "I'll get an ambulance."

"I'll . . . be . . . all right," she sighed, weakly.

"I'm going to get a doctor."

I could feel blood cooling on my skin. My shirt clung to my stomach.

"No!" she protested. "Go! Now!"

I felt exhausted. My muscles ached and my joints felt

swollen, grating against each other with every marginal movement. My chest felt tight, a box of pinched nerves. I wished my swimming vision would settle.

"You don't understand," I tried to explain to her. "You need medical attention."

She slowly shook her head and moaned, "No."

An echo rattled off the damp walls of the car park. It sounded like the swing door of the stairwell being wrenched open. It was followed by a chorus of clicking shoes coming in our direction. I thought I should call out, but didn't. What would they think when they saw me, covered in blood, leaning over the victim?

"There are people coming," I told her, softly. "It's going to be all right."

She tightened her grip on my arm and opened her eyes fully, glaring at me, angry and alert, raising her head off the ground.

"You have to go!"

She had an accent which I couldn't identify.

"But . . ."

"You must go!" she insisted, pushing my arm away. "*Now!*"

I was confused. There was nothing I wanted more than to be far away, with the blood washed from my skin and the event cast from my memory. But I couldn't just leave her.

I began to perspire. Cold beads of sweat broke out all over my trembling skin. My head ached and I clenched my teeth together to stop them chattering.

"Please go!" she pleaded, in a hoarse whisper.

She was offering me a way out. Perhaps it was gratitude. I hadn't fled from the danger. I had saved her and even in her feeble state she could recognize that. Now she was offering me my reward: the chance to slide away and avoid the aftermath. Maybe she could see how out of my depth I was. I didn't know why she was doing this and, whatever the reason, it didn't stop the guilt, but I figured I could live with a little shame.

"Okay," I whispered.

She tried to force a smile and failed. "Thank you . . . thank you . . . *Who?* What is your name?"

"Christian. Christian Floyd."

"Thank you, Christian Floyd."

I rose to my feet, using the Volkswagen van to steady myself. Four men were coming towards us as I took the car keys from my coat pocket. I retreated into the gloom cast by the pillar with 1B painted on it and tumbled into my car. No drunken driver's vision could have been as blurred as mine. I stabbed the key at the ignition slot and missed. My body implored me to stop and recuperate, but adrenalin just managed to keep me going. I forced the key in and turned the engine. I was panting like a sun-scorched dog, clutching the steering wheel for support.

My coordination was shot. My shaking legs could barely manoeuvre the pedals. I lurched forwards like a first-time driver, before grinding into second gear and thumping the accelerator. I flew up the exit ramp, passing the ticket booth. Normally, there was a barrier across it, but the wooden beam lay to one side, smashed in two, surrounded by splinters. The attendant manning the booth had chased the light-blue Toyota into the rain and still hadn't returned. In the rear-view mirror, I saw one of the businessmen running up the greasy ramp, waving his arms. Rain drops splattered on my windscreen. Office block lights pricked the dark. In the final moment before I really gunned the engine and sped out of the car park, I could just hear the excited cries of the man in the mirror.

"Call an ambulance! Call the police!"

I couldn't help but drive like a drunk, knowing that if the police pulled me over, for whatever insignificant reason, I was in deep trouble. There was blood all over me and the car. As a result, I drove with dangerous caution, taking the exaggerated care which is the hallmark of inebriated drivers.

I cleared the area and found a quiet side-street, where I parked and killed the engine. The rain hammered the roof and streaked the windows, diffusing the glow from the street lamps. My energy waned and the sickness rose up again. I opened the door and threw up. Cold rain splattered on the back of my neck as I retched violently. It sapped me of everything. I could barely prevent myself from falling onto the drenched tarmac. When I was through, I slumped in my seat and tugged the door shut. It felt heavier than lead.

There were tears running down my face, over my quivering chin and onto my soaked clothing. If I'd had the energy, I would have cried properly. I felt hysterical but couldn't display it. Instead, I was still. Eventually, like every other resource in the mine of my body, the seam was exhausted. I felt truly empty.

Minutes passed and I gazed through the window without focus, too shattered to do anything but breathe softly. I might even have drifted into a light sleep. I can't be sure.

When the phase passed, I was more rational. I couldn't shake the fear, but at least it was under control. The shock of the moment had robbed me of reason. I hadn't bled because I had no wounds and no one had assaulted me. As for the stain I saw spreading across my shirt, maybe that was a trick of the imagination. Perhaps the woman had been holding me at the time and my mind had somehow erased that fact. All I knew for sure was that I wasn't bleeding and I wasn't wounded.

I was calmer and lit a cigarette. The aching emptiness remained. I'd never felt weaker, but it seemed more like an injury than an illness. There was some perverse comfort in that.

It was hard to think straight. I could see her in the back

of the Toyota, pleading for salvation. I could see her in my arms, bleeding all over me, clutching me like I was life itself. I could see her urging me to disappear. So now what?

I'd fled. That was the choice I'd made and now I recognized that I had to stick with it. I had to distance myself from the assault and that meant not drawing attention to myself. It wouldn't be easy, but I didn't have a choice.

Did the man on the ramp think to note the number plate of my car? How was I going to get rid of the blood? How could I behave normally?

By sheer force of will I didn't allow panic to engulf me. In the relative dark of the car, I felt secure. It allowed me to think. The shaking in my hands began to subside and the numbness faded from my fingers, tingling hotly as it did so.

As I finished my cigarette, I formed a plan. The first priority was to remove the evidence. That meant getting the blood off my body, clothes and car. Getting it off the car would be hardest. After that, there was patience. I would continue life as normal, as though the incident had never happened. I would force myself to behave in character. And the more time passed, the safer I would consider myself.

As a scheme it was childish in its simplicity, but I figured that was for the best: less to go wrong. Ignorance and innocence would make my best defence. I waited until all the shaking had ceased before driving again. I still felt very weak, but at least I could handle the car safely.

It was still raining hard when I drove into my street, just off Notting Hill Gate. I passed over an opportunity to park close to my front door, because the space was just beneath a street lamp and I didn't want the interior of my car illuminated. Instead, I parked fifty yards away, doused the lights, cut the engine and sat in the dark while I composed myself. When I got out, I rinsed my hands and immersed my feet in the dirty puddle which had formed around an over-flowing drain. I hoped the filthy water would wash away the most obvious blotches of blood.

I turned the key and opened my apartment door. Somebody said, "About time!"

The small entrance hall was dark. I looked at my watch. It was nine. Katy should have left for the restaurant half an hour before. She appeared from the drawing-room and I instinctively closed my overcoat, concealing the evidence.

"Christian, where the hell have you been?" cried a different voice, from the kitchen.

That was Charlie Prime. It was his birthday we were supposed to be celebrating. Katy reached for the light switch, but I beat her to it, placing my hand over the panel, before leaning forward to kiss her, hoping my face was blood-free.

"You're soaked!" she exclaimed.

"It's raining."

"You don't say!"

Charlie appeared behind her, sliding out of the kitchen with a brimming glass of clear liquid, probably gin, possibly vodka.

"Happy birthday," I said, as the rain drops spilled off me onto the carpet.

"You're late!" he accused me, with a grin. "I've had to drink your spirits to kill the time. Looks as though you could use some."

"I could. As well as a shower."

"Do you have to?" asked Katy. "We're already late."

I felt light-headed again and leaned against the wall for support. My stomach muscles were contracting.

"Exactly," agreed Charlie. "Besides, the rest of us are anxious to . . ."

"The rest of us?"

16

He nodded. "That's right. In the drawing-room."

That was all I needed. Charlie went to announce my arrival. Katy looked up at me in the semi-dark. "I was all for going on, but Charlie wouldn't hear of it. You know how he is."

I didn't need another surprise that night. Finding a party in my home was the least welcome thing I could imagine. My throat felt blistered. It stung to swallow.

"Couldn't you just dry your hair and put on some fresh clothes?"

My pulse throbbed and I squeezed my eyes shut. She was crying for mercy, watching the blood streaming from her stab wounds. The slim man in the Toyota screamed as his wrists broke. The stain on my shirt was spreading. Katy's touch snapped me out of my reverie and I stumbled away from her. My reaction made her jump.

"Are you okay?" she whispered.

"I *need* a shower," I croaked. "Five minutes, I promise."

I pushed past her and staggered down the hall, through the bedroom and into the bathroom. I locked the door, let out the deepest sigh of relief and slid to the tiled floor. My wet clothes were heavy and cold.

"Behave," I murmured to myself. "Act normally."

I wore a weary smile. How could I possibly act normally after what had happened? Fatigue circled me like a vulture surveying a carcass. Now that I was down on the floor, it would have been easy to submit to sleep. It was the thing I desired most, but I found the will to resist. Somehow.

I scraped myself off the tiles and hauled myself up. The strip light above the mirror was brutal. I began to peel away the sodden layers of clothing, dropping them into a damp and dirty pile on the floor. My shirt was bright pink. I examined myself in the mirror. Some of the blood across my torso had actually dried, despite the rain. It was reddish brown and I could flick flecks of it off, like chipping rust from an old car. My hands were still stained in the lines of each palm. My feet were filthy too, the socks drenched with a mixture of blood and dirty water.

I gathered up my revolting clothes and bundled them into one of the disused cupboards, beneath the basin. It would do for the moment. Then, with damp handfuls of loo paper, I cleared the floor of diluted blood and dirt, flushing that evidence away, before stepping into the shower.

The stinging heat of the jetting water had a revitalizing effect. I wondered where the victim was now. She was probably lying in an intensive care unit, with tubes sticking out of her. I shouldn't have left her, but I had to. It was just too complicated to stay. I tried to convince myself of this, but I couldn't wash away the sense of shame as easily as the blood and grime.

Katy came into the bedroom as I was getting dressed. I didn't feel so crushed, just tired.

"Are you okay?" she said.

"Yes," I lied. "Why?"

"You seem to be acting a little strangely."

The television was on in the kitchen. I could hear voices debating the prospects for the general election. There were a lot of lies and promises flying back and forth.

"I had a terrible day, that's all. Really dreadful. I just needed to wash it away."

I found a relatively clean shirt hanging in a cupboard. Katy handed me a beer. She had light brown hair which fell straight to the shoulders. The few faint freckles across the pale skin of her nose and cheeks were charming to me, but she despised them.

"Christian, you promised me you wouldn't be late this evening and . . ."

"I did phone to warn you as soon as I knew."

". . . so we decided to wait. And the first thing you do,

when you get back, is to run into the shower. You didn't even say hello to anyone."

"I'm sorry. Really, I am."

She didn't look convinced. When I apologized to everyone else, they were more generous. We gathered our coats and stepped into the persistent rain.

"Who's driving tonight?" asked Jorge.

Jorge Sanchez had two cars in London and rarely drove either. The girl he brought with him, who was half Norwegian and whose unpronounceable name had passed me by, clung to him tightly.

"Not me," I replied. "I'm definitely taxiing tonight."

"I'll drive," said Katy. "I don't feel like drinking."

"You don't have to," I said.

"No, really," she insisted, holding out her hand, "I don't mind. Have you got the keys?"

I wanted to collapse into a deep sleep, where warmth and darkness would envelop me entirely. I found it hard to focus on anything. Every sharp edge was slightly blurred.

Charlie said, "If the lady's volunteering, I should accept her offer with grace."

"I would, but the thing's not running properly. It's got to go into the garage in the morning. That's part of the reason I was late."

The lie slipped out so smoothly that no one questioned it, but Katy looked at me suspiciously.

"Like I said, I've had a dreadful day."

We went by taxi.

# Chapter Three

The last thing to go through my mind before waking was the sound of cracking wrists. I watched the ruined hands dangling uselessly from the car, the scratched concrete floor ripping skin off the knuckles while the driver plunged his foot onto the accelerator. The scream which followed echoed through the cavernous car park. I kept hearing the crack, again and again. My eyelids flicked open and I was staring at the ceiling, catching my breath. Katy leaned over me.

"Bad dreams?"

I nodded, slowly. "I had them all night." My throat felt parched.

"I know. You kept waking me."

The breaking wrists left an aftertaste in my thoughts. There was a delicate film of perspiration on my forehead. Katy rose from the bed. It dawned on me that if she was getting up, I was certainly late. Most mornings she was fast asleep when I left for work.

"You'd benefit from a day in bed," she told me.

"How true."

I turned onto my side. Daylight brought relief and it was easier to believe that yesterday was history. There had been no repetition of the haunting cold which filled me in the dank car park, no return of the fire in my hands when she clamped them to her torn skin. The weakness had subsided and the shaking was gone. My vision had completely cleared. I still felt drained but it wasn't an

21

alarming sensation. It was curiously satisfying, like some post-coital lull.

Fear of the unknown remained, but I felt better equipped to deal with it now the night was gone. There was a sense of survival in me.

"Did you enjoy last night?" she asked.

I couldn't recall enjoying an evening less. While the others drank and laughed, I struggled to conquer my exhaustion. Anxiety and fatigue came at me in waves. The aching never ceased and I was dizzy in a way which had nothing to do with alcohol. Fortunately, the intoxication of those around me proved to be my best cover. I said the right things and laughed at the right moments. I got away with it.

"Yes," I lied. "Did you?"

"It was okay," she said, unconvincingly. "But Charlie can be a little ... *tedious* ... when he's drunk, can't he?"

"Sure, but not as tedious as when he's sober."

"That's what Jorge says."

Charlie Prime and Jorge Sanchez made unlikely companions. Charlie came from the north. Two centuries of brewing had turned his family into large landowners with a vast house as the centrepiece of their fortune; a monstrous pile of rubble with wings that protruded like spider's legs.

If Charlie was traditionally English, then Jorge was fashionably continental, equally at home in Madrid, Munich, Milan, wherever. His circle of friends spoke a dozen different languages and married foreigners as often as their own, whereas the concept of marrying a girl who lived south of the Trent had never even occurred to Charlie.

Jorge was tall, athletic, handsome and charming. Charlie was none of these things. He was five nine, fat, prone to insensitivity at all times, and uneasy in the company of women. Since it had been his birthday, Charlie's drunkenness was excusable, though hardly unusual. When sober, Charlie staggered between arrogance and criminal shyness, depending on his wildly fluctuating levels of self-confidence. Alcohol dissolved his numerous insecurities and allowed him to enjoy himself. But more fun for him usually meant less for those around him. That was the inebriation equation which I knew well.

Katy was right. He had been tedious, but we all knew him well enough to make allowances for it. Besides, it had been his birthday. I watched her search for a skirt. She said, "You haven't forgotten about next Thursday, have you?"

"Next Thursday?" I replied, flicking through a mental diary where every page was blank.

"The dance."

"Ah yes," I sighed, without any enthusiasm. The Heart-Shaped Ball, a charity extravaganza that I would loathe and Katy would adore. Her mother was on the organizing committee. She was on *every* committee, it seemed. No charity blow-out was complete without her. Consequently, we ended up attending a disproportionate number of these events, nearly all of which were stupefyingly dull and expensive. The fact that some meagre portion of the price went towards charity was never any compensation. It was one of the drawbacks of dating Katy . . . one of several that often felt like many.

"Don't be grouchy," she said. "Once you're there, you'll . . ."

". . . have a really good time? Sure."

I thought about the victim. A nurse had probably sat by her bed through the night. She would be yawning now, waiting to be relieved. A doctor would be changing the dosage on an intravenous drip. A little green screen with squirming electronic signals would monitor her erratic heart. Outside, in the corridor, an impatient police detective was no doubt waiting for her first drowsy words. Did

23

she have any relatives? Had they been told? Perhaps they were waiting in the corridor with the detective?

The radio crackled. *And if you're listening to this on the M4, I hope you're enjoying it because you're not going anywhere for the next couple of hours!* A talent-free Australian began singing tunelessly to a monotonous backing track.

Katy zipped up her skirt and buttoned her shirt, flicking her hair over the collar. One of the essentials for her job – perhaps the *only* essential – was smart dress. She worked for Polly de Blanche, a humourless interior designer on Walton Street, and it often seemed to me that it was as much a social occupation as a professional one. Polly de Blanche was a certified snob. She didn't speak to people she considered beneath her and that certainly included me. But for fortunes and titles she was glad to prostitute herself.

I hated going in there. De Blanche would be standing in a corner, dressed beautifully, not a hair out of place, sticking her roman nose in the air and making sure she didn't smile, in case it broke the smooth coat of pale plaster-like make-up on her face. She was elegant and utterly sexless.

For Katy, the job was an indulgence, a way to pass the time until I married her. She would never admit it, but her indiscreet friends had confirmed it to me. It didn't bother me, except when she claimed to be working as hard as I was.

"In my line of work," she sometimes argued, "it simply isn't good enough to take their order and then show them the door. We rely on the personal touch and it's not as straightforward as you'd imagine."

Oh, I could *well* imagine! Those power lunches where gossip was top-secret information. The thorny choices that had to be made in a fraction of a professional second. Was it to be the lobster salad or the cucumber soup?

"I'm sorry about yesterday evening," I said.

She turned round. "I thought you had a good time."

"I meant before that . . . you know, when I got back here."

"Oh that!" she replied, dismissing it with a small flick of the hand.

I propped myself up on one elbow. The dizziness was gone too. I was thirsty and hungry. I felt as though there was nothing left inside me. I felt hollow.

I thought about the scarlet stain spreading across my pristine shirt and the points of liquid fire where I touched her body. The rest of me had been ice. There had been so much blood, it didn't seem possible that it could all be hers, and yet . . .

There were no marks on me and it was impossible to reconcile logic with what I'd witnessed. My hands had stung when she clamped them to her skin, but there were no traces on them, nothing to betray anything unusual. My entire body had hurt as though torn apart, but there was no evidence of it. Could it really have been in my imagination? I found that hard to accept and wanted someone to speak to. But that would compromise my safety.

Who was she? Why was she being attacked? Did she know them? Had she survived? Did the ambulance get there in time?

Katy was calling from the kitchen. "Do you want coffee?"

"Sure. Thanks."

I had a quick shower and went through to the kitchen with a towel wrapped around my waist. Katy stepped away when I put my hand on her hip and attempted to kiss her on the cheek.

"I haven't got the time," she muttered, tersely.

"Is something wrong?" I asked.

She looked me in the eye and shrugged. "I don't know. Is there?"

I frowned. "What do you mean?"

"You tell me. It's the middle of the morning and you're still here. Normally, you're in a panic if you're not up by six-thirty. But here you are, having a shower, casually drinking coffee, even making a pass at me."

I let out a sigh of relief. "Is that all?"

"*Is that all?* Usually, it's the end of the world."

"So I decided to take it easy today. Is that a crime?"

"It's not a crime. It's just peculiar. Like your behaviour last night."

I took a sip from my coffee and lit my first cigarette of the day. It was a bitter kiss. "I've never taken so much as a single day's sick leave since I've been at Parke Millen. I've never taken my full annual leave, either. Yesterday was a nightmare and I didn't feel too hot last night, so I thought I might take it easy this morning. Is that all right with you?"

Katy looked at her watch and reached for her keys. "I've got to go. I promised Polly I'd be in early."

"You mean before ten?"

She gave me a sour smile and left.

Once she was gone, I dressed and got rid of all the clothes by putting them in a black bin-liner and dropping it into a builder's skip. Then I took my car to Gary Flowers's garage just off the All Saints Road. For the appropriate fee, Flowers discreetly took care of all vehicular headaches.

"Blood, eh?" muttered Flowers, with his hands on his hips, looking at the stained seats. "Been a bit reckless, have you?"

The forecourt was clean but the workshop was covered in dirt. It was impossible to see the original colour of anything, including Flowers, who was caked in oil and grime. In one corner, a mechanic was using a blow torch on an ancient Capri. Sparks spat furiously off the door panel. On a split wooden bench sat a radio, splattered with paint and grease. Its tinny sound could only be heard when the power-drills rested.

"Well, it won't be perfect. Never is with blood, but it'll be good enough. What's left you'll be able to pass off as something else. Won't be cheap, either. Blood's expensive," he said, turning to me and grinning. His teeth were no whiter than his face. "Especially if you want it done quick, which is what you said, right?"

"That's right."

Before going to my office, I returned to the NCP car park. Both the entrance and exit ramps were sealed by police incident tape. The stairwells were closed too. There were several police officers stopping pedestrians and asking questions. I stood at the corner of the square and smoked a cigarette in the chilly drizzle.

The guilt returned, but there was nothing I could do to change the choice I'd made. I crossed the road and walked past the stairwell I'd used the night before. A policeman stood by the swing-door. When I asked him what happened, he gave me an inaccurate description of events.

As a concerned citizen, I appeared suitably aghast. "How terrible," I said. "Is she going to be all right?"

"She's in hospital. More than that, I couldn't say, although I understand it was a particularly unpleasant attack. Very vicious."

They were looking for a light-blue car which was seen speeding down Moorgate at about eight-thirty with two or three men in it. When he said they were also looking for a second car – possibly a BMW, perhaps silver – my heart skipped a beat.

"Mind you," he added, "looking for an unspecified BMW in this part of the city is like looking for the odd grain out in a bucket of sand. Doesn't narrow it down much, does it?"

By the time I strolled into Parke Millen, it was mid-morning and the plastic coffee cups were already filling the bins. The air-conditioning was poisoning the air we breathed.

"Ah, Floyd! Nice to see you ambling in at the crack of eleven o'clock!"

Robert Poulsen was director of European Trading for Parke Millen Securities. I got on far better with Gordon Rowdy, Parke Millen's number one man in Europe, than I did with Poulsen. The air was frosty when we were too close.

Going back to the car park had sent the shivers through me. I hadn't been able to resist the urge even though it filled me with trepidation. Standing by the stairwell, I could see her again. She was hanging out of the back of the Toyota, wriggling like an eel, pleading for help. And as every instinct in me cried out for retreat, I'd stepped forward. My own reaction still shocked me.

"Fuck you," I muttered inaudibly, looking down at my desk and the wad of overnight telexes and faxes which had come in.

"What was that?" barked Poulsen, leaning over Danny's desk and squinting through his glasses, with their thin, navy-blue frames.

Chantal Loursain, transferred to London from the Parisian outfit and who sat to my right, picked up a ringing phone. Poulsen glared at me. The cracking wrists echoed in my skull.

"ECU. European Currency Unit," I said, waving a handful of faxes at him. "One of the banes of my life."

So much blood. *Too much.* I couldn't understand the strength of her grip, just when she should have been at her weakest. And her insistence that I desert her? It made no sense. I desperately wanted someone to talk to. But that desire was superseded by the necessity to try to act normally, to avoid the merest hint of suspicion.

"Why are you late, Floyd?"

"I was ill."

"And now you're better?"

"Somewhat."

Robert Poulsen really was the last of the yuppies. He was yesterday's man in every respect, married to the kill-or-be-killed work ethic because she was the only whore who would have him. He had an image of himself as a business giant and a social success that was as pathetic as it was absurd. He liked to wear Italian suits from the cutting edge of fashion, never that popular among conservative City folk, who left that sort of dress to advertisers.

His other great weakness was for young girls on Friday nights. Most evenings, Sugar And Spice, a bar-restaurant in Covent Garden, was just a flashy, over-priced pick-up joint. On Friday nights it was a meat-market. Everyone was drunk on a seedy cocktail of drink and lust, usually fortified by some narcotic or other. It was one in the eye for those who thought the eighties were dead and buried in a coffin of moral resurrection, beneath a mountain of debt.

We all knew Poulsen went there. He lavished champagne on young girls, got them plastered and, when they could barely walk, shovelled them into a taxi and took them home. These were his glamorous conquests. Poulsen had somehow convinced himself that this was proof of his animal magnetism. He should have looked in the mirror. On the ladder of sexual appeal, Robert Poulsen shared a rung with the Elephant Man.

"You could have called in sick," he suggested.

"If I'd decided to take the whole day off, I would have."

Poulsen still hankered for the giddy heights of excess that marked the mid-eighties. In the vulgar boom years, he had been a man in his time. That was one reason we couldn't get on. That style of ostentation embarrassed me. I could never claim to be a moral crusader, but I wasn't morally bankrupt, either. As far as I was concerned, trading European securities for my American employers was just a job. I viewed the good pay as compensation for the generally tedious nature of my work and for the long hours I put in. I never bought into the idea of corporate warfare as something heroic.

I despised the synthetic atmosphere generated by people like Poulsen. It was absurdly aggressive, as though we were troops in trenches while sitting at desks.

I don't know why I turned out to be good at my job. It certainly wasn't through love or dedication. Maybe I was just lucky enough to have the knack, but for two years in a row I was the top-rated trader. That meant my seat was secure and this angered Poulsen. But what really tortured him was that he knew I couldn't have cared less about it. He could never forgive me for my blend of achievement and indifference, just as I could never forgive him for his mixture of ambition and absurdity.

Chantal said to me, "Call on two, Christian."

It was Gordon Rowdy, calling from the semi-dark of his monstrous office on the top floor, announcing his intention to send me on a tour of Parke Millen's European offices. I hated these trips.

"Don't worry," he assured me, as he picked up the reluctance in my voice. "It'll be a breeze. Anyway, it's only a week out of your life. The change of scenery will do you good."

"But why me? I'm just a trader."

"I know. And a fine one."

"But this sort of thing . . ."

"I have my reasons."

By the time I finished my call, Poulsen was in his director's office, a small cube of glass that afforded him a view

30

of his traders but which gave him a little privacy if he wanted it.

Danny pulled the tab off a can of Diet Coke. He offered me a Benson & Hedges over the top of his main computer.

"No, thanks."

"Did you hear about the woman who got attacked?" he asked me.

I cleared my throat to hide my surprise and mumbled, "Oh, er . . . somebody mentioned something."

"Yeah. You know the big NCP car park just round the corner?"

I nodded.

"A woman got raped there last night."

"Raped?" I replied, startled by his certainty.

"Well, attacked, but you know how it is: a young woman assaulted by three men in an underground car park. You don't need to be Sherlock Holmes to figure out it spells rape, do you?"

"You'd be a crap lawyer," I told him.

"Wait a minute," said Chantal. "Isn't that the garage you park your car in?"

"That's right," said Danny. "And you were working late last night. You might have seen something."

My blood stopped flowing for a second. Act normally, I told myself. I blinked and looked for my lighter. "I didn't use my car yesterday. I went by taxi."

"I thought you drove your car into work every day," said Chantal.

I patted her on the arm and smiled sweetly. "Doesn't that just prove how little you really know me?"

# Chapter Four

"And what seems to be the problem?"

I'd considered my answer to this inevitable question while sitting in the waiting-room, between a mother with her whining child and an old man whose chest rattled when he breathed. Saturday morning at the surgery was busy. All the seats were taken and the receptionist's phone rang incessantly. The posters warning people off smoking were old and faded and yellow at the edges, as if stained by tobacco smoke. It was airless and quiet. Everyone avoided direct eye contact. While waiting, one could either read old magazines or steal furtive glances at the other patients and try to guess what was wrong with them, and whether it might be infectious and merit a move away.

"Mummy, mummy," moaned a small girl on the other side of the waiting-room, "what's that big red thing on that boy's face?"

She was pointing at a particularly savage boil on an unfortunate teenager's cheek; a volcanic island in a sea of acne. The mother was mortified and roughly took the girl's outstretched arm and tugged it down. The boy, who was painfully self-conscious of his condition, lowered his head even further into an old issue of *National Geographic* and tried to pretend he hadn't heard. The surgery was filled with silent embarrassment. I was saved by the receptionist who called out my name and sent me in to see Dr Wheeler.

Gerald Wheeler had been my doctor ever since I started

work in London, but I had only seen him once before. He had thinning silver hair and wore half-moon glasses.

I really wanted to talk to someone. I was still confused by the possibility of bleeding. The more I thought about it, the more convinced I was that it had happened, but there was no avoiding the lack of evidence. I always believed in the confidentiality of doctors and consequently felt Wheeler was the only person I could safely talk to.

"I'm not sure what the problem is," I confessed. "*That*'s the problem."

"I don't understand."

"Then let me ask you something. Is it possible to bleed without a wound?"

"Of course. Haemorrhage, for one thing. Internal bleeding from . . ."

"Not internally," I interrupted. "*Externally.*"

He frowned. "What?"

"Is it possible to bleed externally without an obvious wound? I'm not talking about nosebleeds or anything, I'm talking about bleeding *through* sealed skin."

He sat back, removed his glasses and held them in his hands, rubbing one lens with a thumb. "I assume this isn't entirely hypothetical?"

"No, it isn't."

He let out a deep breath and nodded slowly. "Then could you be more specific?"

I said, "There was an incident and a young woman was badly injured. I happened to be there and so I went to help, until the medical services arrived. And while I was there, I started bleeding . . . I think."

"You think?"

I nodded. "I can't be sure."

"Why not?"

"Because it doesn't make sense. I was holding onto the woman and when I looked down I saw a bloody stain spreading across my shirt."

"Was there blood around? Was she cut?"

"Yes. Badly. She'd been . . . there was a lot of her blood about."

He looked up from his notes when I checked myself. "And there's no way this blood on your shirt could have been hers?"

"No. I hadn't got that close. Besides, when I looked down, I could actually see it spreading."

"I see," he murmured. "And what did it feel like?"

I thought about it and replied, "I'm not sure. I was too cold to . . ."

"Cold?"

"Yes. I was freezing. Except where I was touching her."

"And where was that?"

"My hands. She held them to her body and the palms were hot. It's hard to be precise. I was very . . . confused."

"Was your stomach hot?"

"No, I don't think so."

"Do you think you bled from any other part of the body?"

I shook my head. "I didn't see anything."

"No blood at all?"

I smiled. "There was masses of blood. It was everywhere. I held her close to me. I was trying to comfort her, so I got covered in it."

"On your hands?"

"Sure. Even in my shoes and on my feet."

"Head?"

"No."

"And the blood on your hands was hers? You don't think it was coming out of you the way blood seemed to be coming out of your stomach?"

"No."

"Despite the painful heat you experienced?"

"I don't think so. Besides, there were no marks."

"And on your stomach?"

35

"No, but I didn't get to look at that until later, so maybe there was a wound and ..."

"And it cauterized, sealing itself, leaving a scar that disappeared in ... what? A few minutes? An hour or two?"

I knew how ridiculous it sounded and so lapsed into silence. He put on his glasses and scribbled words on a pad. He said, "I assume you're aware of the stigmata?"

"Stigmata? I've heard of that, but ... I'm not really sure. It's something religious, isn't it?"

Wheeler smiled tamely. "That depends on your brand of belief, I suppose. Basically, it's a series of marks which broadly represent the wounds of Christ's crucifixion."

I shrugged. "I don't know much about that. All I think I saw was blood on my shirt. I'm afraid I'm not into religion."

This clearly surprised him. Sun slipped through a small window behind his desk and sparkled on the edge of a pristine kidney-bowl. It sat on a trolley at the foot of the examination bench, with its strip of medicated paper laid out along it. Dr Wheeler fiddled with his tortoiseshell pen.

"Tell me something," he said, pursing his lips and looking onto his blotting pad. "You said you looked after the victim until the medical services arrived. So, when they finally did, why didn't you get them to take a look at you?"

I didn't want to admit I'd fled before they arrived, so I said, "I was too frightened."

"Too frightened? But if you were scared of the bleeding, they would have been the best people to help you, don't you think?"

"Probably. I don't know. I was upset and confused. Who can tell how you're going to react in an extreme situation, until it actually happens?"

"Quite," he conceded. "And there were no other witnesses to this?"

I felt a flush of anxiety. "No."

It was easy to see how bad the answer looked. No evidence and no witnesses. He nodded politely and said, "Well, I think I should take a look at you, since you're here."

He examined me for traces of the bleeding but I could have told him it would be pointless. There was nothing to see.

"Well?" I said, tucking my shirt in.

He scratched his chin as he walked round his desk and sat down again. "I'm confused, to be perfectly honest."

"You don't believe me?"

"It's not as simple as that. You seem sincere enough and I'd like to give you the benefit of the doubt, but it's hard. For a start, I can't find even the smallest sign of bleeding. It may be that other, more extensive tests would reveal something, but I certainly can't. The story you've told me is . . . well, it's extraordinary. Extraordinary, but not without precedent. Ever since St Francis of Assisi there have been claims of this nature, some that were discredited and some that were never disproved. But, as I recall, these people were often schizophrenics and hysterics, that sort of thing. We could do some tests, but I'd be amazed if you fell into that category. I'm no expert in this field, I have to confess, but even if I were, I think I'd find your claim tough to substantiate. You must see that. And when you add that to everything that my medical training proposes, I'm sure you can understand my doubts."

I nodded glumly. I didn't mind that he disbelieved me. It was a farfetched thing to expect anyone to believe, especially a doctor. What I objected to was being humoured like an idiot. He went through the motions, asking questions and looking earnest when I replied. He wanted to know if I had a family history of haemorrhaging and I said I didn't, so far as I knew. When he started to question me about my diet, I knew where our conversation was heading. After diet, we dealt with drinking and smoking and finally we reached the last question, the one he had wanted to ask first, and the only one he wanted answered.

"Do you have any experience of hallucinogenic drugs?" he asked, with his head bowed, looking at his pad and delivering the question as though it were no different to any other.

I smiled. As soon as I had first seen the disbelief on his face, I guessed it would come to this. I rose from my seat, still smiling politely.

"Not yet," I replied. "But I'm considering it."

He looked up at me. "Where are you going? I still have more questions to ask you."

"No, you don't. You've just asked the only one you really wanted to."

Gary Flowers opened a tobacco tin and pulled out a hand-rolled cigarette. It was thin and crooked. He lit it, puffed out a measly stream of smoke and shook his head sadly.

"Not easy. Not easy at all. Did you bring cash?" he asked, suddenly perking up, now that his mind had turned to money.

I nodded.

"What about a credit card?" he enquired.

I frowned and then said, "Yes." He had specifically requested cash the previous day.

"Real nice motor you got," he told me.

He led me to the back of the workshop. My car was parked next to an Alfa-Romeo, half white and half red. The red half was still wet. Just beneath the front bumper lay three different number plates. Flowers saw me looking at them and smiled lamely before shouting to a thin mechanic, with spiked peroxided hair and a small dagger tattooed on his right cheek.

"You dickhead! How many times have I got to tell you not to leave this shit lying around?"

The mechanic's long face grew longer and he loped towards the front of the car to pick up the plates.

"Occupational hazard?" I wondered.

"He's a bloody idiot!" muttered Flowers. "It's a wonder he can find his pecker when he's going for a piss."

My car had been cleaned and polished. Flowers opened the door and showed me the interior.

"Spotless, eh?"

It certainly looked so, but we were half in the dark.

"We gave it the full treatment," Flowers explained. "Washed your engine, shampooed the carpeting, cleaned your leather and polished everything in sight. I figured you want the full valet service."

"Very thoughtful."

"You can pay for that on your credit card."

We entered his office at the back of the workshop. A table groaned under the weight of pending paperwork. Flowers started to fill out the credit card slip. The wall was covered in old calendars featuring cars or big-breasted women, and sometimes both. Over one blonde-haired girl, with a painfully heavy-looking chest, somebody had scrawled, in pencil, "Garys Missiz". Beneath that, in red ballpoint, were the words, "Kevins Dad".

"A pleasure doing business," said Flowers, pushing the credit card slip in my direction.

I studied the amount and replied, "I'm not surprised."

"Got a family to look after, don't I?" he said with a grin, as he tore off the top copy.

Two of the mechanics were having a row by the doorway though to the forecourt. I wondered where the Alfa-Romeo had come from and where it might end up, once a licence plate had been selected to go with its new red coat.

"And now," said Flowers, once he had safely pocketed the credit card slip, "there's the matter of the cash."

My heart sank. "You're not going to charge me more than that for a simple cleaning job, are you?"

He looked irritated. "What me? A man of his word? Never! You've paid for the valet service and that's that. Ask around. Everyone knows you can trust Gary Flowers. I'm a man of my word. That's why I'm still in business, and doing good business."

"So what about the cash?"

"I thought you might like to buy something else."

"Like?"

"Come here and I'll show you."

We went back to the BMW and he invited me to take a close look at the leather-work. On careful examination, there were still some light stains where the blood had set in.

"We did our best, but as I warned you, it's not easy."

"So?" I wondered.

"Well, the thing is, they shouldn't be a problem as they are. I mean, nobody would know they were caused by blood, as you can see. It might be coffee, or a can of Coke, or one of a hundred different things. In order to verify that as blood you'd need proper forensic testing equipment . . . you know, like the police use."

His speed of speech dropped dramatically with this last phrase. He radiated a cheeky innocence.

"You're not serious," I suggested.

"I'm supposed to report this kind of stuff to the Old Bill. It's my duty as an honourable member of the public. Crime prevention and all that. But like I said, I got a family to look out for and a decent man always makes his family number one. Know what I mean?"

"But I've already paid through the nose," I protested.

Flowers narrowed his eyes into a resentful squint. His good humour suddenly vanished. "I beg your fucking pardon!" he snapped, looking completely outraged. "Through the nose? I tell you – *mate* – under different circumstances, I wouldn't leave you with a fucking nose to pay through!"

The row in the doorway through to the forecourt had stopped and both participants were watching us. Flowers noticed this and lowered his voice.

"What you paid for is the valet service and up to now the valet service is the *only* thing you've paid for. You tell me it's a little expensive and I tell you I'm not running a fucking charity. Get the picture now, do you?"

There was no point in arguing. I nodded.

"Good. No hard feelings, eh?"

"None at all," I grumbled bitterly. "I'm sure it'll be cheap at the price, a real bargain."

"That's the spirit! My silence is golden, Mr Floyd. You can take it to the bank."

"Yeah, I know. A man of honour, right?"

I pulled away from the garage a poorer man, but a happier one, nevertheless. The bloodstained clothes were gone, lost in a builder's skip. The car was clean of incriminating evidence and Flowers's silence had been bought. From a culpability – or even, criminal – point of view, I was just about in the clear. That was a great relief. There had been no comebacks so far and, as I originally thought, the longer that was the case, the safer I could consider myself. It seemed to me the first twenty-four hours were the most crucial and they had passed without incident.

As for what I thought had happened to me . . . I didn't know what to believe. Nor, evidently, did Dr Wheeler, though he clearly suspected the problem was in my head, not in my stomach. I couldn't be sure where the explanation lay any more, but my concern was eased by the improvement in my condition. Driving back home on that Saturday morning, I felt fine. For the first time since I touched her bleeding body, I felt physically normal. The last drops of fatigue had evaporated.

The combination of feeling well and feeling safe brought on a sense of relief that was uplifting. Unanswered questions were nudged onto the back seat.

When I got back to the flat, I made a sandwich, took a beer from the fridge and sprawled across the sofa, flicking through TV channels. There was a Comedy Classic double-bill scheduled for that afternoon. First up was *Passport to Pimlico*, followed by *Whisky Galore!* Katy came back from a morning's shopping, groaning under the weight of her acquisitions. She dropped the bags by the sofa and sighed.

"It's high time shops considered giving free transport to bulk customers," she said. "By the way, before I went out, Louis called."

"Louis?"

"Yes. He said he'd ring back later."

"Louis who?"

"He didn't give his surname."

"I don't think I know anyone called Louis. Did he say what he wanted?"

"No. Just that he'd call back later."

"Thanks, anyway. What did you get?" I asked, as she sorted through the bags.

"Clothes."

As if I needed to ask. Katy was always trying to persuade me to buy more and I'd come to believe that the reason she did it was so she wouldn't feel quite so self-conscious about the amount she bought. Besides, I liked what I'd bought and I didn't *need* anything else. Katy couldn't understand that mentality.

Similarly, I liked my flat greatly. It wasn't large, but it was perfectly sufficient for two. Yet Katy kept insisting I should buy something larger, preferably a house.

"With a garden," she would usually add, as a premeditated afterthought. "After all, you can easily afford it."

And I would usually insist, "That's not the point. I can afford to pump a kilo of heroin into my veins, but that's no reason to do it, is it?"

But by this stage, she wouldn't be listening. She'd be

thinking about the interior and how Polly de Blanche would decorate it ... as if buying a house wasn't expensive enough.

I finished my beer and went to the fridge for a second one. Katy was looking for something to eat.

"Any plans for this afternoon?" I asked.

"Yes. We're going to the Franz Munzer exhibition."

"Where's that?"

"The ICA, I think. Justin knows."

"Justin? As in Whitehead?" I asked.

"Yes. And Miranda. We're all meeting there."

I asked, "Who is this Munzer?"

"I told you. He's a photographer. He specializes in erotica. Or perversion, depending on your point of view. This is a collection of his work from his Berlin period."

I went back to the sofa and made myself comfortable. "What time are you meeting them?"

Katy poked her head round the doorway. "At three and you're coming too," she said.

"What?"

"We better leave here at about two-thirty."

Looking at a pervert's photos was one thing, but doing it with Justin Whitehead and Miranda Hart was another. I considered my free days too precious to waste on them.

I said, "I thought those two disliked each other."

"They both like Munzer," explained Katy.

"Listen, I'm really not in the mood for any exhibitions. I just want to ... you know ... do nothing. They've got *Passport to Pimlico* and *Whisky Galore!* on television."

Katy strolled into the living-room with a cup of tea. "You want to watch old films all afternoon?" she asked, incredulously. "Don't be tiresome, Christian. Besides, it's all arranged."

"I'm sure they won't miss me. I know I won't miss them."

Katy blew steam from her mug and took a small sip. "Don't be pathetic," she said, like a schoolmistress.

That irritated me. "One afternoon a month to myself is too much to ask for, is it? Perhaps you could jog my memory and tell me when I last did this?"

She looked down at me unsympathetically and said, "You're not the only person who works hard. Other people do too, you know, and they still find the energy to get off their backsides and go out on a Saturday. Miranda and Justin both work and they're going to . . ."

"Be reasonable! Whitehead puts in how many hours a week? A taxing two dozen? And as for Miss Hart, she only cuts dresses for her customers when she isn't too busy having long lunches with . . . with . . ."

My attack petered out and Katy fixed me with a steel stare. She said, "With?"

I shrugged and replied, "Whoever. You know what I mean."

But it was too late and the slip was made. "Yes," she said, acidly, "I know *exactly* what you mean."

It was a prelude to a common argument, but there wasn't time to play out the whole scene. When she left to meet Justin and Miranda, the atmosphere was still heavy with conflict and I was glad to see her go. I didn't feel guilty about that, which was an increasingly common experience since she'd started making obvious moves towards marriage.

I watched *Passport to Pimlico*, flicking over to the other channels during the commercial breaks to get the latest on the sport. While I was making a cup of coffee, the phone rang.

"Mr Floyd?"

"Yes."

"Mr Christian Floyd?"

"That's me."

"I know what you did."

I stopped pouring coffee into my mug. The voice was strained, as though it were badly damaged.

"I don't know what you're talking about," I replied.

"Yes, you do."

I suddenly clicked into gear and froze. Was he one of the attackers? Or one of the businessmen who entered the car park as I was leaving? Or perhaps he was the attendant who had spied me from some concealed vantage point? My throat was dry.

"Who are you?" I croaked.

"You don't know me."

"I don't know what you're talking about, either," I stammered, trying to regain some composure.

He chuckled coarsely. "My name is Louis and I am talking about an incident which happened in a certain car park on Thursday evening."

I felt sweat on my forehead. Katy had said someone called Louis had phoned, while I was picking up the car.

"I still don't know what you're talking about."

"Of course you do," insisted Louis. "You know very well and I suspect you revel in it."

"*What?*"

There was a pause. I needed a cigarette. They were in the sitting-room.

"I know you, Mr Floyd. I know what you are."

"Who are you?"

"You must drive the darkness out."

"What is this? Some kind of practical joke? If it is, then I . . ."

"Does this sound like a joke?" he interrupted, fiercely. "You must plead for forgiveness and beg for help in your battle against the evil which has stolen your soul! It is the only way you can save yourself. And if you won't do what is required, then we shall."

"If you call me again, I'll ring the police."

There was a low laugh down the line, almost a growl.

"Don't be ridiculous, Mr Floyd. You can't contact the police. You *know* you can't. You were seen."

"Who saw me? What did they see?"

"God is a witness to everything."

Fear made me aggressive. "Look, I don't know what you want, but you're not getting it from me, so just fuck off! Otherwise, I *will* call the police and then . . ."

But Louis cut me off angrily. "How ridiculous you are! You don't even know who I am," he said, before hanging up.

# Chapter Five

My taxi was gliding up Moorgate and the sky was purple.
I pictured a light blue Toyota on the opposite side, the
driver wrestling with his steering wheel, a fat man in
the back seat trying to keep his thin friend's hands connected to his arms. It was six-thirty on Monday morning and
drizzle drifted down onto grey London.

I was tired. Since Louis called, sleep had been scarce.
Through the darkest hours of two bleak nights I tried to
imagine who he might be. As I grew progressively weary,
so I entertained ever more colourful possibilities, most
of which were sufficiently alarming to prevent me from
tumbling into sleep. The soles of my feet carved out a
"racing line" on the circuit of the sitting-room carpet,
while I paced through the early hours. I'd contemplated
trying to discuss it with Katy, but couldn't see a way of
doing that without alluding to the attack in the car park.

The call had come just as I was starting to think I'd
escaped any repercussions from the incident. The feeling
of failure at the point of success left me deflated . . . and
anxious.

At seven o'clock I was in Gordon Rowdy's office. The
head of Parke Millen had been in since five. He seemed
to regard sleep as an optional extra he could do without.
Under the circumstances, I was jealous of that.

"Coffee?" he asked, pouring himself a large cup from
a pot on the sideboard.

Gordon Rowdy had a proper office: it had walls, not

sheets of glass. He handed me a cup and saucer which, in terms of their size, were really a bowl and plate.

"I hope you're not one of these wimps who drinks decaffeinated coffee."

Nearly all his countrymen at Parke Millen drank decaffeinated coffee. I never did. Nor did Chantal, who once told me, "To decaffeinate coffee is to rape it", while Danny couldn't tell the difference between Colombia's finest and the rusty water dispensed by the vending machine.

Gordon Rowdy was a balding Bostonian. His remaining hair was jet black and oiled to the scalp. I looked around his office. There were no photographs of his family, if indeed he had one, no mementos from the past, no paperweights with sentimental significance, nothing personal. He did have a tiny silver pennant with "Boston Red Sox" inscribed on it, which stood by one of his phones, but that was all. He slid a manila folder towards me.

"This is your programme for next week," he said.

I looked at the details. The five-day trip incorporated meetings in Paris, Frankfurt, Madrid and Zurich. I was supposed to return to London on the Friday evening.

"It's not as bad as it looks," Rowdy told me.

I flicked through some of the papers beneath the travel schedule. There were copies of new trading regulations set out by the government and outlines for new working practices within Parke Millen.

"Excuse me for saying so," I said, "but why am I doing this? This isn't the sort of . . ."

"I know, I know," he interrupted, anticipating my query. "The thing is, I don't want this done by fax. It needs a human touch to make sure the changes are understood. Then they can be implemented properly and smoothly. I want to hit the ground running on Day One."

"I can appreciate that, but . . ."

"Everybody knows who you are," he went on. "You're

the number one trader here, for the second year in a row. It'll sound good coming from you. Besides, it'll give you a chance to meet the right people from some of our other offices. In Paris, you'll be meeting several members of the controlling board in New York. They've specifically asked for you to be there. You won't be a trader for ever, Christian. These people are your future. If they like you, you'll be a shooting star . . ."

He let the sentence hang in the air. I engineered an appreciative smile and wondered what Louis looked like. If the face matched the voice, what horrible flaws would there be?

"You okay?" asked Rowdy.

"Just tired," I replied. "I've had trouble sleeping."

"Guilty conscience, huh?"

I looked up at him. "What?"

He smiled and said, "Take it easy, Christian. I was just kidding."

Danny and Chantal had arrived for work by the time I got back to my desk. As usual, Danny was a wreck. When he arrived at work to start a hectic day, he always looked as though he'd just finished one. His hair was chaotic, his tie knot was halfway down his chest and his sleeves were rolled up above the elbow. Chantal was always elegant, even in a crisis. She chose her clothes carefully, always coordinating her colours and sticking with the ones which suited her best: dark greens and blues, mostly. She liked to strike a balance between conservative and chic.

The weekend had been a strain and I was relieved to be back in the sterile but secure surroundings of my office. Just as the call from Louis had rattled me, so the sadistic images of the Munzer photographic exhibition seemed to inspire a mood change in Katy. She was at her most antagonistic on Saturday night. Justin Whitehead, who also went to the exhibition, arranged dinner for a dozen of us at a Greek restaurant in Brewer Street, where he pretended he was best friends with the owner. Katy was snide all evening. My anxiety about Louis made me mentally frail and so I was all the more vulnerable to her verbal poison.

On Sunday we drove down to Wiltshire to have lunch with her parents. Peter Donaldson, her father, was a misogynist. Half this condition was genetically inherited and his wife, Louise, was to blame for the rest. She was a tedious alcoholic, a truth that was strenuously denied by Katy. When her parents weren't bickering they were oblivious to each other. He was nasty and she was a bore, especially when intoxicated. Being in their company was draining, unless you were in the mood for menace.

The subject of marriage hung heavy in the air, like a pregnant cloud waiting to split into a storm. I was glad it didn't because nothing could have been further from my distracted mind than marrying Katy. Even in lighter times, I'd come to regard marriage with deep-rooted suspicion.

Before my mother was killed, she and my father argued incessantly, when they weren't too busy having secret and not-so-secret affairs. That stopped the day she forced a lover's Maserati under the wheels of an articulated lorry, near Aosta, in northern Italy.

It was a couple of years since I'd actually seen my father, but I wasn't bothered by that. Neither he nor my mother had been good at marriage or parenting and I can't really pretend I was fond of either. It was primarily their example which had led me to the conclusion that I'd probably be a bad husband and a hopeless father.

So, with these matters in mind, marriage was a difficult subject for me to consider with any great enthusiasm. Katy's ideas on wedlock seemed to be entirely concerned with dresses, flowers, houses, decorations . . . anything that could be acquired by credit card, and little to do with the spirit of the union. Sunday with the Donaldsons had done nothing but reinforce the beliefs I'd held before.

I changed the price page on my screen. All things considered, my professional life seemed more attractive by the hour; going to work at six-thirty on Monday morning was beginning to look appealing.

"You had two calls," said Chantal. "One from Fengel and the other from Felipe Massaga in Madrid."

Gunther Fengel lived in Essen where living was terminally easy; you could die for lack of life's daily frustrations. It was very clean, efficient and civilized. Fengel and Massaga were two of the constants in my real life: my professional life. They were anonymous contacts with whom I had simple, antiseptic working relationships. I always found work much easier to deal with. The rules were clearer and, although I had no love for my job, it was, in many ways, a more comfortable thing than my personal existence. All I ever wanted out of life was to achieve the right balance and maintain it. Before Thursday night, I seemed to have done that, but what happened in the car park threatened me with chaos. And the introduction of Louis only compounded that.

Just before eleven o'clock, one of the receptionists at the front desk called on the phone.

"Miss Fiorini is here to see you," she said.

"Thank you."

"Would you like me to show her into a meeting-room?"

"No, I'll come out myself," I replied, before putting the phone back.

I walked out of our division and through the long hall of money-dealers. They would move down a floor when the new dealing rooms were ready. The project was two months behind schedule and they still couldn't control the air temperature down there.

The first thing that occurred to me, as I reached the reception desk, was that Miss Fiorini's appointment was actually scheduled for Tuesday, not Monday. And I was sure that we were supposed to meet at Credit Suisse, not at Parke Millen.

The small waiting area was just past the reception desk, with its pair of immaculate receptionists, who sat in front of gold letters on dark wooden panels, announcing "Parke Millen Securities". It was a small recess, opposite the lifts, where light tumbled into soft pools from concealed spots. The day's newspapers were on a low, central coffee table, around which were three leather sofas, two side-tables with lamps, and a couple of sprawling pot plants that had been sprayed with the luminous green polish.

The second thing that occurred to me, as I entered the recess, was that Miss Fiorini was, in fact, married. The receptionist had definitely said "Miss" but I knew Maria Fiorini was married, to Umberto Fiorini, the renowned pianist. I looked at the woman who rose from the leather sofa and didn't recognize her. That was when the third thing occurred to me: the lady I knew at Credit Suisse wasn't Fiorini at all. She was *Fucini*. Mrs Maria Fucini. Her husband was Umberto Fucini, not Fiorini. It was an easy mistake to make, when you were speaking to six people at once. I presumed the lady before me *was* Miss Fiorini, but I couldn't be sure. I'd never seen her before.

"Miss Fiorini?" I asked, cautiously.

She nodded. "Yes. Gabriella Fiorini."

"Good morning. I'm Christian Floyd."

"I know."

We shook hands politely. She was about five eight in height and wore a long overcoat. Her shoulders were flecked with rain drops. A pair of black sunglasses concealed her eyes.

"Do we have an appointment?" I asked.

Her mouth stretched into a wry smile. "Do I need one?" she enquired, removing her glasses. Her eyes were a stunning green.

"Well, normally, yes," I replied, a little disarmed by the way she was looking at me.

She looked a little surprised herself and said, "You have no idea who I am, do you?"

I looked again. She had a broad mouth and lovely, smooth cheekbones. Her hair was an auburn cascade and her skin was exotic; even if you'd seen it on someone called Mary Smith, you'd never believe she was English. It wasn't especially dark, but it looked richer than anything I knew. I took a step back. She was easy on the eye, but not on the mind.

I smiled hopelessly, held out my hands and said, "Sorry. You've got me."

She bit her lip and nodded. "Well," she concluded, "there could be no greater testament to what you've done than that. You saved my life on Thursday night."

I could feel gravity's pull weakening. For a moment, I couldn't think of a single thing to say. I wanted to ask her if she was sure. I thought she looked so different, but now that I cast my memory back to the confusion of the event, I found I hadn't got a face in my mind at all. It could have been her. The light had been poor in the car park. Were the amazing emerald eyes the same ones? Maybe . . . but then maybe not.

Had it not been for the wounds, I might have believed her. But the stabbing had been so severe, I was convinced she couldn't have been discharged from hospital so soon. And hadn't there been bruising and grazing on her face? Where had that gone?

I felt awkward and jittery. Not wanting to deny her claims too bluntly, I said, "I don't understand. You . . . you're so much . . ."

Her expression changed from mild surprise to outright astonishment. I looked around. Both receptionists were watching with growing curiosity. I directed her deeper into the recess, out of their line of vision.

"You do look sort of ... I don't know ... well, a bit like her, I suppose. But what about your injuries?" I whispered. "The woman I pulled out of the car was battered and bleeding. She had knife wounds. Serious ones! I mean, I thought she was going to die."

Gabriella Fiorini now looked utterly shocked. She took a few unsteady steps backwards and clumsily sat down on one of the sofas.

"Are you okay?" I asked.

She put her hands together and gasped, "Oh my God! You don't even know!"

I swallowed and my Adam's Apple felt like a tennis ball. "Know what?"

She was trembling when she whispered, "You saved my life!"

"I don't know about that," I countered. "I just pulled you free of the car and ..."

"No! You saved me! You *healed* me!"

"What?"

She looked up at me in wonder and amazement. "I don't believe it! You saved my life by healing me and you had no idea, did you?"

She smiled humourlessly and shook her head in exasperation. That was when I remembered the woman in the car park had carried a strange accent. So did Gabriella. I couldn't be sure if it was the same one, but ...

I looked at her blankly. "I healed you? How?"

She rose from the sofa, took hold of both my hands and said, "With these."

# Chapter Six

She wasn't lying to me. Gabriella Fiorini believed what she was saying. All the doubt was mine.

The reception area at Parke Millen was not the ideal place to be. Two men, who were waiting for lifts, pretended not to notice us, but stole furtive glances when they could. The receptionists were whispering.

"I'm so sorry," said Gabriella, quietly. "I promise you, I would never have come if I'd known. I just assumed . . ."

"We should talk," I told her. "But not here. Somewhere else."

Outside, a turbulent slate-grey sky rolled above us, making a ceiling that was so low it seemed just out of a raised hand's reach.

"How did you find me?" I asked.

"You told me your name. Remember?"

"Vaguely."

"So I went through the phone book. I got your flat this morning and a woman gave me your work number."

That would be Katy, I thought. We went into a café. Since it was mid-morning, it was empty; the breakfast rush hour was over and the lunch hour was yet to come. A lot of the greasy-spoons in our area had been forced out of business by cleaner and smarter places, or been blown to smithereens by IRA bombs. We ordered two coffees and sat at a small table with a chipped, yellow Formica top, by a window of condensation.

Gabriella wouldn't remove her overcoat, even though the café was warm and humid. She peered through the wet window and onto the drab street outside. Her eyes were aimless.

"Miss Fiorini?" I interrupted, trying to break the blank stare, as I offered her a cigarette.

She sniffed. "What?"

Our coffees arrived. The owner slapped them onto our table and half the beige liquid slopped onto the saucers. I pushed the packet of Marlboro towards her.

"No, thank you," she replied. "And please, call me Gabriella."

"Okay."

"You don't believe me, do you?"

I said, "I'm not sure what to believe."

"Do you even believe I was the woman you rescued?"

"The fact that you know about it proves something, but the injuries were . . ."

She nodded with resignation and ran a finger around the smooth edge of the saucer. "I understand."

Once again, I saw the crimson stain spreading across my shirt and felt the icy sludge creeping through my veins. My palms were soaked and scorched. She was clamping my hands to her body with an unnerving ferocity. Even in those moments when I was convinced the bleeding had happened and I was searching for an explanation, I never came up with such a fantastic theory.

When the silence became embarrassing, I said, "So, where do you come from?"

"Italy. Rome."

"How nice. My father lives in . . ."

"Is that why we're here?" she interrupted, looking up at me from her coffee. "For small-talk?"

I took a drag from my cigarette and studied her face. It annoyed me that I couldn't make a match. The cracking wrists echoed in my head.

"Why were you attacked?" I asked.

She shrugged. "I have no idea."

"They just appeared from nowhere?"

"More or less. They took me by surprise."

"As you were getting in your car?"

"You mean the blue one?"

"Yes."

"That wasn't mine. It was theirs. I don't have a car."

I frowned. "You don't? So what were you doing in a car park?"

Gabriella smiled, then took a sip from her cup and grimaced. "Suddenly, you sound like a policeman."

I relaxed a little. "I've been compared to many things before, but never a policeman."

"In answer to your question, I was using the car park as a sort of subway. I was heading for the Underground and I had to cross the square. Since it was raining so hard, I figured I might as well use the car park to keep dry."

"You work in the City?"

"Not yet."

"I'm sorry?"

She smiled. "I was on my way home from an interview with a firm of lawyers. I'm a linguist and they needed someone who was fluent in English and Italian."

I took a sip from my cup. It was lukewarm and disgusting. Gabriella's grimace was well deserved. A gust of wind whipped a slice of rain across the plate-glass window.

She looked down into her coffee cup when she asked me, "Do you think I'm crazy?"

"No."

"But you still don't believe me?"

"It's not that simple," I admitted.

I tapped some ash into a gold foil ashtray. She leaned back and flicked some hair out of her eyes.

"At the hospital there are confused doctors looking for an impossible solution to an improbable problem. I'm sure they would be very interested to meet you and hear what I have to say."

"*They* might think you were crazy," I pointed out.

The owner of the café was trying to scratch some dirt off a cup. Steam rose from a scrubbed metal tea-urn.

I said, "Assuming what you say is true, what happened to you after I left?"

"There was confusion. Someone raised the alarm and an ambulance crew came shortly after. I remember hearing the siren scream as we raced towards the hospital. The lights were flickering overhead when they rushed me into the building. It's hard to recall with any clarity because the drugs made me drowsy. But I vaguely remember being in a room of bright lights with several fuzzy faces looming over me. Their worried whispers turned into gasps of amazement. There was so much blood everywhere, they must have expected to find the most horrendous wounds ... and of course, they found none."

She paused and looked up at me when she said this. I looked away and started to trace letters in the film of condensation on the window. The café owner tuned his radio, moving through bands of static until he found his channel.

"The next thing I remember was waking up in a clean bed in a small room. I was the only patient in there. It was daylight. I could hear voices mumbling in the corridor outside. My mind was still cloudy with the hangover from the drugs, but I had a pretty good idea what was going on. Whenever a doctor or nurse came in to attend to me, I could see the look on their faces."

"The look?"

"Yes. Part suspicion, part wonder, I suppose. They tried to behave as though nothing unusual had happened, but they looked at me like some sort of grotesque circus attraction. They were courteous and remote, but no one asked me a direct question about it, until the afternoon, when three doctors came to see me and asked for my version of events. There were two police detectives with them and . . ."

I stopped drawing. "The police?" I said, sharply. "Did you give them my name?"

She shook her head, and replied, sadly, "Only now are you interested!"

"I'm sorry. I didn't mean to . . ."

"Don't worry. I never mentioned you. For one thing, I was afraid of saying what really happened because I knew it would sound absurd. So I lied."

"What did you tell them?"

"That I was hit over the head and knocked unconscious. I said I never saw who did it and couldn't remember anything until I was in the ambulance. The police wanted to know if I was alone, and when I said I was, they asked me about the blood. I told them I didn't know how it happened. By this stage, they'd run a test on it and matched it to a sample they took while I was unconscious."

"Jesus Christ!" I muttered, stubbing out my cigarette. "What did they make of that?"

"The doctors were obviously mystified. The police were quite aggressive. Perhaps they felt awkward at being out of their depth; I don't know, but they implied that a woman walking through a London car park gets what she deserves. I mean, it may not have been the smartest move of my life, but they actually made me feel ashamed to be the victim. Can you believe that?"

"Unfortunately, yes."

The sudden realization of what was happening made me shudder. Gabriella hadn't noticed it. She was too engrossed with her narration. Contrary to what I might have expected, or ever wanted, I found I was beginning to believe her. So far.

"There was chaos, by this stage. The ambulance crew who collected me from the car park reported that I had been bleeding but they hadn't seen proper knife wounds.

They said I was covered in strange blemishes, all of which were cauterized. There were no open wounds. One of them said they looked like fresh scars. They also remembered that I was badly bruised. But by the time the doctors and detectives came to see me, there wasn't a mark on my body. The ambulance crew were questioned again and they confirmed everything they'd seen the previous night. So you know what they did?"

I shook my head. "What?"

She smiled and said, "They brought in the ambulance crew to check that I was the person they'd retrieved, in case there was a mistake in Admissions. It was a joke! The doctors and the ambulance crew were arguing with each other about possible explanations, and the police were stuck in the middle without a clue!

"In the end, I think the doctors discharged me because they were embarrassed at their inability to explain the discrepancies between the ambulance crew's report, the report supplied by Admissions, and what they could see for themselves."

The door swung open and an old lady wobbled into the café, making her way to the gloom at the back. Her shoulders were round and her head was half hidden by an olive-green woollen hat. Gabriella waited until the woman was out of earshot before continuing.

"I don't know what would have happened if I'd tried telling them the truth. I guess they would have kept me there. Maybe they would have run some tests. And I suppose the police would have tracked you down, looking for answers to all the wrong questions."

The prospect was not appealing and it must have showed on my face. Gabriella smiled kindly and said, "That was really why I kept silent. After what you did for me, it would have been unforgivable if I'd given them your name. I just wanted to get out of hospital quickly, so I could find you and thank you in person. Of course, I assumed you knew what you'd done."

I shrugged apologetically. She was finally warm enough to remove the overcoat, draping it over the chair next to her.

"You're still not sure, are you?" she said.

"Can you blame me?"

"Not really, but I feel bound to try and persuade you. You have to know what you are."

"And what is that?"

She was about to rush into an answer and then checked herself. After a considered pause, she replied, "I'm not sure what the name is, but it's something very special. Something *vital*. It's far too precious to be shrouded in ignorance, Christian."

I bit my lip. I said, "You're really convinced, aren't you?"

"I *know* what happened. You saw the wounds yourself. I could show you there are no marks there now."

"I'm sure you could but that wouldn't solve the problem. For one thing, I knew about the bleeding. Or I thought I did."

"What do you mean?"

"When I was holding you, I saw blood spreading across my shirt. But afterwards, there was nothing to see, no marks of any kind. Besides, I hadn't been hurt, so how could it be? And since I didn't want to be involved – I was frightened and wanted to forget – it was easier to bow to logic than ask awkward questions. I told myself it was the mind playing tricks on me, at a time when I was scared and stressed."

"That's understandable."

"I knew it wasn't right, though. I guess I was hoping that if I ignored it long enough, it would just go away."

She smiled sympathetically. I tore open a sachet of sugar and poured it into my cup, hoping it would mask some of the taste. I recalled the lacerations on her body, all similar in size and shape, pumping blood over her rich skin, staining her clothes and mine.

"Even now," I continued, "I still have doubts. Bleeding is one thing, but healing is quite another."

"Of course you have doubts. You're *right* to have them. But if you've made the leap of faith in accepting the bleeding, you don't have much further to go to accept the healing."

"I haven't accepted anything yet."

I took another Marlboro from the pack and lit it. If I had bled without wounds, there had to be a reason for it. Could it be healing? It seemed ridiculous, but under the circumstances, would any suggestion seem reasonable?

"What did it feel like?" I asked.

She put her elbows on the table, interlocked the fingers of her hands and rested her chin on them. She looked upwards for a few moments.

"Well," she said, slowly, "it was an odd mixture, really. Firstly, it was incredibly hot, especially where your hands touched my skin. And then there was a sort of . . . I don't know quite how to describe it . . . a sort of *pouring* sensation. I could feel something flowing in me. It was like molten lava coming through your hands. It filled my entire body; a brilliant burning. The whole experience was very painful, and yet . . ."

Gabriella bit her lip and considered the memory. Outside, on the pavement, a three-legged dog stood uneasily on the kerb and watched the traffic passing by.

"It was painful but I never wanted it to end," she said. "It was simultaneously agony and ecstasy. The intense heat completely superseded the pains of my injuries and, when it was over, I couldn't even feel where I'd been stabbed."

She had been so hot and I had been so cold. A phone was ringing from the back of the café. The old woman asked the fat owner if he was going to answer it, and he told her to shut up and mind her own business.

"I have a suggestion," said Gabriella.

She took a deep breath and leaned forward, spreading her hands over the Formica. The café owner was turning down the volume of his radio as he reached for the phone.

"Don't answer too hastily," she told me, "and don't laugh."

I nodded. A taxi's tyres squealed in the rain as it stopped at a red light.

She said, "Why don't you try to do it again?"

The words fermented in my mind for a moment. I nearly did laugh, but not out of amusement, more out of surprise.

"You're not serious, are you?" I asked.

"Why not?"

"Because it's absurd."

"Why?"

"Well," I began, "it's . . . it's . . . well, it just is!"

"Not at all," she insisted, confidently. "It's an excellent suggestion because you have nothing to lose. Think about it."

I smiled. "I don't need to think about it to know it's crazy."

She took my hand and said, "The only reason you say it's stupid is because you're frightened of discovering the truth."

Gabriella was right, of course. I was terrified of the truth. We sat in the café drinking more of its grim coffee and braving a little of its cooking; grey chicken and a weary salad, decomposing on a fractured plate. All she asked of me was that I consider her suggestion and allow her to make contact again, in a few days, to see if I had come round to her idea. I agreed to the request because I needed time to think.

When I returned to Parke Millen, real work was impossible. I went through the motions, unaware of the few trades I made. I expect I lost money for my clients, but they could stand it. I'd made plenty for all of them in the past.

In my dehumanizing office block, I felt strangely secure. Countless questions shimmered before me, but I didn't feel overawed by them, as I had done at certain times since I chanced across Gabriella in the car park.

I no longer had any realistic doubts over her claim to be the victim. In fact, I found myself in the curious position of believing her entirely, and yet not believing in my power to heal, despite that being an integral part of her story. It felt like she was talking about a different Christian Floyd.

Just as I believed she was the victim, so I now fully believed I'd bled. Yet despite this, I couldn't make the final leap to accepting I could heal. It was like the end of the rainbow: I reached for it and it edged further away, always just out of my grasp.

I kept asking myself the same question that had bothered me ever since the bleeding: Why me? And the answer was so obvious. Why not? Being part of a crowd is no guarantee that you won't get singled out. Someone has to be.

I tried to imagine what would happen if, in fact, it turned out that Gabriella was right and that I had healed her. How would my life change? The possibilities were too numerous to calculate. The uncertainty of it excited me. Given my strong preference for security and order, contemplation of the unknown was bound to make me nervous.

The rest of Monday was pointless. I couldn't concentrate on anything else. At three-thirty, I rose from my desk to leave.

"Where are you going?" asked Danny.

"Home. I can't do ... this. Not now."

Danny and Chantal looked at each other. This was

something shocking for them; the workaholic dismissing his drug. She said, "Are you feeling ill?"

"Not ill. But . . ."

The prospect of investigation became more tantalizing the more I considered it. I barely noticed Katy that evening and she decided to go back to her own home, down in Wandsworth. I slept like the dead that night, not waking when my alarm rang at five-thirty. I called in sick and took Tuesday off; a new experience for me.

The bleeding's terrible cold had dazed me. My memories of that phase were indistinct. The glaciers had crept through me and my hands smouldered on her torn skin. Bleeding and healing. I'd done one, but as for the other . . .?

On Wednesday, I felt more together and returned to work. By now, something else had occurred to me. Why had Gabriella urged me to abandon her in the car park? I'd previously assumed it was out of some notion of gratitude for rescuing her. That had never been a satisfactory theory and now I had a better one: she realized what had happened to her and foresaw the trouble ahead. That made more sense, provided I accepted that I had actually healed her.

I'd had several days of almost continuous contemplation of the matter. By Wednesday evening, I was entertaining the possibility that she might be right. There had to be a reason for the bleeding and I hadn't come up with a better one than hers.

Thursday night, exactly one week after my adventure in the car park, was the night of the Heart-Shaped Ball, for which Katy had organized two tables of a dozen. I couldn't deny that these events raised important sums of cash for charities which certainly deserved the attention, but I often wondered what percentage of the ticket price actually made it to the good cause. For my own part, I would rather have donated the entire ticket price straight to the charity concerned. And if it meant I didn't have to actually attend, I'd probably write a cheque for twice the amount. But any complaint from me would be greeted with a guaranteed reply.

"You love it once you get there!"

This wasn't even hopelessly optimistic. It was just wrong. Some people like train-spotting, some don't. Some like charity balls, some don't. But the suggestion that enjoyment of a fund-raiser might be subject to individual personal preference was greeted with derision by both Katy and her mother.

"Ridiculous! Everyone has an absolutely *wonderful* time!"

So, I'd learned to grin and bear it because the price of dissent was too high. I kept my opinions to myself for the twenty-four hours on either side of an event, wore an air steward's plastic grin and went through the motions.

Katy looked elegant in a ball-gown of a blue so rich it was almost purple. Her mother gave it to her for her last birthday, in addition to the silver choker and the week at a remote health farm. Louise Donaldson won that in a raffle but since alcohol was prohibited, she'd passed on the prize to her daughter. The choker clung tightly to Katy's neck, accentuating its slimness and delicacy.

I stood in front of a mirror, adjusting my tie, humming "I Want To Marry A Lighthouse Keeper" and thinking of *A Clockwork Orange*. It was the same whenever I heard "Singin' In The Rain". I never thought of Gene Kelly in the street, but rather of Alex, the teenage teara-way, singing it in the bath. He made compassion seem like a terrible weakness. I always envied Alex for his purity.

The phone rang and Katy answered it. "It's for you," she called out.

I went over to the phone and picked it up. "Hello?"

"Christian? It's Gabriella."

I could still hear the hard echo from the phone in the living-room so I said, rather pointedly, "Thank you, Katy."

There was a click. Gabriella sounded amused. "And that was?"

"Katy," I replied. "She's a . . . friend."

It sounded clumsy and deceitful and I felt embarrassed. "Of course."

"This is quite a coincidence," I told her, quickly trying to move the conversation on.

"It is?"

"I've been thinking about what you said. I can't get it out of my mind. All day and all night . . . it's all I ever think about."

"And have you come to any conclusion?"

"I decided I should be a little more open-minded."

"Meaning?"

"Meaning you might have a point. I can't find a better explanation for what happened to me than what you've suggested. God knows, I've tried. I've exhausted every wacky theory you could possibly imagine and none of them are better than yours."

"But you've still got doubts?"

"Plenty."

"So what about trying to do it again?"

"I don't know, Gabriella. If something came along and I . . . and I felt I might somehow make a difference, then maybe."

There was a moment's pause before she said, "That's good news, Christian. It really is. Just to consider it is a step forward. I'd really like to see you, to talk about it."

I cleared my throat. "Fine."

"There's still so much to discuss that we can't share with anyone else. Could we meet this evening, perhaps?"

"I'm busy. How about tomorrow night? Can you make that?"

"For sure."

"Good. Listen, I'm rather rushed at the moment, so could . . ."

"Oh, I understand," said Gabriella, sounding almost sly. I imagined she was grinning.

". . . could we talk about this tomorrow? I'll call you from the office, or you can call me."

"I'll give you my telephone number," she said, "in case you want to beat me to it."

I put the phone down and continued to wrestle with a stubborn cuff-link. Katy appeared in the doorway, holding a long-stemmed glass of wine. From the living-room I could just make out Bryan Ferry singing "In Every Dream Home A Heartache".

"Who was that?" asked Katy, as though she wasn't really interested and might just as easily have asked any one of a million other questions.

I could excel at indifference too. "No one in particular," I said, making a play out of searching for my second cuff-link.

Katy leaned forward and gave it to me. "No one?"

"Her name's Gabriella. She works in our Italian office in Milan. She's over here for a few days."

Anything was better than the truth. I succeeded with the second cuff-link, strapped on a watch and looked for my jacket.

"Do you know her well?" enquired Katy.

"Well enough. We speak on the phone quite a lot."

"And you see her when you're in Milan?"

I couldn't resist a smile and that irritated Katy, just as it would have annoyed me had our positions been reversed.

"Really," I insisted, "there's nothing to worry about. She's a twenty-five stone Jehovah's witness, you know."

"She's got a sexy voice," said Katy, flatly.

"So have you, when you're angry."

I tried to imagine how Katy would react if she knew the truth. Suppose she saw me down in the dirt, clutching

Gabriella's limp body to my chest, leaking boiling blood over her ripped flesh. If I told her what I'd felt, would she listen? Could I trust her with the truth? Since it wouldn't be convenient, probably not.

I moved through to the kitchen where I began to pour vodka in a glass. A stiff drink would be the least of my requirements to see me through the night. She appeared in the doorway.

"You look lovely," I told her.

"Thanks," she said, while she adjusted an earring. "By the way, my parents are bringing some friends of theirs that they want you to meet. So please be polite and charming."

I forced a slim smile across my lips and said, "Of course."

I watched Katy as she retreated towards the bedroom, but I was thinking about Gabriella screaming for help.

# Chapter Seven

Red and silver hearts filled with helium rose towards the ceiling but were anchored by multi-coloured ribbons. The balloons looked like monstrous flowers of foil. There were hundreds of them throughout the ballroom.

A light shone vertically onto the floral arrangement at the centre of my table. Plumes of blue cigarette smoke twisted and climbed in its beam. I always believed it was rude to smoke while others ate but, having tried the chicken, I felt the duty to abstain lay with the eaters. Looking around the table, it seemed I was not alone. The overcooked chicken breast had been drowned in a tasteless cream sauce. The new potatoes were under-cooked and the carrots were almost soup. The white wine was warm. The red wine was too acidic. I ordered a vodka and tonic with a handful of ice.

The Heart-Shaped Ball was in full swing. The guests ranged from twenty-one to ninety-nine. There were aristo-crats, actors and actresses. There were too many minor television celebrities, plenty of gossip columnists, and an army of photographers. Bloated captains of industry held whisky tumblers to their swollen bellies, chomped on thick, soggy cigars, and exchanged views on the upcoming election. The "artistic" contingent air-kissed too much. Media personalities introduced themselves forcefully, before anyone ever had the chance to ask, "And you are . . .?"

I saw a crusty duke having his photo taken with a crusty rock 'n' roll dinosaur. It was hard to tell who gained most pleasure from the experience. Both had survived the ravages of drink, drugs and tabloid journalism. The middle-aged superstar was accompanied by an under-age partner. She stood to one side, admiring the way light danced off the large diamond bracelet which encircled her wrist like a handcuff.

Laughter was the aural wallpaper. Sometimes it bellowed, sometimes it twittered but wherever you were, it was inescapable. It filleted conversations, reducing them to meaningless clusters of words.

Katy sat at the other table she had organized, along with the pick of her guests. She was having such a good time. At the table where I sat, merriment seemed to be taboo. Given my mood, that suited me fine. As we entered the ballroom, Katy had put her hand on my shoulder, kissed me on the cheek and said, "I've placed you between Morag McDurrie and Julia Graham. Is that all right? Please look after Julia. Johnny brought her and she doesn't know anyone else. We met her once, a couple of years ago. Plain girl. Remember?"

I didn't *need* to remember. The pleasure in her voice said it all: I was to be sandwiched between Morag McDurrie and whoever had been persuaded to accompany John Cartwright. Since his reputation as a social leper was undisputed, I couldn't look forward to sitting next to his partner with any great relish.

Had Morag McDurrie been appearing on *Mastermind* her chosen subject would have been "The Man On My Left". I was on her right. On the few occasions I did turn to speak to her, I was presented with her unattractive upper-back and bony shoulders. In the end, I gave up even trying to be polite.

Julia Graham, on the other hand, was a bonus and a mystery. Katy's idea of her as a "plain girl" took a beating as soon as I saw her. She was tall and slim with long blonde hair. In a clinging turquoise dress which raised many a bushy, greying eyebrow, she cut a striking pose. As it transpired, her attitude was made to match. She had a refreshing talent for plain-speaking. All in all, she wasn't the dull disaster I had every right to expect and that was the bonus. The mystery was what she was doing with John Cartwright.

He was a man with the physical appeal of a spider. When he moved, he scuttled. You didn't have to touch his skin to know it was clammy; you could see it in the white glow. But his unattractive appearance was actually his greatest asset. The really killing element of Cartwright was his character. He was King Bore. Even the kindest souls were exasperated by the effortless ease with which he could butcher the most lively gathering, reducing it from fun to funereal with a phrase. Julia Graham and John Cartwright made as natural partners as Germaine Greer and Bernard Manning.

Julia put a cigarette between her lips and I lit it for her.

"Thanks," she said, shifting away from the man on her right. She gave a small backwards flick of the head and asked, quietly, "Who is he?"

I took a look and shrugged. "No idea."

"Well, take it from me, it's not worth finding out. He's about as tedious as . . ."

"As John Cartwright?"

She smiled and took a drag from her cigarette. "You're Christian, right?"

I nodded.

"Julia Graham," she said, extending a hand. "Forgive me for being so rude, but I couldn't get him to be quiet."

"That's all right. I was fine."

"Really? It didn't look as though you were getting much joy from your left."

"Oh, I don't know. Sometimes, silence can be golden. I don't know who she's talking to, but he must be an expert on fox-hunting or something, otherwise Morag wouldn't . . ."

"*Morag?*"

It was my turn to smile. "Lovely, isn't it? Morag McDurrie. Have you met her two sisters, Spatula and Brake Fluid?"

Julia said, "Her parents must have wanted a son really badly to give her a name like that."

I laughed and lit a cigarette for myself. Somebody on the other side of the table knocked over a glass of red wine. The liquid tumbled into the lap of a girl in a cream taffeta dress. My collar felt too tight around my throat.

Julia and I tumbled easily into casual conversation and my mood brightened significantly. She had a sharp wit and I imagined getting into an argument with her would be a miserable experience. The steel core was never far beneath the inviting surface. But our attitudes were compatible that evening and we took pleasure from the vicious things we said about those around us. In view of what I felt about Katy, I revelled in the bitter fashion of our flirting.

"So how come you ended up here?" I wondered.

"Because John invited me."

"Is that a good reason?"

"Probably not."

"How do you know him?"

"We grew up together. Our parents were friends."

"I see. And so you jumped at the opportunity when he offered you the chance of enjoying his company for the evening?"

"I wasn't doing anything else this evening, so I thought, why not? Then I remembered why not, but by that stage, it was too late. And once the man on my right had given me half an hour of his stimulating thoughts on the nature of the computer virus, I really thought I'd made a terrible mistake."

I nodded in sympathy. "I can see that."

"But who knows?" she said, breaking into a sly smile. "The evening may not be a total loss, after all. Excuse me."

Julia rose from her chair and walked towards the cloakroom. I got another drink. While she was away, Jorge came over to talk to me.

"Is that Katy's 'plain' friend?" he asked.

"That's right."

"She must be out of her mind putting you next to her."

"What do you mean?"

"Come on! Even from over there, where I'm sitting, it's obvious. She wants you for breakfast."

I wasn't about to declare that it was mutual. Not even to Jorge. I broke a bread roll in half and said, "It's just games."

"Oh yeah? Well they look like the kind of games I wish I was playing. Anyway, the reason I came over was to say goodbye."

"You leaving already?"

"I need the sleep. I'm going to Madrid in a few hours. Remember? I've got to be at the airport by six-thirty and I haven't even started to pack, let alone sober up."

"When are you coming back?"

"I don't know yet. But I'll be there next week, when you're passing through. So give me a call and we'll have a good time."

"Sure."

He rose from Julia's chair and then leaned forward, putting his hand on my shoulder. His good humour had suddenly evaporated.

"By the way, Katy tells me you've been arguing again. What you two do in private is your own business, but you might try and discourage her from making it public."

I looked up at him and said, "What?"

He nodded sadly. "It may be the drink, but she's been a little bitchy, and for the people around the table it's been ... well, it's been embarrassing."

I drained my tall glass. A fat lady with a dog collar of pearls around her jowly neck got up onto the stage. Jorge gently shook me by the shoulder to recapture my attention. He must have seen what I felt; the blood draining away.

"It hurts me to even say it, Christian. I'm only telling you this because I'm a friend. I'm not trying to interfere."

"I know. And thanks."

"You should sort it out."

I lit a Marlboro and looked up at him. "Don't worry," I assured him. "I will. You can count on it."

Jorge left and I sucked the cigarette's poison into the very deepest part of my lungs. The lights dimmed and the fat lady on the stage tapped the microphone to make sure it was working. The clinking of her jewellery echoed through the ballroom. The metallic amplification of her voice cut through my head like a blow-torch through butter.

"Good evening to you all and, on behalf of the committee, may I say how lovely it is to see so many old friends here tonight, and to be making so many new ones. As many of you know..."

I wasn't sure whether news of Katy's verbal indiscretion left me angry or sad. Our disintegration was becoming painless. I found her at the back of the ballroom, by one of the bars. She clutched a glass of champagne in one hand and Justin Whitehead in the other, hanging onto his arm for support. She was kissing him on the cheek as I appeared from behind an urn crammed with red roses. I felt peculiarly indifferent to her embarrassing display.

"There you are, darling!" she exclaimed, turning to me unsteadily. "Are you having fun?"

"Not yet. And you?"

She raised her glass to me, spilled half the drink onto the carpet and replied, "Naturally."

"You're drunk," I told her, flatly.

Justin Whitehead looked uncomfortable with the tension. "Maybe I should leave you two to it?" he suggested.

"Nonsense!" replied Katy. "Christian won't mind if you stay while we . . ."

"No need," I said. "I'm the one who's leaving."

"God you're a bore!" concluded Katy, rolling her eyes upwards.

The more drunk she looked, the more sober I felt.

"Perhaps, but at least I'm not an embarrassment."

*"What?"* she snapped, lurching dramatically. Only her grip on Whitehead appeared to save her from the humiliating fall which would have underlined my point so well.

"I understand you've been entertaining everyone at your table by cracking jokes at my expense, but no one's been laughing. Perhaps if you'd been a little less inebriated, you might have recognized this and changed tack."

Katy's mouth opened but she couldn't force the words out. Justin Whitehead seemed equally stunned.

"But all's not lost," I continued, dryly. "If you were to shut your mouth for the rest of the evening, you'd give the poor bastards at your table a chance to resurrect some party spirit. Do you think you could manage that?"

Whitehead looked outraged, but before he could utter a syllable, I pointed a finger at him. "Don't say a word!"

"You bastard!" hissed Katy, through clenched teeth. "You really are the fucking worst!"

"Probably," I conceded. "At least in that, if in nothing else, it seems we were made for each other."

The three of us stood in a silent triangle. Katy and I looked into each other's dead eyes. Instead of throwing champagne, tantrums or slaps, we stood still. For a few moments, nothing happened and then Katy turned away.

A round of applause filled the ballroom as the speech from the stage came to an end. The lights dimmed further and the twelve-piece band burst into life with "Take The 'A' Train". I pushed past corpulent figures who filled their clothes to bursting point. The hazy ceiling of cigar and cigarette smoke hovered just above head-height. The air was hot and sour. Patent leather shoes ground dying cigarette butts into the carpet. Fat lips slobbered over baggy cheeks. Insincerity ruled and I made my way for the exit.

"That was quite a performance between you and your intended," declared Julia Graham. I stopped and looked down. She was sitting on a sofa outside the ballroom, relaxing in relative tranquillity with a cigarette. She rose slowly, smoothing away a few imaginary creases in her dress.

"She's not my intended."

"You could have fooled me."

"Evidently."

She smiled and said, "So, where were you heading at such speed?"

"As far away from here as I can get."

She stubbed out her cigarette. "How about a drink?"

Our eyes met and her gaze seemed to confirm what the offer suggested. It sparkled with intent and I succumbed to the adrenalin rush. I said, "A drink?"

As the taxi pulled away from the kerb, I watched the hotel recede and then kissed Julia. She moved her body closer to mine, sliding over the seat and threading an arm around my neck. I briefly caught the driver's eye in his rear-view mirror. His overhead radio crackled.

We came to a halt, just off Eaton Square. Julia Graham lived on the fourth floor of a five-storey house which had been converted into flats. Marble steps rose from the pavement to the entrance; a beautifully polished door, flanked by two tall, narrow windows with a black wrought-iron grille over each. A security-camera looked down on the doorway from a bracket above the left window.

I paid the driver.

"Thanks, mate. Have a good evening," he said, as I handed him a generous tip.

"I'll try."

As I approached the door, Julia was looking for the key in her purse. I put my arms around her waist. She turned round and we kissed on the top step.

"Feeling good?" she whispered.

"I'm feeling something," I confessed, with a grin, "but I'm not sure I'd call it good."

She ran a finger over my lips. "You know something? I'm surprised you're even here."

"Because of Katy?"

"Of course."

"She's not a good argument against infidelity. At least, not tonight."

Julia smiled. "How fortunate."

She turned round to unlock the front door and I had my one moment of doubt. All the wholesome reasons to resist rose up in front of me. I was haunted by notions of decency, fidelity, honesty, propriety and morality. But I thought of Katy's drunken bitching and then I looked at Julia. Lust blasted away all my reservations. I'd leave them for the morning.

Her key produced a thick clunk from the heavy lock. As she pushed the door slightly, she peered through a side-window and muttered, "Oh, shit!"

"What's up?"

"It's Mr Leonard. He lives in the apartment on the ground floor and he's the nosiest old fool you've ever met. He spends all day waiting for people to come and go. He listens for the front door and then comes out to stick his nose in. He *especially* disapproves of late-night visitors, so please be quiet."

I ran three fingers down her spine as she pushed the door open and we stepped into the warmth. A chandelier hung from the high ceiling, sparkling brilliantly. I noticed another, smaller security-camera covering the hall. There was a cage lift at the far end, around which a staircase rose in a squared spiral. Two large prints in gilt frames hung on the right wall. On the left, there was a large oval mirror in an elaborate bronze frame, above a small table with a marble top and curved legs of polished mahogany. Dried flowers of magenta, rust and mustard rose from a china vase. There was a deep blue strip of carpet which stretched from the front door to the lift. At the foot of the stairs, on the left, there was an apartment door, which was partially opened.

"Who is it?" croaked a voice that had been brutalized by smoking.

"It's me, Mr Leonard. Julia Graham."

"Ah, Miss Graham," said the voice. "It's rather late in the evening, isn't it?"

Frail fingers appeared round the edge of the door, gripping the wood for support.

"I'm that sort of person, Mr Leonard. A night person."

"That makes you sound like a vampire!" he replied, with a fragile chuckle which seemed to rattle his ribs.

Julia turned to me and I frowned because I couldn't quite understand what was happening. She blew me a kiss to complicate my feelings.

Mr Leonard appeared from behind his door. A pair of thick-framed glasses masked his eyes. The lenses were tinted. He had a beak for a nose and skin which looked dehydrated. A hand of protruding sinews and long, crooked fingers moved slowly over a tanned scalp with its thin blanket of pure white hair. He didn't look at me.

Julia pressed a button on the brass panel and the doors to the cage lift lurched open, clinking as they parted. She stared at me and mouthed the words "I want to fuck you". I could feel myself blushing and glanced at Mr Leonard, who was as motionless as a statue. Julia was delighted by my confusion. She hitched up her dress and wriggled slowly out of some shamefully insubstantial underwear, which pooled around her ankles. It was a wicked and delightful performance. And under the circumstances, I found it completely shocking. My mouth turned to dust. It was only then, when I looked across at Mr Leonard, that I realized. She was in his view, but he hadn't even flinched. It seemed he was totally blind.

"Are you alone?" he asked Julia, completely unmoved by the display.

"No," she admitted. "I've got company."

She picked up her flimsy underwear from the floor. My evident bewilderment contributed to her glee. She could barely suppress the giggles which were rising to the surface. I didn't know whether to be amused, annoyed or outraged.

"Is your guest a gentleman or a lady?" he enquired.

"A gentleman," she announced before moving into the lift and pressing herself against the back of it. "A cousin, in fact."

"What a large family you must come from to have so many cousins who visit you," he exclaimed, turning his head left and then right.

If Mr Leonard was hoping to make me feel like a sexual convenience, then he partly succeeded. It didn't seem to worry Julia, though.

"That's Catholicism for you!" she replied, waiting for me in the lift, like a hooker who'd already started the clock. But I couldn't follow her.

Fate took delight in scuppering my lusty ambition. Pure desire urged me to join Julia in some sticky union, starting in the lift and ending up somewhere in her apartment. But that wasn't what happened.

Mr Leonard looked mean, like those miserable old men who scare young children. His cheekbones were angular, leaving shadows for cheeks. Without any warning, I removed his glasses, plucking them free of his beak-shaped nose before he could get his hands to his face. His useless eyes bobbled in their recessed sockets. Even without the glasses, it was hard to see his pupils. The chandelier sent sparkling rods of light through the hall and their brilliance hurt him. He blinked furiously.

"What ... *what* are you doing?" he cried, in a trembling voice.

"I'm going to touch your eyes."

Julia pushed her head out of the lift, as I placed Mr Leonard's glasses on the marble tabletop and took his head in my hands. I didn't really know what I was doing, but I submitted to some strange guiding instinct. My thumbs slowly moved into the cave cast by his protruding brow. I found the eyeballs crouching in the dark at the back, frightened to come out into the light. I sensed their wild movement beneath the tissue-thin skin of his eyelids. One good thrust from both digits and Mr Leonard would have no eyes to heal, and I would have warm jelly dribbling over my wrists.

"Jesus Christ!" yelped Julia. "What the hell are you doing?"

That was when the cold spirit entered into me. Or maybe it had always been there, concealed and dormant, and I simply shook off its lethargy. However it happened, the ice flowed through me for the second time and, like the first, it filled me completely.

The coldness hurt. As if I'd just plunged into an icy sea, my lungs were shocked into semi-paralysis. But a prickly heat started to spread across the palm of each hand. They grew wetter and hotter. I felt liquid soaking my socks and shoes. It oozed between the toes. A sudden sharp pain in my side made me wince and I felt the scorching streams start to flow. The blood seeped freely from the wounds. In my mind, I was staggering through an emotional blizzard.

Julia stumbled backwards with a hand across her mouth. Mr Leonard started to groan as my fingers pressed more deeply. His frail hands held my wrists, but instead of trying to reject me, he was forcing more pressure onto them. The discomfort started to make him cry out, but his encouraging grip grew stronger. My thumbs felt as though they had pressed past the eyeballs and were embedded in the clay of his brain. I couldn't feel the floor beneath my feet.

"Stop it!" screamed Julia. "For God's sake, Christian, please stop it!"

"*No!*" gasped Mr Leonard.

She was too frightened to intervene. I pressed my hands together so tightly I thought I would crush the frail porcelain of his skull, compressing bone, blood, flesh and skin into a wafer-thin disk.

Julia's panic-stricken screaming gave way to straightforward sobbing. She collapsed onto the stairs, with her head in her hands and tepid tears spilling onto the deep blue carpet.

I don't really know how long it lasted, but when the freezing ceased, reality and clarity began to return. I examined my burning hands. Blood was ebbing out of the creases on the palms. On the back, there were ugly blemishes, swollen bruises which rose up out of the flesh.

I reached for the wall and slid to the floor. I was shaking as my clumsy fingers wrenched my shoes and socks off. Both feet were drenched in blood and there were marks on the top and sole of each, similar to those on the back of my hands. They didn't look like proper flesh wounds, but more like weeping scars; blood leaking from the rough skin of cauterized lacerations. While I watched and felt the fluid oozing out, there was no pain at all. I rose unsteadily to my feet and ripped open my stained shirt. My left side was bleeding profusely and I prodded the area gently. It felt vile and rubbery. The heat was amazing. My fingers tugged my shirt further back, so I could get a proper look at it.

"Oh no! Oh my God!" shrieked Julia, when she looked up and saw the wounds.

She was sitting on the third step of the staircase. Above her, on the half-landing, stood two men. One wore a silk dressing-gown with an olive paisley design. The other had pulled on jeans and a sweatshirt. What they saw rendered them speechless. Mr Leonard lay on the floor, with his head propped up by the bespattered wall. He was crying blood. Scarlet tears rolled over his jagged cheeks. He wasn't moving at all. His left arm was pinned beneath his twisted body.

I was desperately short of breath. My damaged vision made me unsteady. I wanted to lie down and sleep for a decade. The icy tide was receding, leaving a peculiar numbness in its frigid wake.

"Christian!" howled Julia. "What have you done?"

"What's going on down there?" yelled a woman from upstairs. "Shall I call the police?"

The two men on the landing were dumbstruck, still unable to comprehend the scene. Mr Leonard groaned and coughed as he tried to free his trapped arm.

"Mr Leonard?" said the man in the jeans.

The old man slowly rolled onto his side and started to wipe away the blood from his face. Nobody else moved. His glasses were still sitting on the marble tabletop. There were drops of blood on the left lens. His efforts to clean himself just seemed to smear the hot liquid across more parched skin, like some morbid moisturizer. He blinked like before, as though the light was still hurting him. Julia's wailing subsided and she lapsed into the silence of shock. She peeped through the mask of thin fingers which covered her face.

Mr Leonard was on all fours by now, slowly going through the stages to standing. He was hunched, with his head drooping, as though he were about to be sick. Drops of blood fell from the tip of his nose, exploding on the marble. He put a finger through a puddle and raised it to his face, squinting fiercely as he did it.

"Blood," he sighed, softly.

He blinked again before brushing his face with his sleeve.

"What?" breathed Julia, disbelieving her ears, just as Mr Leonard found it hard to believe his eyes.

He lifted his head and stared right at her. A nervous smile cracked across his mean mouth. He looked left and right, up and down, and then back at Julia.

"That's a . . . lovely blue dress . . . you're wearing, Miss Graham," he said in a faltering voice.

The two men on the half-landing looked at each other. Julia's make-up had run down her cheeks in grubby, uneven lines. She ran the back of her hand across her face.

He watched her do it and whispered, "I can see!"

Julia froze. "What?"

"I can see."

"What's going on? Is this some sort of joke?" snapped the man in the dressing-gown.

"No," insisted Mr Leonard, cautiously. "I *can* see. I can see both of you standing up there, and I can see Miss Graham and I can see . . . ."

He looked up at me.

"I don't believe it," muttered the man in the jeans.

"What have you done to my eyes?" whispered Mr Leonard.

"*What* can you see?" I asked.

"Everything. It's a little blurred but I can see colour and shapes and people and . . . everything."

The smile spread across his bloody face. I felt fatigue clawing at me like extra gravity, dragging me down towards a coma-like sleep. My eyes stung with the futile effort of trying to find perfect focus.

Mr Leonard looked around in amazement and said, "I never imagined you'd look the way you do, Miss Graham.

You're such an attractive young lady, even more than you were in my head. And blonde too! I always pictured you as a brunette."

I stretched my arms out and dropped my head back, letting out a deep sigh to release the tension. I looked at my outstretched arms under the chandelier's dancing light. The blood glistened beautifully on me. I closed my eyes and concentrated on the natural warmth returning to my veins. The sticky streams were drying up, cloying on my skin. The rage in my mind had calmed, leaving a post-storm lull, a sense of tranquillity. I was complete.

I stepped into my shoes and said, "I don't know what happens now, Mr Leonard, but you should probably get some rest."

He looked at me with a sense of urgency in his repaired eyes. "Are you out of your mind?" he muttered. "I can't rest now! I've too much to see!"

"Trust me, you won't relapse. You'll have plenty of time to see everything you want."

I wasn't sure how I could be so confident about that, but I was.

"Wait!" said the man in the jeans, as I turned for the door. "You can't just leave! I mean, shouldn't we get a doctor or something? What about a check-up? Or the police? What do we do?"

"Do whatever you want to do. I'll tell you one thing, though: this hall needs a cleaner more than Mr Leonard needs a doctor."

Julia raised her eyes from the carpet to meet my gaze. I held out my hands apologetically and said, "I'm sorry."

"Please don't go!" cried Mr Leonard, as I pulled the door open. "I ... I ... thank you. I don't know ... what ... I ..."

"It doesn't matter," I told him.

"But how did you do it?"

I shrugged and said, "I don't know." Then I left.

The streets were largely deserted because it was wet and late. I couldn't go home. Not now. I staggered to a pay-phone and dialled the number Gabriella had given me before I went to The Heart-Shaped Ball. She was sleepy and muddled.

I was slumped against the edge of the phone-box, afraid that I'd collapse. "I need to see you," I said.

"Do you know what time it is?"

"Please! It's important."

"What is it?"

"You were right."

"*What?*"

She gave me her address. Half an hour later, she greeted me on her doorstep. I opened my coat to reveal my shirt and then held up my hands so she could see the stained palms.

# Chapter Eight

"Oh my God!" she exclaimed, taking a step back into the gloom.

My muscles felt like soup. Gabriella quickly tried to regain her composure. She stepped into the drizzle and gently took hold of my hand. I was shaking; a combination of physical exertion and the fever of fear.

"Are you okay?" she asked.

I opened my mouth but didn't say anything. My throat was dry. I stared at her and shook my head. She was wearing torn jeans and a black cotton shirt. She tugged the cuff absentmindedly. I could see the concern she was trying to hide. She guided me out of the rain.

"It'll be all right," she assured me.

She led me into a narrow hall and up some creaking stairs. The damp plaster was crumbling off the wall and onto the worn carpet. Gabriella's flat was the top two floors of a house in Pimlico. It wasn't a large building, but the landlord had still found space for two more apartments beneath Gabriella's. At the top of the staircase, she ushered me through her own front door and then into the kitchen. The harsh glare of fluorescent lighting revealed my true condition.

Only now was I starting to appreciate the true significance of what I'd done. Rescuing Gabriella had been an act which left uncertainty in its wake . . . until the moment I reached out and touched his eyes. Healing Mr Leonard was all the proof I would ever need. And now that her claims had been confirmed, I was terrified. I didn't know how it had happened, why it had happened, or, most worryingly, what was *yet* to happen.

My shaking grew worse and I felt tears welling in my eyes, further blurring my vision. Gabriella led me to a frail chair by the kitchen table. I buried my head in my hands and tried to stop myself from crying. She touched my shoulders softly.

"I shouldn't have done it," I muttered to myself.

"Done what?"

If I'd left him alone, I could have avoided whatever was now going to befall me. I could have got on with my normal life and written off the incident in the car park as a freak adventure, a once-in-a-lifetime aberration. And even though I'd always know that wasn't entirely true – that there was something more – I'd still be able to live with it. A little self-deceit would have been an acceptable tariff, a price well worth paying. But that was no longer an option.

"What did you do?" asked Gabriella.

I mumbled into my hands, "I healed a blind man."

"What?"

"I reached out and touched his eyes and . . ."

She'd moved round to face me. I looked up at her through my bloody fingers. She put her hands on her hips, cocked her head to one side and tried to lighten the mood. "You said you were too busy to see me this evening, and now I know why."

I shrugged hopelessly. "What the fuck am I going to do?"

I wanted to cry, shout, run away, get drunk, tear my hair out, something, *anything*. Instead, I sat there trembling, trying to light a cigarette. I dropped the pack and the cigarettes spilled across the floor. Gabriella bent down to pick them up and handed me one.

"You've got to calm down," she said. "You'll never . . ."

"Calm down? *Calm down?* How am I supposed to do

that? *Jesus Christ!* I just healed a man. Like in the bloody Bible! How can I possibly . . .?"

"You healed me too. Remember?"

"I don't know what to do!" I cried, my hands clenched into fists. "I'm desperate! What the hell have I done? *What am I?*"

My fingers couldn't operate the lighter. Gabriella knelt before me and eased it out of my grasp. She flicked the switch and brought the yellow flame to the end of my quivering cigarette. I sucked heavily on it. I held my breath for a second and then stepped back from absolute breakdown.

She appeared so calm, it was disarming. She put her hands on her knees, looked up at me with kind eyes and said, "What you've done is something marvellous. Whatever else may happen, never forget it. *Never.*"

I was as jittery as a drug-starved junkie. I scratched the wooden table at my side, gathering small splinters beneath the fingernails. I didn't notice them. I bit my lip while my eyes darted around the kitchen, resting on nothing. I was tired but I was restless; the body was shattered, but the mind was in overdrive.

Gabriella said, in as soothing a tone as she could muster, "What exactly did you do?"

I thought about it as I watched the smoke slinking upwards from the orange tip of the cigarette. "I healed this man. He was blind and . . . and I just . . . I'm not sure."

"What do you mean?"

I frowned as I tried to remember. "Well, I took off his glasses and I touched his face and then . . . it was . . . it was *automatic*. It was instinct, I guess. My fingers were sliding over his eyes and there was blood and . . . screaming."

"Screaming?"

"There were people there."

Gabriella averted her gaze and then stood up. She took

a saucer from the drying rack by the sink and offered it to me as an ashtray. "Would you like some coffee?"

"That's going to be a problem, isn't it?" I said.

"What is?"

"Witnesses."

She came back to me and took hold of my hand. "Aren't you getting a little ahead of yourself?"

I forced my weakest smile. "Maybe."

I could feel her relief. She said, "Why don't you have a bath? You can clean yourself up and try to relax. While you're doing that, I'll see if there's something in the flat you can wear, when you get out."

"I think I might be a size or two larger than you."

She led me out of the kitchen. My coordination was still impaired and I felt as unsteady as a drunk.

"Don't worry. They won't be mine. There's all sorts of rubbish in this flat. I'm sure we'll find something for you. Whenever anyone lives here, they invariably leave behind half the things they brought with them. They're usually in such a hurry to disappear! Just a couple of days ago, I got back to find the two girls who'd been living here for the past six months had gone. They left a scribbled note on the kitchen table and ten pounds towards this month's rent. Ten pounds for both of them! Can you believe it?"

She was looking for a towel in a cupboard. I felt dizzy and reached for the wall. My head ached.

"They were three weeks late with last month's rent so I guess I should have seen this coming. Anyway, if I don't find replacements for them quickly, or get some extra cash, I'm going to be in trouble. My landlord has no pity. Or shame. Every time I have trouble making the rent, he suggests I get into his bed to work off the debt."

"Nice," I murmured, hoping my swimming vision would stabilize.

"There's nothing on this planet that could get me into

*his* bed. I occasionally have a food-free week to save money, but it's better than the alternative and . . ."

She reappeared and stopped talking as soon as she saw me. I felt her arms moving around me for support.

"I'm okay," I told her. "Just a little light-headed."

She sat me on a small bench with my back against the wall. I closed my eyes and heard the wrench of the tap, followed by the harsh splatter of hot water smacking the bottom of the bath. Then her fingers were fiddling with my blood-drenched shirt.

"What are you doing?" I asked.

"Undressing you."

I sighed wearily and murmured, "I don't even know you."

"In that case, there's no need to be embarrassed."

I could feel the steam filling the bathroom, warming my skin, making me yet more drowsy. "I've got to sleep."

"After you're clean, you can."

Gabriella left me soaking in the steaming tub. The door was open so she could make periodic checks on me. I drifted into a semi-sleep where there was no gravity. It felt like I was floating. My frantic mind began to settle.

Eventually, she pulled the plug and provided me with the bottom half of a tracksuit which had faded from black to dark grey, and a navy blue sweatshirt. I dressed and joined her in the kitchen, where she had just finished making a pot of strong black coffee. I knew I still needed some deep sleep to help me recuperate, but the doze in the bath had taken the edge off my distraction and exhaustion. She poured us both a mug and I heaped two spoons of sugar into mine. Then we moved into the living-room.

I sat on a sofa with broken springs. There was a fireplace which was coming away from the wall. A crack rose in the plasterwork from the mantelpiece to the ceiling.

"So what now?" she asked.

"I don't know," I replied. "I don't know what I *want* to do or what I *ought* to do. And when I find out, what's the betting the two will be totally incompatible? There are so many questions which need answering. Is this ability permanent, or just temporary? Do I exploit it, or ignore it? Should I shout it from the roof-tops, or should I carry on as normal and go into work a few hours from now, just like on any other weekday? And what happens if I'm strolling down Moorgate and some arthritic beggar asks for money? Do I give him a fiver and a free healing?"

Gabriella sat in an armchair by the television set. There was a sickly pot plant on top of it and three small vines drooped over a corner of the screen. The blue digits on the video timer flashed on and off. Several cassettes were piled on top of the machine.

"You know you can count on me to help you in whatever way possible," she declared.

"Well, thank you, but . . ."

"Don't say it was nothing. You saved my life. In time, that may become as normal to you as brushing your teeth but for me . . ."

I could feel myself blushing. "Please!" I protested. "Don't keep saying that. It makes me feel ridiculous. Besides . . ."

I paused and then shook my head.

"What?" she said.

"I was going to say that anyone in my position would have done the same."

She smiled. "I know what you mean."

I said, "The point is, you shouldn't feel any debt to me. You don't owe me a thing. I'd never do it for gain."

Gabriella took a sip from her mug and brushed some hair out of her eyes.

"You should be careful about making statements like that."

"What do you mean?"

"If people hear about you, there are bound to be some who try to exploit you. They'll want you to do this and that, influence these people and discredit those people. And that'll be quite apart from the healing itself."

"Then they'll be disappointed. I won't be coerced into doing something I don't believe in."

She flicked some light dirt off the armchair. It looked like powdered plaster from the ceiling.

"You're being a little impractical," concluded Gabriella. "If somebody wanted to exploit you badly enough, they'd probably find a way."

I frowned. "How can you be so sure?"

"Because I can see how naive you are."

I sat back and smiled at her. "It doesn't happen like that in the real world, Gabriella."

"Don't you understand? As long as you can heal people like this, you're not going to be living in the real world. You won't be *allowed* to."

When I finished my coffee, I left. I still needed some proper recuperation, but at least I wasn't as broken as I had been when I arrived. She offered me a bed, but I said I felt strong enough to return to my own flat. I thanked her and set out in search of a taxi.

When the outer door to my apartment block clicked shut behind me, it was just after five in the morning. On the carpet in the main hall lay a crumpled sheet of paper with my name on it, which appeared to have been thrust through the letter-box with unnecessary force; it was dirty and torn. I went into my flat, shut the front door behind me and turned on the light before unfolding the paper. Katy's handwriting was familiar, if larger than usual. *Where are you, you bastard?*

A succinct message that no doubt communicated just what she felt when she wrote it. Perhaps it was better that I had not been there to receive it. I might have responded in a similarly pointless fashion.

I went into the living-room and emptied my pockets onto the coffee table. The contents consisted of loose change, a scrap of paper with Gabriella's number and address, a book of matches from the hotel and a business card that had been thrust into my hand before dinner by someone whose face had already faded from my memory. I changed out of the clothes that Gabriella had given me and got into more comfortable ones of my own. I dumped my bloodstained dinner shirt into a laundry basket.

It was cold, damp and black outside. I pulled on an extra jersey and turned on some more lights. I scoured the fridge for something edible. Katy usually kept it well stocked but that habit had recently fallen by the wayside like everything else of value in our relationship.

The answer-phone's red message light was winking at me. I hit the "play-back" button and turned on the television, reducing the sound to a whisper. The TV screen flickered with enticing images of Key West. It was a documentary on the town.

*Beep.*

"Hi, Christian. It's Danny. Poulsen wants you in early tomorrow morning to discuss your trip to Europe next week. He's worried about you getting your orders direct from Rowdy... he's paranoid of being bypassed. He thinks he's about to lose his bloody job! So do the whole department a favour when you come in tomorrow by doing absolutely fuck all to reassure him!"

*Beep.*

"Christian, it's Jorge. I just got back from the ball. Looking forward to seeing you on Thursday in Madrid. Remember, *you* may be working, but I might not be, so don't call too early! Also, I'm ringing up because I'm curious about how you got on with our 'plain' friend. I'll bet you took her number, right? I wonder who's listening to this message! See you Thursday."

I smiled. *Beep.*

96

"Hello? I hope this is the right number for Christian Floyd. It's Julia Graham. I ... er ... we ... where are you? I need to speak to you. Please call me."

The next message was also from Julia, giving me the telephone number she forgot to supply with her first call. I made a note of it.

"Where are you?" started the fourth call. "I came round to the flat and you weren't even there! You left the ball hours ago! Just what the hell are you up to, Christian?"

Katy sounded hysterical. I paused the answer-phone and dialled her house in Wandsworth. A sleepy voice answered but it wasn't hers. I couldn't tell which of the two girls who also lived in Katy's house was speaking to me. She looked for Katy and reported that she wasn't even there. I apologized for waking her and put the phone down. It was twenty past five. Where was she? I restarted the tape.

"Hello? It's Julia Graham again. Please answer the phone! I have to talk to you. Everyone's very confused and upset and excited and everything. Mr Leonard is desperate to speak to you! We all are! How did you do it? Where have you gone? There are just so many things, so please, *please* call me!"

*Beep.*

"I'm hoping I've reached a Mr Christian Floyd. My name's Lloyd Pratt. Sorry about the hour, but it looks like you're not in anyway, so no harm done, right? You and I have a little mutually beneficial business to discuss, so please give us a bell when you get in and ..."

Mr Pratt never hinted what form our "mutually beneficial business" might take. The nudge-and-wink tone in his voice suggested something dishonest.

"For God's sake, please answer the phone! It's me again! Julia Graham! Remember? The one you wanted to sleep with only a few hours ago? *Now please speak to me!*"

*Beep.*

"What's wrong with you, Mr Floyd? Perhaps you thought I was a fool?"

The voice was horrible and I knew I'd heard it before.

"Did you think I'd forget you so quickly? Did you think I'd forgive you so easily?"

Louis. That was his name. Louis the lunatic. He was the one with a voice which sounded as though he was recovering from throat surgery.

"I meant what I said when I spoke to you last. And what did you do about it? *Nothing!* You never even tried to make amends. And now you have spread your evil again."

I frowned and it was as though Louis could sense this through the answer-phone because he continued by saying, "Oh yes, I know all about it. I know what you did. Does that confuse you? Are you wondering how I found out so fast? Does it feel like I'm watching you?"

Louis broke off his monologue to cough. It sounded a painful business, as though he burst stitches with every gasp.

"Perhaps you will now start to show me a little more courtesy. Or is that too much to expect?"

I stopped the machine and considered fast-forwarding to the next message. But after a moment, I pressed the "play" button again.

"That you would come was never in doubt. It is written. For years, we waited for your identity. We were taught that the challenge would come and that some of us would have to rise to meet it. So we chose this path, forsaking all other choices. We have dedicated ourselves to the protection of the Word. The truth must never be shrouded in deceit. And now you're here among us, dripping your fraudulent poison over the innocent. Our wait – all our sacrifices – are at an end.

"You've been seen. There's nothing you can do that can escape the all-seeing gaze of God. No crime you commit will go undetected, no action will go unpunished. I know what you are. I've been told. You won't succeed because we shall protect Him. And if you try to interfere, we shall destroy you. You cannot win. We would sooner die than let that happen.

"You know what you have to do. You must repent. Renounce the corrupting spirit which has stolen your soul. Beg for forgiveness with all your heart and you shall receive it. It's not too late. Mercy and compassion are open to those who reject evil and embrace salvation without reservation. Purge your heresy and free yourself from eternal damnation!

"If you persist in your vile corruption, we shall meet you, confront you and destroy you. You will not be allowed to succeed because the penalty for our failure is too high."

The message ended in a throaty cough. "Fucking fruitcake!" I muttered to myself, in a private display of bravado, hoping it would ease the chill I suddenly felt.

*Beep.*

"This is Lloyd Pratt calling again. You do lead a busy social life, don't you? Come on, mate, do us a favour and give us a call. The number's the same as before."

That was the last one. I replayed the message from Louis several times and then sat in silence, watching seductive pictures of Key West on the television screen.

*That you would come was never in doubt.* Was he talking about me, specifically, or in more general terms? And how did they discover my identity? How did he know what I'd done? Was he one of the two men on the half-landing? And at the car park too? That seemed too farfetched for even the wildest extravagances of coincidence.

Who was he? And since he didn't appear to be acting alone, who was with him? Did he know what I was? Because I didn't.

The phone rang at seven. I let it ring and waited for

the answer-machine to pick up the message. I braced myself for another maniacal tirade from Louis but, instead, found a journalist leaving her name and number, asking me to call her back as soon as possible. I looked at my watch. It was just a few hours since I'd been with Julia Graham and Mr Leonard. Ten minutes later, another journalist called, leaving a similar message.

At seven-thirty, I rang my office and spoke to Danny.

"Morning, sunshine!" he chirped. "Where the bloody hell are you? I left a message on your phone, telling you to get in early."

"Yeah, I know."

"That doesn't mean seven-thirty, my friend. Six-thirty would have been all right."

"Well, I won't be in by eight-thirty, either. Or eleven-thirty, for that matter. I'm ill."

"Again? That's not going to make you very popular."

The outer-door entry-phone was buzzing.

"No, but who cares? Listen, I'll call you later to find out the news. I've got to go."

The entry-phone was still ringing. I picked it up and a woman spoke to me. She started politely, apologizing for the early hour and wondering if I could spare her five minutes for a few questions and a photograph.

"You're a journalist?"

"Yes, but . . ."

"No."

I put the phone back. It occurred to me that she might, in fact, be working for Louis. How could I be sure? He seemed to have an eye on me and wasn't working alone. I peeped at her through a tiny crack in the closed curtains. The gap was minute but I was still able to see all of her bulk bursting out of a navy anorak. She was sharing a joke with a thin man who wore three cameras around his neck. They were both leaning against a silver Vauxhall

Cavalier. I didn't care whether they were journalists or not; I didn't want to see them. I didn't want to see *anyone*.

Sleep began to stalk me again. Gabriella had insisted I stay calm, but the messages on my answer-machine and the vultures on my doorstep made that difficult. I didn't know who they were, but I figured that if there were already two, it wouldn't be long before there were more. I changed into some clothes of my own and packed a small bag.

Before leaving my flat, I took one last look through the curtains. There were now four of them on the pavement, in animated discussion. The two newcomers were both men. One looked distinctly ill, standing in the drizzle with his balding head slumped between coat-hanger shoulder blades. He was grey from head to toe. The other was puce in the cheeks and dressed in a luminous green bicyclist's cape. And as I retreated into the dark, a van pulled up carrying at least three more. I was tired but nevertheless primed myself for one final effort.

I double-locked my front door and retreated into the building, taking the stairs down to the basement which opened onto the garden. By climbing over the seven-foot wooden fence, I dropped into a narrow alley which connected with the road parallel to my own. I arrived on the street and broke into a run. No one followed.

Nevertheless, it was only when I reached Notting Hill Gate that I stopped running. I found a payphone and rang Katy's number. This time, there was nobody home at all. Next, I tried Julia Graham. After a single ring, she answered. "Christian?" she said, before I had a chance to announce myself.

"Yes."

"Jesus Christ! Where the hell are you? What have you done? What . . .?"

"Julia, please!" I protested, sharply.

There was a short silence. When she spoke again, she was calmer. "Where are you?"

"I'm calling from a pay-phone."

"What's going on?"

"You were there. You saw what I did," I replied, flatly.

"I know what I saw, Christian. But I still can't believe it."

The phone-box didn't seem secure. I felt vulnerable, like an exposed target for a concealed sniper. I thought the sooner I was off the street, the safer I'd be.

"Listen, Julia, I can't talk now. I just wanted to know if you'd been contacted by anybody from the press or . . ."

"Contacted? They're all over the place. They're speaking to everyone and . . ."

"Have you spoken to them yet?"

"No. I didn't want to. At least, not until I'd spoken to you. I wasn't sure what I'd say."

"Would you mind keeping it like that? I'd really appreciate it if you wouldn't say anything to them. Not yet, anyway."

"Sure, if it matters. But what about . . . ?"

"Thanks. I've got to go."

"Wait! Don't hang up. There are so many things I've got to ask you, that I *need* to ask you."

"I know, but not now. I'll call you later, when things have settled down. I promise."

I terminated the call and dialled Gabriella's number. Her voice was sleepy.

"Have I woken you again?"

"Christian?" she said, through a yawn.

"None other."

"What are you doing? I've only been asleep for . . ."

"I know and I'm sorry about that, but I've got a real problem. You know you said you'd help me if . . ."

"What is it?"

"I need somewhere to stay. *Badly.*"

There was a pause and I could hear her moving in the bed.

"Did your friend kick you out?" she asked.

That Gabriella had brought up Katy in a moment like this almost made me laugh. "No, it's nothing so simple. I wish it was. Some psycho's left a message on my answer-phone, threatening to do God-knows-what to me. I don't know if he's serious, but I don't want to find out. Not only that, but it looks like the press have got hold of the story. They're all over my doorstep. I just need a place where I'll be safe, while I try to figure out what I'm going to do. Can I come over?"

"Sure. Are these people still hanging around your flat? I mean, how are you going to get out without being seen?"

"I've already taken care of that. I'm calling from a pay-phone in Notting Hill Gate. I've tried to get hold of Katy but she's nowhere to be found. Listen, I'm really sorry, but do you think you could . . .?"

"Of course," she interrupted. "No problem. I meant what I said. Come straight over. And one more thing: try to relax. We'll work it out. Take a taxi and calm down. I'll see you soon."

"Thank you, Gabriella. I owe you," I told her.

"Hardly."

# Chapter Nine

*IT'S A BLEEDING MIRACLE!* That was how the front page of the *Sun* described my encounter with Mr Leonard. There was a fuzzy black-and-white photograph of me, standing in the hall with my arms outstretched and my head thrown back. The blood looked like black ink. Mr Leonard's crumpled body could just be seen on the floor. The wall was stained by dark streaks.

Somebody had to be making money because this shot was repeated in most of the newspapers. Whoever owned the tape from the internal security camera which recorded the healing was going to make thousands of pounds. Nearly all the newspapers reproduced the same provocative image; me in crucifixion.

I had no idea at the time how it would look, or even that I was being recorded. But no one would believe that now.

It was Saturday morning. Friday had been spent at Gabriella's flat. As soon as I was safely ensconced in the sanctuary of her apartment, I had allowed myself to unwind. Sleep wasn't far behind.

"You should rest," she'd told me.

"I will," I replied, "but before that, there's one thing I have to do."

I called Robert Poulsen at Parke Millen. He was furious that I was calling in sick. He threatened to have me fired or, at the very least, disciplined. I reminded him he couldn't.

"You were powerless to fire me last week," I told him, "and you're even more powerless today."

By fuelling his paranoia I felt I'd done more than a good day's work for Parke Millen.

Gabriella spent most of Friday at her language school. It seemed to me she was wasting her money. Her command of English was far better than most Englishmen's. Maybe she was trying to eliminate her mild Italian accent, which would be a pity, I thought, since it made English sound so much sweeter.

I was still asleep when she returned home, laden with food and wine for the evening. I awoke about an hour later and found her sorting through the groceries in the kitchen.

"How do you feel?"

"Weak and thirsty," I said. "But apart from that, not too bad."

"You do look a little pale."

As a token of appreciation, I cooked. In retrospect, I should have offered to wash up. The veal was like toast by the time we ate it. Gabriella was almost diplomatic.

"You're probably too busy to do much cooking," she suggested.

I couldn't judge Gabriella against my first impression of her because no one who's bleeding to death on a damp concrete car-park floor is at their best. But as we talked through that Friday night, Gabriella redefined herself in my mind. She was far stronger than I'd initially realized. Her parents had tried to bring her up wrapped in the stifling cloak of Catholicism. Despite their failure in this, it had nevertheless left her with a powerful and personal sense of morality. Every now and then, her diamond core sparkled; if she was adamant, it was final.

When she was quiet, which was most of the time, she had a peculiar look, which seemed to detach what was going on behind her eyes from anything in front of them.

It made her seem docile and meek and, most of all, vulnerable. But the truth was well disguised. I wondered how many men had regarded her as easy prey, moved in for the kill and only realized, when it was too late, the magnitude of their error. She would shoot them down in flames with a look. I could feel it. She wouldn't take pride in it – indeed, she might not be fully aware of it – but it was easy to picture her butchered suitors wondering how they could have got it so wrong.

I was probably more relaxed that evening than at any time since I discovered her in the back of the light blue Toyota. We hardly discussed the healings. When I tried to, she said it could wait. And she was right.

There were two bedrooms in Gabriella's flat. I slept in the one vacated by her former flatmates. My bed was uneven and sagged in the middle, but I was tired and slept soundly into Saturday morning.

Gabriella came back from an early excursion with an enormous pile of newspapers. I think she bought everything except the *Financial Times*. The only newspaper which didn't comment on the incident, or publish a photo, was the *Independent*. On their front page they displayed a photograph of two policemen feeding pigeons in Trafalgar Square.

The coverage was mostly absurd. The reports were so wildly inaccurate I began to wonder if I'd been there at all. The *Sun* kept talking about the hysterical crowd of onlookers who were baying for more, as blood "jetted" all over Mr Leonard. Where was this crowd? The only observers had been the two men on the half-landing and Julia Graham. Maybe the *Sun* meant crowd in terms of "two's company but three's a crowd".

The grains of truth were so obscured by the imagination of the journalists that they might just as well have written their accounts *before* the healing happened. They all got my name right, but estimates of my age ranged from twenty-five to thirty-four. Parke Millen was variously described as a ruthless trading operation, a Yank bank, a cut-throat stockbroking outfit, a sanctuary for well-heeled wheeler-dealers and, in one wayward tabloid, an old firm of respectable lawyers. My reported salary was regarded as generous, excessive, amazing, distasteful and criminal. Some quoted figures, starting at forty thousand and escalating to an absurd five hundred thousand. My company car was a Mercedes, an Alfa-Romeo, a Porsche, a Ferrari. In one instance, it was even a BMW; a rare island of fact in an ocean of invention.

I read all these potted biographies of myself and couldn't recognize the subject. The character the papers called Christian Floyd was a disgusting creature, a spiritual twin for Robert Poulsen. He bore no relation to the man I saw in the mirror.

Gabriella looked up from her paper and laughed.

"I can win a car," she announced.

"What?"

"This paper is offering a free Ford Fiesta to the person who tracks you down."

"You're joking!"

"I'm not. Look."

There was a colour photograph of a crimson Ford Fiesta with a peroxide blonde in a G-string sprawled across the bonnet. Underneath, the paper cried, "Be a detective for a day and win a Ford Fiesta! You could be the proud owner of this superb top-of-the-range Ford Fiesta!"

None of the newspapers, it seemed, were about to let anything as trivial as the facts interfere with their reporting.

"So, how does it feel to be famous?" asked Gabriella, circling the table in the kitchen.

"Unreal . . . quite literally. None of the papers look real at all," I told her. "I remember when I was a child you could get a faked front page of *The Times*, blown up into poster size, with your name and photo on it. It would say something like 'Christian Floyd, aged six, becomes the first man to land on Mars' and it would give details of your heroic space voyage. It was the sort of thing you got given for a birthday present to stick on your bedroom wall. Well, that's what these newspapers look like. But it'll pass soon enough. In a couple of days, they'll have found another freak story to chase. The English press have no stamina; nothing holds their attention for long."

"I wouldn't be so sure. I've been here long enough to see what a paper can do if it wants to. And for your information, this country doesn't hold a monopoly on imaginative journalism, you know."

"Ah, but it's quality that counts," I told her, flicking through the pages of one tabloid. "Listen to this, for example: 'In my opinion, he's lost about a quarter of his blood, so he must have a highly efficient replenishing system,' said Professor Anthony Savage, an expert in haematology. 'I would imagine he has his own private blood-bank.' Can you believe *that*? An expert? He hasn't got the first clue what he's talking about."

"If it's in that particular tabloid, he probably doesn't even exist."

I looked at the largest print of the most popular shot. It was taken at the moment I released the tension which had built up inside me. From the angle at which the camera caught me, it did look remarkably like a crucifixion pose, which was an unfortunate coincidence.

Gabriella ran her fingers across the page and said, almost inaudibly, "The full stigmata."

"The full stigmata?"

I remembered Dr Wheeler mentioning it, but I hadn't paid it much attention. Gabriella nodded. "It's incredible. I mean, I knew you bled when you healed me, but only now, looking at this picture . . . well, it's amazing!"

"And I thought bleeding happened to everyone."

She shook her head. "You don't understand the full significance of this, do you?"

"I know enough."

"I don't think so. When you heal, you're bleeding from the wounds of Christ."

I frowned and held up my hands, as if to distance myself from the subject. "Listen, I'm not religious. It's not my thing."

"It is now. Through history, there have been various cases of people who experienced stigmata. The bleeding on the hands and feet corresponds with the nails which pinned Christ to the cross. The bleeding from the torso is where the Roman soldier stuck his spear in. Bleeding around the head represents the scratches from the crown of thorns."

"I haven't bled around the head," I pointed out.

"It doesn't matter. In many of these cases, only one or two of the marks were observed. St Francis of Assisi, who is generally regarded as the first documented case, was supposed never to have bled from the head. But on the other hand, he was supposed to have carried permanent marks on his body for two years after he got them, until he died."

"How come you suddenly know so much about this?"

"I had a very strict Catholic upbringing. My parents are devout to the point of fanaticism. This sort of thing isn't news to people like them . . . like *me*. It's a crucial part of the history of our Church."

The notion of being associated with anything religious made me uncomfortable. Every night on the news, I saw what religion was doing to millions of unfortunate souls. "Look, Gabriella, I'm a lapsed Anglican which makes me about the most godless thing on this planet, so . . ."

"It doesn't matter what denomination you are. It doesn't matter what you believe. It's what you *do* that counts."

"So what are you saying?"

"That I understand your position, but that you're going to have to understand the position of everyone out there who reads this sort of thing."

She left me alone with my sensational press. Where before it had been a source of some amusement, it now inherited a more sinister overtone. When she returned, she was carrying a small radio. She put it on the table and told me to listen. It was a phone-in show on a city FM station.

". . . You can call me about anything you want in today's news. The government intend to cut the basic rate of tax by three per cent. With an upcoming election, does that sound like a bribe or what? Tell me what you think. And, of course, if you've read any of today's newspapers, you won't have failed to notice the stories about this so-called healer. Do you believe in this sort of miracle-working? Is he for real or is he a fraud? Call me, Mike Foster, and tell London what you think."

Gabriella leaned against the kitchen sink and folded her arms.

"On the line now we've got . . . John, from Maida Vale. What do you want to discuss, John?"

"Hello, Mike. It's this bloke in the papers, the one who's done all this healing stuff."

"What's your point?"

"Well, it's rubbish, ain't it? What kind of healing is it where you start bleeding all over the patient, eh?"

"So you don't believe in him?"

"No way! The fact is, he's having the whole world on, ain't he? He's probably raking it in, selling his story to all the papers. Money for lies, that's what it is."

"How do you know he's lying?"

"Stands to reason, don't it?"

"Not without proof, John," said Foster, before abruptly

cutting him off. The next caller was Mary from Streatham, who took a different view.

"I think we should be jolly careful, Michael. Who's to say he isn't a legitimate healer? Perhaps he really is blessed with the spirit of the Lord. In fact, one could go further and ask if he might not be . . . *divine*. In the proper sense, of course."

"That's a bit strong, don't you think?" said Foster.

"Why?" snapped Mary. "Everyone seems to assume it would be impossible for a prophet to come to earth in such godless times, but really, what better time could there be?"

"Are you suggesting this man might be . . . *holy*?"

There was a pause. "Well, why not?"

"You'll forgive me for saying so, but it just seems highly unlikely. A prophet working for an American bank who does healing in his spare time? Come on, Mary."

"Your attitude is highly regrettable, Mr Foster. The Lord faced similar rejection when He first trod the earth. I don't see why it should be any different when He returns."

I lit a cigarette and held up the packet for Gabriella to see. "If people start believing I'm some sort of reincarnation of Jesus Christ, how much do you suppose Marlboro would sponsor me to smoke their cigarettes? I mean, it's ridiculous!"

Gabriella shrugged. "Some people *want* to believe in things. They need to have faith to give them strength. Their minds are up for grabs. Maybe she's one of them. And if she is, and you appear on a billboard smoking a Marlboro, she'll stop at the nearest newsagent and buy a carton."

I rose from my seat and flicked the switch on the kettle.

"What about you?" I asked. "After all, you've had the direct experience. Who do you think I am?"

Gabriella said firmly, "I don't think you're the second coming of anything. You're an ordinary person with an extraordinary talent. It's as though somebody somewhere *had* to inherit it, and it could have been anyone on this planet. In the event, it turned out to be you."

"You make me sound like I'm the sole winner of a global lottery."

"Something like that. As far as you're concerned, only time will tell whether the prize is a blessing or a curse."

When Gabriella went out to buy food, I made a couple of calls. One of them was to Katy in Wandsworth. She didn't sound thrilled to hear me.

"How are you?" I asked her.

"Where are you calling from?"

"Well . . ."

"And just what do you think you're doing? I've been trying to get hold of you since Thursday night, and now . . ."

"That's what I was calling about. I assume you've seen the papers."

"I certainly have. What is this? Some kind of practical joke?"

"No. It's the truth."

Silence was all she could offer. It was no surprise. Katy knew me as well as anyone, and this was as far from her version of the true me as she was ever likely to get.

"The truth!" she scoffed, eventually. "You expect me to believe that?"

"I know it's hard, but . . ."

"Hard? It's impossible."

"Well, put it like this: why on earth would I make up such a story? What would I gain? Am I the sort of person who'd seek insane national publicity? Of course not. Exactly the opposite."

"Christian, I don't believe you. I mean, when did you first realize you had this wonderful talent?"

"The night of Charlie's birthday," I said, too quickly.

"What?"

It was a mistake to mention it. But having started, I

couldn't easily retreat. She demanded an explanation and I gave her the undiluted truth, which was met with an inevitable verdict.

"Absolute bullshit! You mean to say that having rescued some girl from certain murder, and then healed her wounds, you came home and casually went out to dinner with the rest of us?"

Who could blame her for her incredulity? I said, "It's what happened. Don't you recall how strangely I was acting that night? That's because . . ."

"What happened to your bloody clothes, then?"

"They were ruined. I threw them away the following day."

"How convenient."

"Katy, I know it sounds crazy but . . ."

"It doesn't sound crazy. It just sounds like the shabbiest set of lies I've ever heard."

"I understand that! But you've seen the picture in the newspaper and what the witnesses said. So why can't you . . .?"

"They never mentioned anything about you saving some girl from murder in a car park."

"That's because I never . . ."

"Were you busy saving Julia Graham from certain murder too? Is that why you ended up at her place? You stumbled across some plot to kill her, so you saved her and just happened to heal a blind bystander at the same time?"

"For God's sake, Katy!"

There was a long pause, which she eventually ended by asking, "What were you doing there?"

"Where?"

"At Julia Graham's place."

"Please, Katy, not now! In the light of what's happened . . ."

"To be honest, Christian, I don't give a fuck about that. Not any more. I just want to know about Julia Graham."

114

"I can't believe this."

"I'm serious."

"I know. That's what I can't believe."

"What were you doing there?" she asked, flatly.

I took in a deep breath and slowly let it out. "Grow up, Katy. You know perfectly well what I was doing there."

I waited for the storm. Matters had degenerated so badly that the vicious truth couldn't make things any worse. I felt better for telling her, but not happier.

"How can you say that so lightly?" she whispered.

"I'll tell you how: in exactly the same way that you can dismiss what I've done so lightly."

"In that case, since we seem to be in the mood for confessions," she said, "I might as well tell you where I was when you were trying to contact me on Friday morning."

My stomach lurched. "You don't have to."

She ignored me and said, "I was with Justin."

"Whitehead?"

"Yes."

All I could say was, "Oh."

"That's right. After I found you were out, I went round to his flat. He was considerably more receptive than you've been recently. Just like you, I had infidelity on my mind. Unlike you, I didn't take time out to heal passing strangers."

If Katy had been standing in front of me, I wasn't sure how I would have reacted. Maybe I would have hit her as hard as possible, willingly breaking my own fingers if it meant fracturing her teeth. Or maybe I would have reacted no differently to the way I behaved at that moment of confession. I was powerless to respond. I just sat there and let her run riot, while I tried to imagine how she looked at the other end of the line.

". . . Did I forget to mention that it wasn't the first time? Certainly not! We've been . . ."

I'd heard enough so I replaced the receiver onto the cradle, while she continued to spill poison into her mouthpiece. That our affair finished over the telephone seemed, somehow, suitably tacky. In time, I came to accept that it was as dignified a death to our relationship as we deserved.

I called Julia Graham, but got her answer-phone. I put the receiver down before the end of the recorded message. I owed her an explanation. Indeed, I'd promised her one. The trouble was, I didn't really have one. Maybe it would be easier to leave a message. That way, at least I could pretend I'd tried and I wouldn't have to answer any awkward, direct questions. It was a little shabby, I knew, but I could live with that, so I redialled and waited for the tone.

"Julia, it's Christian Floyd calling and . . ."

I was suddenly an actor who'd dried. I couldn't think of a word to say. For a moment, I considered putting the phone down.

"I . . . I don't know where to begin. Or what to say. Does 'sorry' cover it? Probably not. But what else can I say? I can't explain this to you because I don't know what it is. What you see is what you get. I had to do it because I had to know. Up until then, I wasn't really sure whether I had this . . . this *ability*. So when I saw Mr Leonard, I knew I had to try.

"I'm truly sorry for the chaos I've caused you, Julia. It was obviously never my intention. I mean, you *know* what my intention was, right?

"I'm sure this isn't exactly what you had in mind when I promised to call you, so I'll try to get hold of you again sometime. But if I can't . . ."

I left it at that.

Gabriella dumped three brown paper bags on the kitchen table. She pulled bread out of one of them and looked up at me.

"Trouble?" she enquired.

"How do you mean?"

"Your face. It looks like it."

"And there I was, thinking what a complex animal am I."

Gordon Rowdy had been surprised to hear my voice on a Saturday morning. He was even more surprised to learn why, since the papers he took were the *Financial Times* and the *Independent*; the only two to ignore me. Naturally, he was incredulous when I told him which story was dominating the others.

"And is it true?"

"Yes, it is."

Rowdy hummed to himself down the phone. "I see. And how long have you known about this?"

"Not long at all," I replied.

"You're not pulling my chain are you, Floyd?"

"No."

"Jesus!" he exclaimed. I waited for him to carry on. I heard him sigh and then say, "Listen, I'll take your word for this, for the moment, but what do you want to do about it?"

"Well, I think Europe's out of the question, don't you?"

There was another, long, awkward pause, before he said, "If I didn't know you better, I might think this was a scheme dreamed up by you to get out of the trip, seeing as how you weren't very enthusiastic in the first place."

"All you have to do is buy any other paper than the two you've got. But generally speaking, if you feel I'd be an embarrassment to Parke Millen then I'd understand and I'll hand in my notice, but . . ."

"Of course you're going to be an embarrassment. Jesus Christ, Floyd! What do you goddamned expect? But then again, what you do in private has nothing to do with us."

I could just hear him chuckling down the line as he said

something indistinct to his secretary. Rowdy was a totally unpredictable man.

"I don't care whether you're Lord God Almighty or Lucifer," he continued. "I want to keep you on. Like I told you the other day, there are people investing their time and effort in your future here. You know me . . . I'd hate to think I was wasting company resources on a non-starter. But in the short-term, maybe you should take some time off, until you sort this thing out."

I could have asked for nothing more from Rowdy and gratefully accepted his offer.

"That was the more fruitful one, I assume," said Gabriella.

"Correct."

"And the other?"

I took a deep breath. "Well . . ." I sighed, stretching it into a word lasting a couple of seconds.

"You don't have to tell me, if you don't want to."

Gabriella was placing three cans and two small jars in a cupboard above the toaster. Her auburn hair tumbled down her back as she stood on her toes. She was peering into the crowded cupboard, looking for space. The flat's rundown condition gave it a student-like feel, but it was far too well stocked for that.

"Katy and I lit our funeral pyre."

Gabriella lowered herself back onto her heels and looked at me. "You mean . . .?"

"Yes."

She put the jars and cans on the worktop by the sink.

"I'm sorry. It wasn't any of my business."

"It doesn't matter. Really. It's goodbye and good riddance, as far as I'm concerned."

She looked a little cross and slowly shook her head. She said, "You don't mean that."

I felt ashamed. "You're right," I conceded. "I don't."

"Maybe a little time will pass and the two of you will . . ."

I raised my hand to stop her. "No. It gives me no pleasure to say so because most of the time Katy and I shared was great, but recently . . . well, what's happened now puts reconciliation out of reach. In fact, the only satisfaction I can take from this is that we've done the right thing."

Gabriella tried to smile.

"Well," she said, cheerily, "at least it sounds as though you split up amicably. That's good. Acrimony is so unproductive."

If only she knew. "Yes," I replied, forcing a polite, unconvincing smile, as I imagined Whitehead and Katy screwing the living daylights out of each other, and wondering about just how much bitter pleasure Katy had derived from breaking news of her infidelity to me.

If Katy and I *had* got married we would have been Mr and Mrs Spleen before the honeymoon was over. Gabriella opened her mouth to speak but stopped and then frowned.

"What?" I asked.

"Did you hear something?"

"What was it?"

"I'm not sure."

She moved across the kitchen floor and there was a heavy clunk from outside. It sounded like the front door.

"Hello?" called out a male voice.

I searched Gabriella for a flicker of recognition but there wasn't one. She poked her head round the kitchen door.

"Who the hell do you think you are?" she demanded. "Get out before I call the police! How did you get in here?"

I joined her and saw a man standing by the front door. His short, flabby body was squeezed into a pale, powder blue, single-breasted suit, which he insisted on doing up, thereby drawing attention to his monstrous gut. His skin was dark, more Latin looking than Gabriella's. His jet black hair was very thin over the scalp and he had oiled it back. It glistened under the naked bulb hanging over him. He wore no tie and I could see a cut-off mark where a razor had prevented the hair on his chest creeping up his throat and turning it into a carpet. He peered through large glasses with tinted lenses. I could tell he was one of those people who broke into an oceanic sweat as soon as May arrived.

He looked up at me and it was as though he were staring at his long-lost brother. He grinned and turned back to Gabriella.

"I made my entry into this flat," he explained to her, "just as one of my employees made their entry into Mr Floyd's flat. Illegally and cleverly."

"What?" exclaimed Gabriella.

"What?" I repeated.

"Allow me to introduce myself," he said, handing me a business card with a podgy hand weighed down by two vulgar rings and a gold bracelet. "Sammy Price."

I studied the card. Samuel Z. Price.

"You broke into my flat?" I asked.

"I didn't, no. One of my employees did."

I felt the first flush of anger. "What the hell for?"

"To find you."

"Oh, I see! And here you are?"

"You left Miss Fiorini's address on a scrap of paper, on your coffee table. If you were hoping to keep it a secret, you were rather careless."

I made a move forward but Gabriella clutched my arm and restrained me. She said, "So you broke in here to see him, not me?"

Price smiled in an oily fashion. "That is correct, Miss

Fiorini, although had I been aware of your beauty, my motives might have been..."

"What do you want, Mr Price?" I muttered. "Your business card doesn't say what business you're in."

"In my professional circle, it doesn't have to."

"Well, we're obviously not in the same line of work, then. What professional circle are we talking about?"

"I'm an agent, Mr Floyd."

"An agent?"

"Yes."

"A theatrical agent, perhaps? A secret agent? Maybe you're a cleansing agent? What kind of bloody agent?"

Price frowned. "Perhaps we could all move inside and I could explain everything?"

"I wouldn't bank on it."

"Maybe we should at least listen to him," suggested Gabriella.

"He still hasn't told us what type of agent he is."

"I represent ... *personalities*. If you were famous, you'd know me. My reputation speaks for itself."

"I'll bet it does," I replied bitterly, studying his clothes and jewellery.

"Now could we please find somewhere more civilized to talk?"

Gabriella ushered us into the living-room. Price flopped onto the sofa and promptly killed any springs that hadn't already expired. As his whale-like body sank into the mushy sea of worn fabric and stained stuffing, he said to Gabriella, "Couldn't brew us some tea, could you, love?"

He rescued himself, but before he could start his pitch, I asked, "What about my flat? What have you done to it?"

"Nothing. My lad assured me that he left it just as he found it."

"I don't believe this!"

"Listen, Christian – can I call you Christian?"

"Not yet."

"Let me get to the point. Are these reports in the papers true?"

"What's it to you?"

"Look, we won't get anywhere until you start being a little less obstructive. So just answer the question, all right?"

I took another drag on my Marlboro. The ash was an inch long. I tapped it into the clay pot which was home to a sickly looking plant with yellow and brown leaves that hung limply from its puny branches. I was sure a large selection of far coarser contaminants had poisoned the soil long before I added my ash.

"Yes, it's true. Well, most of it's crap but the essence of it is true."

"And how do you do it?"

"I don't know."

"Can you do it whenever you like?"

"Maybe."

Samuel Price leaned forward, resting his elbows on his knees. His fat-fingered hands clasped each other.

"I'll get straight to it," he said. "I'm offering my services to you. I wish to represent you."

I smiled, leaned back and took a final drag from my cigarette before stubbing it out on the damp, black soil.

"Not interested."

"Do you know who I have on my books?"

"No, and I don't give a shit, either."

He wasn't going to allow my indifference to knock him out of his stride.

"I've got bands like Another Way Down and Tulip Assassins," he announced, proudly. "I manage film stars like Christopher Steel and Richard McRae, and then there's England's favourite footballing son, Kevin Connor. Heard of them? There are more. Johnny Raleagh, the crooner? My client list reads like a bloody *Who's Who?* of the people who make the news. My actors and actresses

122

have got Oscars coming out of their collective arses! The footballers on my books have amassed the greatest collection of medals since the battle of the Somme! Do you understand?"

I wondered if Price used this technique on all his prospective clients.

"It's hardly relevant to me, is it?"

Price sighed wearily and ran a hand over his head, as if to check that every hair was still firmly glued to his scalp.

"If it wasn't relevant, I wouldn't be here, would I? Don't you get it? Your gift is far rarer than anything they've got. Think of it as a mineral resource. You own the rights and I own the mining equipment. Together, we extract it, market it and everybody gets happy."

"Including you?"

He sat up straight, wounded by my attitude.

"Well, it is true that agents do take a very small percentage of what their clients earn, but it would be so . . ."

Gabriella entered the room carrying a tray with three mugs. She handed one to Price and told him, "You can have coffee."

He obviously wanted tea but Gabriella's stare persuaded him to nod meekly and accept what he was given. She looked at me and I said, "Mr Price wants me to earn a fortune from my healing. Correct me if I'm wrong, but haven't you and I already discussed this?"

"Yes."

"Perhaps you'd care to tell him what I promised you."

"With pleasure," she said, sitting next to me and facing Price. "He assured me that he would not allow himself to be exploited in any way."

"Why does he need to assure you?" Price wanted to know, looking increasingly exasperated. "I mean, excuse me if I'm out of line, but who are you anyway? I came here to speak to Mr Floyd, not to you."

"You are out of line, Price," I said. "Way out."

Gabriella and I looked at each other. I caught myself wondering about the nature of our bond. All the excitement concerned my healing of Mr Leonard. No one knew about Gabriella. Not even Katy, although I had tried to tell her. Apart from her, Gabriella and I hadn't uttered a word to anyone. Not even the businessmen who raised the alarm in the car park knew; they hadn't seen me. The staff at the hospital could only guess at what had happened. All of which left the relationship between Gabriella and me open for misinterpretation.

Price saw us looking at each other and thought he saw the link, making the most obvious guess. He exhaled like a mistral.

"Oh I get it," he cried, raising his hands and slapping them down on his fat thighs. "You two are ... well, you know ..."

"It doesn't matter what we are," I said.

"Well, I'm sorry anyway. But getting back to business, let me explain something to you, Mr Floyd. Either you stay in hiding for ever, or you come out into the open. It's as simple as that. Maybe you intend to spend the rest of your life as a hermit, but if you don't, you're going to have to consider how you cope with the attention when you reappear. And when you do reappear, take my word for it, you'll be deluged. How are you going to handle the press? Do you have any experience in this area? *Do you know what they can do to you?*" he asked, lowering his voice into a whisper and leaning forward.

Gabriella didn't look very impressed.

"Go on," I said.

"I know every last trick when it comes to media management. Dealing with all forms of the press is really what I do best," he said. "Here's what I'll do. I'll manage you through the whole thing ... for free."

"For free?" I said.

"That's right! For free. I know what you're thinking. Where's the catch? I mean, me?"

"So where *is* the catch?" asked Gabriella, very dryly.

Price cleared his throat and then took a small sip from his coffee. He grimaced and knew he wasn't going to get round Gabriella as easily as he might have got round me. He gave her a hard stare before admitting, "The publicity I would receive from representing you would be beneficial to me. I can't deny it. But remember this: I'd still be doing you a great favour."

Gabriella said, "You're not interested in favours. You dress up profitable business as charity. By waiving what you call a commission, you're really hoping to buy first-class publicity on the cheap. You can see a way of getting your name and photo everywhere, in a fashion that would normally cost you a fortune. If that's your offer, then make it, but don't dress it up to be something it's not. You insult us and you make yourself look pathetic!"

Price turned towards me. "What the hell does she do? Lecture professors at Harvard Business School? I came here to negotiate with you. Do I *have* to go through her as well?"

I looked at Gabriella, who remained as calm as ever, and then back at Price. "Yes."

"But why?" he demanded, holding his fat hands apart.

"Because she's the only person I know who doesn't seem to be interested in taking me for a ride. I like that and I like her. And I instinctively dislike you. So if her contribution makes your job any harder, then that's probably good."

# Chapter Ten

Stigmata. The word made a home in me like a virus. Sometimes it ran rampant and sometimes it slept, but it was always there. And it would never go away.

It was night. Gabriella and I were alone again. There hadn't been enough time to digest what she said about stigmata before Price's arrival. But since his departure, I'd thought of little else. The result of this contemplation was doubt and anxiety.

"What does it mean?" I asked.

She smiled kindly at me, but shrugged her shoulders. "I don't know."

"I can understand the healing part. You hear stories about people who can do it. Personally, I've always been a little sceptical about them, but they're common enough, right?"

"Yes."

"But the bleeding . . . the stigmata, as you call it, that's rare, isn't it?"

"It's more than rare."

"So why me?"

"You know the answer to that already: why not?"

I nodded in frustrated agreement. "I know, I know! But I still don't understand! Why does it happen, Gabriella?"

"For you? I can't say."

"Then for who?" I asked.

"Well, I remember being taught about it when I was a child, but that was a long time ago and . . ."

"How did it happen?"

"As I recall, it often occurred during prayer."

"I haven't prayed in years."

Gabriella nodded. "Well, none of them worked for American banks, either. It doesn't prove a thing."

She was right. "Okay, point taken. So what happened to them?"

"Like I said, they're all different. But often the marks would come during intense prayer or contemplation of the Passion. And when this . . ."

"What passion?"

"*The* Passion."

"What's that?"

Gabriella seemed surprised by my ignorance. If she'd known more about my background in religious education, she might have understood.

"It's the suffering of the Lord, between his betrayal and crucifixion."

"So these people would be thinking hard about this, really focusing on it, and then . . . then what? They started to bleed like me?"

"Stigmata isn't just bleeding. It's more to do with marks associated with the crucifixion. Bleeding is the most dramatic form of it, I suppose, but it's not the only one. When St Francis of Assisi was actually dead, there were people who saw shining nails rising out of his hands and feet, bleeding fresh blood."

"Even though he was dead?"

Gabriella nodded. "That's right."

"But that's just . . . it's just the way they used to write about those things. That's not to say it *actually* happened."

She was amused by this and said, "People will say the same when they read about you, whether it's today, tomorrow, or in a hundred years. They'll think it's hysterical exaggeration. I can't say whether new nails rose out of his flesh, but I've always had an open mind on the matter. And now that I've seen what happens to you, I'm more inclined to accept it than before."

I reached for the wine bottle and refilled our glasses. "So did St Francis also bleed while he was healing?"

Gabriella frowned. "As far as I'm aware, he didn't heal."

"But the stigmata?"

"It's not the property of people who heal, Christian. The cases I learned about involved people who were in prayer, or were suddenly struck by a vision, or something like that. They weren't healing."

"*What?*"

She said, "I'm sorry, I thought you realized."

"No, I didn't. I had no idea about that, just like I've got no idea about anything else, Gabriella. I don't understand a bloody thing!"

I pictured Julia Graham playing the whore, deriving maximum pleasure from my confusion. And then there was the moment when Mr Leonard held a wet finger in front of his face and saw blood. I looked at Gabriella and said, "My life is falling apart so quickly there's nothing I can do but watch. Who can help me?"

"I'm afraid I don't know. A priest, perhaps?"

"No. Absolutely not. I'm as close to religion right now as I ever want to be. Who knows what kind of insanity I'd end up getting involved with if I put my trust in some priest?"

"It needn't be like that."

"No organized religion, Gabriella. I don't believe in it. It's just corruption on a cross. You don't think they'd try to exploit me like Price? Of course they would. At least with him, it's only one man, not a whole Church."

"We might find someone who's done research into this sort of thing. Or a doctor, maybe."

I shook my head and felt the fear rise again. "No," I muttered. "It's too dangerous."

"Why?"

"They'll use me as some guinea-pig or something."

"Don't you think you're being a little paranoid?"

I looked her in the eye and nodded. "Don't you think I've earned the right to be paranoid, Gabriella? You of all people should understand that."

She rose from her seat and came over to me. She put her hands on my shoulders and said, "I know. I'm sorry. So what about Louis?"

I ran a hand through my hair and sighed, "Jesus, I don't know! He's probably some harmless nut-case, but on the other hand . . ."

"You have no idea how he could have found out what you did?"

"No. That's the very thing which gives him credibility. I've replayed each scene a hundred times in my mind and he's just not there. He couldn't be."

She came back from the fridge and offered me some chocolate, which I refused. She broke off two chunks for herself.

"Fuck it!" I snapped, more through exasperation than anger. "I just wish I could get it back the way it was." I drained my wine glass and slumped in my chair. "But I can't, right?"

Gabriella smiled sympathetically. "I'm afraid not." There was real kindness in her dazzling emerald eyes. I suddenly remembered how struck I was by them when I first met her in the reception area at Parke Millen. She had been so shocked when she realized I had no idea of what I'd done. In that moment, we'd been equal: stunned by revelation. Since then, she'd been level-headed, supportive and protective. I shuddered to think what state I might have been in without her. It made me wince.

She saw the face I instinctively pulled and asked, "What's wrong?"

"I was just thinking about what you've done for me."

"Well, don't. Think about what you did for me . . . and for the blind man. Whatever happens, Christian, remember that you have nothing to be ashamed of. No matter how chaotic it gets, what you did was wonderful, not crazy or criminal. Never forget that. You have good on your side."

"I have *you* on my side. That's what I'll remember."

The sound of a disturbance woke me at ten past three in the morning. I guess I'd only been asleep for an hour. We'd gone to our respective beds earlier, but my mind had still been too busy. There was too much to consider. At some point, though, when my cluttered thoughts started to make no sense, the energy faded and I began to slumber.

In other cities, people would still be spilling in and out of restaurants and nightclubs. Pavement drinkers would have to shout to make themselves heard over the traffic. But not in London. At this time of the morning, you could whisper across Piccadilly Circus and be heard by the partially deaf.

Now that I was awake, my startled senses tried to pick up further signs of whatever it was that had snapped me out of my sleep. I lay in the dark, feeling my pulse pumping the accelerator pedal. I hoped what I'd heard was in the safety of the dream, and not with me in the precarious environment of reality. I picked up the distant hiss of a car cruising down a neighbouring street. Two cats screeched at each other, disputing the territorial rights of an overflowing dustbin.

Just as my eyelids began to feel heavy again, there was a dull thud. Closed doors and poorly plastered walls muted the noise, but it was still sharp enough to shock in the quiet night. Something bumped against a fragile wall and the entire apartment seemed to quake. I thought I heard whispered expletives, but I couldn't be sure. Silence followed.

I strained my ears and couldn't hear a thing. I considered calling out to Gabriella, but then decided not to. Very cautiously, I rose from my bed and pulled on a pair of trousers, going to agonizing lengths to keep quiet, waiting for a creaking floorboard to betray me. All my ears could detect was the gentle snore of the city and my own shallow, fractured breathing.

As I reached for the door handle, I heard a muffled grunt, followed by the scuffed signature of a struggle under repression. Somebody was muttering, but trying to keep it quiet. There was a crack and a muted groan. Unusually, my bedroom door opened onto the landing and not into the room itself. This was a stroke of luck, for as I threw it open, I caught one intruder in the face, propelling him backwards down the staircase. I only saw a glimpse of him, as he tumbled into the darkness with a fading cry.

I charged into Gabriella's bedroom, but was barely through the doorway when a blow to the ribs sent me crashing to the floor. I never really saw it. A large shape moved in a lightning blur and suddenly I was on my way down with fire in my chest. Unable to suck air into my lungs, I grunted uselessly and curled into the foetal position. The true pain began to register. I looked up and saw Gabriella being restrained by her attacker, while another man stood by the door, holding a long, black truncheon in his right hand.

Her captor yelled, "Calm down!" at her, but she wouldn't. He wore a ludicrously inflated jacket of black satin with a bold silver logo across the back which read "COMMITTED TO EXCELLENCE", and carried the emblem of the Los Angeles Raiders on each arm. He had pale skin and thick copper hair. He sported a baseball cap which cast a shadow over his eyes. At first, I thought it was a match for his jacket because it was also black and carried a silver emblem on the front. But instead of a Raiders badge, there was a silver triangle standing on a point with the letters CDS squeezed inside its three lines. The man by the door was wearing an identical cap. Beneath his thick black cotton shirt, he wore a white T-shirt. He had racing gloves on his hands and chunky boots with metal toe-caps on his feet. My head was on the floor, just eighteen inches from his left boot. I could see my reflection in the polished steel tip. He leaned over and jabbed me in the ribs with the rubber-coated stick.

"Where's Paul?" he demanded.

"Paul?" I groaned.

"There are three of us."

"He's downstairs," I told him, aware of the growing ache that radiated from my stomach to every other part of me.

"Downstairs? What's he doing there?"

"I don't know. Why don't you go and ask him?"

I felt a sharp prod in the back.

"Jesus Christ!" I protested.

"Christian!" cried Gabriella, from the other side of the room.

My attacker crouched over me, stared at me venomously, and hissed, "Don't take the name of the Lord in vain."

"Then don't fucking hit me!" I replied, bitterly.

He struck me again. "Profanity is the Devil's tongue."

The realization dawned on me as explosively as the discomfort. While I tried to catch my elusive breath, I looked up into his face. There was no compassion in it.

"Let her go," I muttered.

He said, "First you'll listen to me and then – *maybe* – we'll talk about letting her go."

I looked at her and then back at the man above me. "Louis?" I asked. "Are you Louis?"

I didn't think it was, because the voice was different. But the name produced a reaction. He straightened himself and let out a condescending laugh.

His partner was having great difficulty in keeping control of Gabriella. She refused to stop struggling. Her hand clawed his arm and she had shredded several strips of black satin from the sleeve of his jacket. Her feet continued to stab back at him, occasionally catching him on the toes or on an ankle. The fear in her face made her look crazy. If he knew what had happened to her in the car park, he wouldn't have been so surprised at the strength of her resistance. Then it occurred to me that he probably *did* know. Louis knew and there seemed to be a connection.

"Well, if you're not Louis, who the hell are you?"

My attacker prodded me again and said, "Watch your language."

Gabriella tried to bite into the arm around her throat, but was prevented by a jerk of the shoulder which snapped her head back.

"We are members of his congregation," declared the man standing over me. "The man you call Louis is the dear leader of our Church and he . . ."

"A *Church*?" I spluttered.

"The Church of the Divine Science," he added, in a tone which suggested that the name was an explanation in itself.

I slowly pushed myself onto my knees. The ache was everywhere. I felt sick. The copper-haired man ordered Gabriella to behave and she drove her heel into his ankle.

"Can't you control her?" snapped the truncheon-wielder.

"You try it, then!" came the acidic reply.

I smiled to myself and tried to ignore the discomfort just below the ribs. "What kind of church goes round doing the three o'clock knock and beating the crap out of people with truncheons? It sounds more like the sort of thing Stalin used to go in for."

If I hadn't been kneeling, the boot might not have hurt as much. As it was, it caught me in the chest. I groaned and rolled over onto my back. He was slapping the truncheon into the palm of his hand.

"The Church of the Divine Science is dedicated to the elimination of all evils that might threaten the birth of the Word. Our salvation shall be the Word. We are the protectors of the Word and, when the day comes, we shall be the bodyguard of the embodiment of the Word."

It was as I was looking up at him that I tied in the baseball cap's logo. CDS. The Church of the Divine Science.

"I see," I gasped. "That's all very interesting, but what does it actually mean?"

"It means the Lord is coming. It will be our job to shield Him when He arrives."

This caught me off guard and I looked up. "The Second Coming? Is that what you're talking about?"

"We in the Church of the Divine Science have a specific mission. We must protect Him from persecution. We all know that and we accept the challenge, no matter what the cost. Even if it means offering up our lives. We won't be deflected by ridicule. We won't be distracted or dissuaded. We have one purpose only and we shall see it through to the end."

"And that's to protect the Lord when He comes back to Earth?"

"Yes."

I shook my head. "So what are you doing here?"

"I know what you are."

"Oh, really? And what's that?"

He opened his mouth to speak and then paused before eventually saying, "You were seen. We were told what you did."

"Who told you? *What* were you told?"

"Our leader told us everything."

"Your leader? You mean Louis?"

It was at this point that Gabriella broke free, shaking off the grip around her throat. She twisted to one side, threw her right hand over her shoulder and dug her fingers and nails into the face of the copper-haired man. He cried out and released her, nursing the fresh cuts and scratches with both hands. Gabriella turned to face him and jerked her right knee upwards with astonishing brutality. He collapsed in wide-eyed amazement with a pathetic whimper, no longer knowing where to put his hands.

Stunned, still and silent, the man who'd bludgeoned me watched Gabriella destroying his colleague. Finally, he lumbered forward, raising his truncheon to hit her. I jumped up and intercepted him. For a few moments we were locked in a stalemate struggle. I slid my fingers round his throat and squeezed as hard as I could, while his hands punched my aching sides.

"Christian!" cried Gabriella, suddenly. "Shut your eyes!"

"What?"

Too late. There was a hiss and a scented cloud filled my face. She was actually directing the contents of a deodorant aerosol into *his* face, but we were too close and the jet of the spray was too imprecise. We both caught it in the eyes. The burning was immediate and savage.

We fell away from each other, clutching our faces. I thought I was suffocating. My eyes started to fry in the perfumed gas. To touch them was unbearable, to leave them alone was worse.

"Jesus Christ!" I screamed. "I can't see!"

I felt Gabriella taking one of my hands and dragging me to my feet. "Come on!" she urged me. "We've got to get out of here!"

"I can't see!"

"You don't need to. I'll lead you."

The copper-haired attacker groaned and slowly started to move. Gabriella pushed and pulled me. Her grip on my left hand was strong as she hauled me through her bedroom and onto the landing. With my right hand, I frantically wiped away the streams of stinging tears that were flowing freely down my face. The pain was getting worse. She helped me into a shirt. I could hear somebody else moving.

"I haven't got any shoes!" I pointed out, as she brought me to the top of the stairs.

"We don't have time. Besides, you've got feet, haven't you?"

"Yes."

"Well, you can run on those!"

The stairs were difficult to negotiate. I stumbled repeatedly but maintained a firm grip on the banisters. At the bottom of the staircase, we came across Paul, the third attacker. His matching CDS baseball cap was cocked to one side and slung low over his brow. His speech was indistinct. I assumed he was drunk on concussion.

"My ankle," he mumbled. "It's gone . . . my ankle . . . is broken."

Gabriella helped me stagger over his prostrate form. His ankle was indeed twisted into a sickening position.

"What . . . what . . . you say?" he slurred. "Doc . . . doctor . . . call a doc . . ."

Gabriella's hand felt as though it were welded to mine. Upstairs, we heard the copper-haired attacker imploring his friend to get off the floor because they had to pursue us.

"Come on!" she urged me. "We've got to run!"

The cool air hit my eyes and made them stream even more than before. So I closed them as much as I could and let Gabriella drag me into the night.

*

My feet were cold and my eyes were hot. The smell of damp garbage was really beginning to bother me. I looked up into the bleak sky.

"We're probably okay now. They'll have stopped looking."

"Do you think so?"

"If I was in their shoes I would have."

I looked down at my naked feet and rubbed the right one, hoping to drive some of the cold from the toes.

"I'm sure you would have," she replied, critically. "But what about them?"

"Well, there are only so many times you can drive around in a circle without drawing attention to yourself. As long as we don't go back to the flat, we should be fine."

"So where do we go? Your flat?"

"Absolutely not."

"Exactly," said Gabriella, before preventing me, yet again, from rubbing my injured eyes. "How are they?"

"They still hurt like hell, but they're not getting any worse."

"Does it still hurt to open them?"

"Like hot needles."

"You should really go to a hospital, Christian."

"No way! It's too risky."

"But your eyes are too precious. You can't take a chance with them."

We'd been huddling between dustbins down an alley for more than half an hour. It felt like a week. From where we squatted, we could see the main street. Or rather, *she* could. Occasionally, black silhouettes shuffled by; nocturnal nomads with hanging heads and banana-curved shoulders.

Gabriella had wanted to run further away from her flat but my blindness held her back. I'd stumbled like a drunk, unable to see and barely able to breathe or stand. So she took the decision to lie low, steering us into the alley, which was close to Victoria Station. I was impressed that I'd got that far. She sat me down in the slime, with my back against a weeping wall and told me not to touch my eyes.

"That's easy for you to say," I'd moaned.

"They're in a bad enough state without you rubbing dirt into them."

Not touching them seemed even worse than the pain itself. It was as impossible as eating a doughnut without licking your lips. The half-hour that had passed since we ducked into the alley was the longest of my life.

Just after four-thirty, Gabriella led me onto the street. We found a café for early-risers, not far from the station. The owner took one look at my filthy, bare feet and tried to prevent us from entering, by filling the doorway with his body.

"Do you have a washroom?" Gabriella asked.

The owner looked at her and then back at me, saying, "Yes, but you can't . . ."

"We need to use it," she said. "He needs cold water."

Before the proprietor could protest, Gabriella had barged past him, taking me with her. There were only three people in the café. Two men whispered at a corner table and a young woman with greasy blonde hair sat near the back in a cracked leather jacket, fingering a cup of milky tea. The owner took hold of Gabriella's arm.

"Wait a minute!" he growled. "He can't come in here with his feet like that."

She retorted angrily, "I need to clean his eyes. Can't you see that?"

With my bleary vision, I saw the man peering at me and then grimacing. He jabbed his finger towards the rear of the café.

Gabriella locked the door of the washroom, sat me on a wooden box and bent my head back over the edge of the basin.

"Any further back and you'll break my neck."

"Stop complaining."

She started to scoop handfuls of water over my face. The sensation of icy liquid splashing onto sizzling eyes was excruciating. I half expected steam to rise from the pupils.

"I feel like one of those beagles in a shampoo testing laboratory," I told her.

"Don't worry, you'll be all right," she assured me.

We reappeared ten minutes later and took a table near the rear of the café. The owner came over to us and I think he was going to ask us to leave. But Gabriella spoke before he had the chance.

"Thank you so much. He was attacked and we needed to wash the stuff out of his eyes. We're really grateful. Thank you so much. You're so kind."

"Oh, well . . . that's okay, but . . ."

"Two coffees, please," she added.

"What happened to you?" he asked me.

"Some lunatic sprayed an aerosol in my face."

"Looks painful."

I said, "Believe me, it is."

"And what happened to your shoes?"

"That's another story."

He looked at Gabriella, who smiled sweetly and nodded, and then he retreated. I had some small change in my pocket, which I spilled onto the table top. A cigarette was what I most wanted and didn't have.

"I'm sorry," said Gabriella. "I tried really hard not to get you in the face."

"I know. Don't be sorry. If you hadn't intervened, I'd probably be dead meat on a hook by now."

She looked up from the plastic table top. I noticed that I was shaking slightly and said, "So what do we do now?"

"I don't know."

When the two men who had been whispering left, we took their copy of the *Daily Mirror*, which was lying on the table. Samuel Price was on the front page. Gabriella and I looked at each other. We were surprised. Except that having seen the kind of animal Price was, we weren't *that* surprised.

"Fast work," I said.

"Even for him, I expect."

Gabriella and I read the "exclusive". Naturally, it was all about his latest coup: *me*. The picture which dominated the front page was absolutely Samuel Price; his arms held outstretched and a broad, self-satisfied grin filling his fat face, while his belly bulged out of his jacket. In the sycophantic article which accompanied the photographs, Price made great capital of the fact that there was no money involved in the arrangement.

"This lad is totally unprepared for the publicity which is being generated," he told an over-eager journalist. "Somebody has to help him and since I'm the best in the business, it's only natural it should be me. And since it's such a worthy cause, I'm only too happy to do it for free."

I said, "He's really full of it, isn't he?"

"Up to the ears."

"He's taken a real liberty here. But on the other hand . . ."

Gabriella saw the look spread across my face and said, "What?"

There was a pay-phone in the back of the café, just opposite the door to the washroom.

"Do you realize what time it is?" grunted Price, when I finally got through to him.

"I wouldn't be calling at five in the morning unless it was important."

"Five in the morning? Is that what it is? Jesus Christ! This better be good!"

"Oh, believe me, it's a real peach," I assured him.

When I finished narrating the details of the assault, all he said was, "Well, that's most unfortunate, Christian.

141

Very unpleasant indeed. But what do you want me to do about it?"

I took a deep breath. "You probably haven't seen today's papers yet, have you?"

There was a cautious pause, before he said, "Of course not."

"I have. You're all over the front page, grinning like a mortician at a motorway pile-up. If you're as concerned as you make out, I'd have thought a little effort on your behalf might be appropriate."

"Don't blame me for that. We agreed I could milk the publicity so long as there was no money involved."

"We didn't *agree* anything. We discussed it ... briefly. That's all. And even if we had come to an arrangement, this kind of article would certainly be breaking the spirit of it."

Suddenly he was alert. "So, what are you saying?" he asked, in a guarded fashion. "What do you want?"

"I want someone to come and collect us. Within half an hour."

"What?"

"Within half an hour. I'm still in pain, Price."

"You're taking advantage of me!" he protested.

"That's funny, I thought it was the other way round. That's certainly what it looks like in this article, anyway. But don't worry. If Gabriella and I are still here in thirty-one minutes, you won't have to worry about me taking advantage of you."

"What do you mean?"

He couldn't hide his panic and that made me even more suspicious. What was he frightened of losing?

"You work it out."

"Okay, I hear you," he said, adopting a conciliatory tone. "Just sit tight and I'll get someone to you."

I gave him the address. "Half an hour," I reminded him, before hanging up.

While we waited, Gabriella washed my eyes again. She smiled as she swept water off my face. "I never realized you had such a ruthless streak."

"I didn't, but I've been watching you."

# Chapter Eleven

A silent driver in a red Ford Mondeo collected us from the café near Victoria Station and took us to Samuel Price's huge house in St John's Wood. On the way, we stopped at a twenty-four hour chemist and Gabriella got the driver to lend her some cash for a bottle of eye-drops. She administered them in the back of the car and then we drove on.

Price's house was a triumph of wealth over taste. He lived in a luxury compound, surrounded by a ten-foot wall to keep undesirables out. It might just as well have been constructed to shield the public from the raging vulgarity on the inside.

If I'd ever really believed that notions of taste were a personal matter, Price's house convinced me otherwise. The large entrance hall had a stone floor which was partially covered by a selection of zebra-rugs and lion skins. To the right, on top of a six-foot column, which had been marbled in a flesh tone, a laser pyramid emitted rods of sparkling light which danced on the ceiling. Piped music oozed out of concealed speakers. The central staircase plunged into the ground floor with a flourish. Its maroon carpet looked ankle deep. Two huge bronze eagles sat on the expanded, curved bottom step. Price had drenched them in gilt.

As he greeted us, he took one look at me and said, "Jesus Christ! You look like a rabbit with myxomatosis."

"Thank you."

"And where are your shoes?"

"Not on my feet," I replied, tetchily.

He led us to a bathroom. There was a circular bath set into the floor. The shower had a head cast in the shape of a shark's mouth. There was a small Sony television mounted on a wall bracket. I cleaned the grit out of my feet. Gabriella bathed my eyes again and sprinkled more drops into them.

Considerably cleaner and slightly refreshed, Gabriella and I sat in Price's study, on a snow-white, leather sofa. I was getting used to a pair of shoes borrowed from the cook. Price was behind a large kidney-shaped desk with a black stone top. One wall was covered by identically sized framed photographs, which all featured Price with the rich and famous.

"We'll find these bastards, don't you worry," he reassured us. "What did you say their organization was called?"

"The Church of the Divine Science."

"We'll see what we can dig up on them. I've got all sorts of contacts."

I didn't doubt it.

"Meanwhile," he continued, "I think it would be much better if the two of you stayed somewhere secure. Just until everything's calmed down."

"Secure?"

"Some place where we can protect you from these people. And from the press. You obviously can't go back to either of your homes."

"So where?" I asked.

"Don't you worry, I'll take care of it."

And that was how we came to be gliding south from St John's Wood in a stretched black Mercedes with dark windows. The interior was all smooth leather and thick carpets. As a pedestrian, I often wondered who travelled around the city in cars like this.

"You wouldn't believe the people who've been in here," he boasted, "or what they've done in it."

This was evidently a source of some pride. He told us a lurid tale of some overnight sensation who had sex with a prepubescent groupie all over the polished leather upon which we were sitting.

"They were on their way back from Wembley Arena to the Mayfair Hotel, right? Suddenly there's a collision in the road and the driver does an emergency stop. So these two kids – who are going at it like a train – get thrown forward. My boy broke his hand. Cracked it on the TV set. Naturally, everyone thought it was hilarious, except for me and the mother of the girl. She was outraged, I can tell you. Tight bitch! Cost me ten grand to stop her going to the police. Turned out the daughter was only thirteen," he sighed, wistfully. "And me? I lost a fortune because he couldn't play the guitar with his busted hand. Had to cancel his European tour."

At traffic lights I saw people looking at the car, as I usually did, and no doubt thinking the same thought that invariably went through my mind: who's the fat cat inside that?

The Church of the Divine Science. Where did they get their information from? How did they know what I'd done? Where was Louis? What did they think I was? Some kind of devil?

Price said, "What about giving an interview?"

"What about it?"

"I think you should. I could organize one with a sympathetic newspaper."

"Sympathetic?"

"I'd ensure the interview took place under controlled circumstances."

I shook my head and said, "I don't think so."

"Sooner or later, you're going to have to say something to someone, aren't you?"

"Probably, but not to a tabloid. Not after the junk they've already printed."

"They only do that because they've got no hard facts to go on. If you spoke to them you could . . ."

"That's bullshit and you know it."

We drove down Park Lane, turned left into Mount Street and, a moment later, came to a halt at the Park Street entrance to the Grosvenor House Hotel. I looked at Price.

"Your new home," he explained. "In there, to be specific."

He was pointing to the Flats Entrance. Price picked up the key from the desk clerk and we took the lift to the fourth floor. The apartment was comfortable. There was a bedroom on the right and a living-room on the left. Sandwiched between the two were a pristine bathroom and a diminutive kitchen, barely larger than a cupboard. A cooker, a fridge and a sink were somehow squeezed in there, which was quite an achievement.

"Could be worse," I said.

"Make yourselves at home. If you need something, ring room service and charge it. You'll be fine in here and just to make sure, I'm going to have a couple of my lads out in the corridor."

Anyone who gets disturbed at five in the morning is entitled to feel grumpy, but Price's character change between then and now was something more fundamental than a mere mood improvement. It was more like metamorphosis, and since I'd come to the conclusion that he probably never did anything without a profitable motive, this sudden cordiality made me suspicious. I assumed there was a reason for it and I was right.

"By the way, before I go, there is one suggestion I'd like to make."

The carefully manufactured air of inconsequence amused me. I'd never heard an off-hand sentence sound so contrived. It was almost embarrassing. I tried to restrict my smile to reasonable proportions. "And that is?"

"It's just occurred to me," he lied. "Television."

"Television?"

"Yes. Live television. It seems to me that your main concern is people misquoting and misrepresenting you. If you went on a live TV show, you'd get around that problem."

It was clear he'd anticipated my rejection of his suggestion to speak to a newspaper. What he was now saying seemed logical, so I nodded and murmured, "Maybe."

"I'll tell you what," he continued, warming to the subject, "we could pick a show outside prime time, maybe one late at night. That way, we can use it as a tester. We can see if you come across well. If it's a disaster, we get away without serious damage and if it's a success, we can use it as a stepping-stone to something more substantial."

I played along. "Good thinking."

"The other advantage of picking a small show is that we could lay down our terms. It would be a big coup for them to get you on their programme, so they'd be bound to make concessions for us. We could arrange it so you'd feel comfortable with the format. We'd have control."

It was so obvious he'd had it all planned out in advance. I wondered when he thought it through. After coming to Gabriella's flat? Or before that, perhaps? Maybe it was as soon as he first saw me bleeding on some front page. I smiled and said, "That's not bad. I'll think about it."

"There's no need to rush into a decision. Take your time and we'll talk about it later."

When a man like Price was sweetness and light, you had to raise your guard, not drop it.


My natural inclination was to dismiss this latest suggestion out of hand. Indeed, despite telling him I'd consider the matter, I gave it no further thought that day.

Gabriella and I had a long, lazy lunch and watched a black-and-white movie on the television in the early afternoon. Later, I came across an absurd article in one of the tabloids; an interview with Robert Poulsen. It should have been hard to believe he'd sold his story to the papers, since he certainly didn't need the money, but it wasn't. It merely confirmed what a cheap character he could be.

Reading the article, one could be forgiven for thinking that Poulsen and I were the closest of friends. He made us sound like Siamese twins. He said that ever since he first met me, he sensed I possessed extraordinary qualities which would always mark me out in life. I couldn't resist calling him. His excuse for selling his story was even more pathetic than the interview itself.

"Don't tell me you're not milking it!" he snapped, when I accused him of being a gutless mercenary.

"And that's your justification for this, is it?"

"I don't *need* justification," he replied.

"That's lucky for you, then, isn't it? Life must be so easy without the burden of a sense of shame."

It was low, even by Poulsen's gutter-friendly standards. Furthermore, I couldn't imagine Rowdy being amused by it. I was slightly surprised that Poulsen seemed to have ignored that angle.

When night came, I slept on the sofa in the living-room. Gabriella thought this was funny because she said she didn't mind sharing the double bed with me. I thanked her, but declined. She said that living in Rome, dealing with persistent pestering from lecherous males was an occupational hazard, so my reluctance was unexpected.

"I can assure you that this rejection is a curious first and a refreshing change!"

"Well, I hate being predictable."

"That's one thing you're not. All the same, I really don't mind. I trust you."

"A dangerous mistake," I assured her.

It was the following morning when I changed my mind about Price's suggestion. If I hadn't turned on the radio, I probably wouldn't have deviated from my original thinking on the matter.

Gabriella was in the bath, singing a peculiar version of "La Vie En Rose". I made myself a cup of coffee in the cupboard-sized kitchen and took it into the sitting-room. I turned on the radio before sitting down to read the morning's papers. It was the same FM talk show that Gabriella had been listening to at her flat.

"This is me, Mike Foster, asking you to call in and discuss whatever you want. Tell London what's on your mind. And now, on line two, we've got . . . Peter."

"Good morning, Mr Foster."

"Morning, Peter. What do you want to say?"

"I'd like to talk about Christian Floyd."

I knew something that Foster didn't. The caller's name wasn't Peter. The radio was a cheap portable which produced a tinny sound, but the voice was so distinctive, I recognized it immediately. The sound of the cracked voice trying to wrestle words out of the throat sent a shiver through me. It was Louis calling.

"Ah yes," said Foster. "He's the so-called healer who's been so much in evidence in the papers in the last couple of days."

"That's right."

I had no doubt it was him.

"What do you make of it all?"

"It's evil."

There was a pause before Foster said, "You think it's evil, do you? Why?"

"He makes the claims which fuel the hopes and prayers of the sick, and then he hides. Why does he do that?"

"I don't know. Why do you think he does it?"

"To cause confusion and despair among the hopeful. And when their pain is almost intolerable, he'll return."

"Why would he do that?"

"To appear as a saviour at the peak of their crisis. Then they'll be his."

"I see," murmured Foster, clearly in some doubt as to whether to persist with the call. "So you accept that he can heal?"

There was a moment's silence. "The power to heal does exist," Louis said, eventually.

"So we're being told. After all, he *did* heal a blind man, didn't he?"

"The blind man was healed," conceded Louis.

"Well, that can't be considered evil, can it?"

"Not in itself, no. But if it were a prelude to something greater, then it might be."

"I'm not sure what you mean."

"The act of healing may not be evil, but the healer himself might be. The healing – which appears good to you – may be part of a larger design with evil as its heart."

"This is what you believe, is it?" said Foster.

"This is what I *know*," said Louis.

Fearing a religious rant, Foster cut Louis off and went into a commercial break. Gabriella was still singing in the bath. She had a good voice, but then again, even I had a good voice when I was in the bathroom.

I lit a cigarette. My eyes were better, but still sore. I had several bruises on my ribs, in various shades of purple and black, with yellow tinges. In another day or two, I'd be able to walk and not feel the cuts and grazes on my feet. Who was Louis to lecture on right or wrong?

It was impossible to know what would have happened to us had Gabriella not broken free and incapacitated her attacker. Was the assault intended to be a warning, or something more sinister? The more I thought about Louis and his miserable Church, the easier it became to take the decision.

Gabriella reappeared, as I finished my coffee and reached for the phone. I dialled Price's number and told her, "I'm going to do it."

"Go on TV?"

"Yes."

"Are you sure? Yesterday you were set against it."

"I know."

"What changed your mind?"

"Screwy Louis did."

She frowned, but before I could explain it to her, Price arrived on the line.

"I've thought about your suggestion," I told him, "and I'm ready to do it."

"Excellent!"

"But before you go ahead, there are a couple of things I'd like to straighten out."

"Sure."

"I don't want any cheap surprises or tricks ... I don't want to go on one of those shows where the host simply does his best to try to take the piss out of his guests. Also, the interviewer's got to stick to the subject of healing. I don't want any personal stuff being raked up."

"Of course. You can take that for granted. This'll be a professional operation, Christian. I don't deal in second-raters or anything that's cheap and nasty. It's all above board with me."

"I'm sure it is. But I just wanted to be clear."

We were told it would take a couple of days to set things up, so we had time to kill. Gabriella and I were mostly restricted to staying in the flat. Price discouraged us from venturing out, so we watched TV, read the papers and Gabriella even tried to pass on some of her culinary expertise to me.

Price supplied us with four minders, who split the day in two and worked in pairs. Nigel and Steve were the sulky duo, probably because they drew the night shift. They rarely spoke, except when asked a direct question. But between eight in the morning and eight at night, we were in the charge of the other pair. Brian Bradfield had been a middle-weight contender in the seventies, but a car accident left him with serious head wounds and he couldn't get a professional boxing licence after that. He'd worked for Price ever since. Bradfield had a weakness for neatly-tailored suits and kept himself in good shape. Although he lacked obvious physical menace, and despite his conservative dress and courteous manner, you always had the feeling that if it came to the crunch, he'd kill anyone who tangled with him, without raising an eyebrow or creasing his jacket. His partner's qualities were more obvious. Jackson was an Antiguan who stood six and a half feet tall but seemed much larger. People who can't see their toes are usually fat. In Jackson's case, it was his chest which blocked the view. He had a gold crucifix dangling from an ear and a deep two-inch scar on his right cheek. He was terror itself. Brian Bradfield told us that ninety-nine times out of a hundred, Jackson simply had to stand still and stare to get tough men to behave.

"And the reason this works," he explained to us, "is that it's no empty threat. He's a slaughterhouse once he gets going. I've never seen nothing like him. Makes Mike Tyson look like Grace Kelly."

On the few occasions we strayed from our comfortable cell, we were accompanied. Brian went with Gabriella and Jackson stuck with me. Brian decided that if we were venturing out, Gabriella and I should not go together. Jackson drew stares wherever we went and it surprised me that it didn't bother him.

"I'm used to it," he murmured, in his rumbling voice.

"Besides, they're just little people. I got better things to worry about."

On the second evening, Gabriella and I were alone in the flat. Price had just left, after an hour-long visit to explain the sequence of events for my interview. Gabriella sat at my side throughout and I noticed that Price kept looking at her. He appeared much more concerned with her opinion than with mine. So, once he'd gone, I asked her what was going on.

"What do you mean?" she responded, innocently.

"It just seems to me that you and Price are on some sort of wavelength that I can't tune into."

She smiled. "That almost sounds like jealousy."

I shook my head and replied, "I just feel I'm missing something."

Gabriella leaned back against the writing desk. "In a sense you are and that's why he keeps checking with me. Because I'm not missing a thing, and he knows it."

She was wearing an old pair of jeans and a new shirt. It was rich green, several shades darker than her eyes.

"I don't understand."

"No, you don't," she agreed. "You understand so little. I've never met anyone as naive as you, Christian. You shock me. You hold a responsible job, you're well educated, you've travelled plenty, you're clearly intelligent and yet you've got gaps in you that I could drive a tank through."

I felt embarrassed and held open my hands in a useless gesture. She mimicked it and said, "Hands open and nothing to say. I'm sure you know your own little world really well, but it's a million miles away from where the rest of us live. It's a tiny sphere of privilege and pleasure. And now that you're outside it, and having to face some sort of reality, you're like a nun in a brothel. You don't know where to look or what to do."

"What do you mean?" I demanded, indignantly.

155

Gabriella sighed.

"You're completely out of touch and Price can see that. The two of you are opposites. He's street-wise, but stupid and ill-educated. You, on the other hand, have the benefits of a fine mind that's been well tutored, but you can't cross a busy street. If I hadn't been around, Price would have had you on a prime-time magic show by now, performing vulgar tricks under coloured spotlights. But I can see him for what he really is, and he knows it. That's why he keeps checking with me. He knows I won't let him take you for a ride."

Her accusations stung. I said, "Why bother? And don't tell me it's because you owe me."

"You idiot!" she said, breaking into an exasperated smile. "Can't you see anything? Everyone else can. Price, Brian, Jackson ... they all think we're about to get married."

"*What*?"

"Don't worry, I put them straight. But it does make the point."

"So why are you doing it, then?" I asked.

It seemed to me the most obvious question, but it appeared to catch her off guard. She looked at the carpet and said, rather unconvincingly, "Because I like you."

"And that's it?"

"No. That's not the only reason. I'm also doing it because nobody else is going to help you ... and you *do* need help."

"You make me sound like a real basket case."

"Not quite," she purred.

Now she was leaning against the sitting-room door-frame. I looked up from the drinks tray, which was close by, and stared into her amazing eyes. Our gazes clashed and locked, where before they had always averted. She was close enough to touch. I picked up her scent. My pulse quickened. She never broke her bold stare. Her fingers were trailing the edge of the sideboard. It would have been no effort to reach out and gently take her hand. The prospect of a kiss sandpapered my throat.

The phone rang. Her eyes continued to bore into mine. I had the choice and made the wrong one. I picked up the phone. It was Price, checking that we were all right. I wanted to yell at him for his atrocious sense of timing, but instead fielded his tedious questions as politely as I could. When the call was finished, Gabriella still seemed in a good mood, but the moment had definitely passed.

She said, casually, "Why don't we eat in the restaurant this evening? I'm already getting bored with room service."

"Sure," I agreed. "A good idea."

"I'd like a bath first, though."

"Okay. I'm just going to get some cigarettes."

Brian and Jackson were standing by the lift, waiting for the night-shift to relieve them. Jackson offered to accompany me.

"I'm only going downstairs for cigarettes," I told him.

Strolling through the lobby of the hotel, with my two packets of Marlboro, I suddenly felt a hand clamp my shoulder. I shuddered in dreadful anticipation and turned round.

"Christian! I thought it was you."

It was Charlie Prime, squeezed into his favourite double-breasted suit. His cheeks and chins struggled out of a tight, striped shirt. A gold pin kept a spotted tie firmly in place. I'd been expecting some maniac from the Church of the Divine Science, or at least a vulture from the press. My heart lurched.

"Jesus Christ!" I exclaimed. "Don't do that!"

He grinned unreservedly and said, "What the hell are you doing here?"

That was a tough one to answer so I said, "What the hell are *you* doing here?"

"I'm taking Miranda out to dinner. She's working in South Audley Street at the moment, so we arranged to meet here."

"Still chasing that dream, are you?"

"I'm afraid so," he said, before looking at his watch. "Actually, I'm rather early. Fancy a drink? I haven't seen you for ages."

"Not since your birthday," I corrected him.

Running into Charlie was a terribly timed coincidence. My heart was beating a drumroll. I should have turned down his offer of a drink, but out of a sheer sense of relief, I allowed him to persuade me. We went into the bar, sat down at a table and Charlie ordered two vodka and tonics. Once the waiter had gone, there was an awkward silence.

"So, how is Miranda?" I finally asked, when the ice was begging to be broken.

"Oh, she's well."

"And are you any closer to capturing her heart?"

He laughed. "I'm still having a bit of trouble there. I can't persuade her that my money makes me worth marrying. She's looking for extras like companionship and love."

"Well, look on the bright side. If she ever relents, it'll be for all the right reasons. What about everyone else?"

"Jorge's still in Madrid. He probably doesn't even know about you yet. And Katy . . . well, Katy . . ."

Charlie's voice trailed off.

"Yes?" I prompted.

"Well, the thing is, Katy and . . . and Justin . . . well, they've been . . . *seeing* each other."

"Seeing each other?"

"Yes."

"You mean sleeping with each other?" I said, bluntly.

Charlie cleared his throat and said, "That's right."

"It doesn't surprise me. It's happened before."

His eyes widened. "Really?"

"So she says."

"That's hard to believe. It's just so unlike her."

"Perhaps she was simply trying to make me look like a fool," I suggested.

"She needn't have gone to all the effort," he laughed. "You've done a perfect job all by yourself."

Charlie stopped himself and the smile disappeared. I sipped my drink. It was beautifully chilled. An elderly Japanese lady was trying to make herself understood at the bar.

"I'm sorry," he murmured.

"That's okay. I'm getting used to far worse things being said about me. In time, I may even develop a thick skin."

Charlie smiled falsely, took a deep breath and said, "Everyone's talking about you."

"I can imagine."

"It's quite embarrassing really."

"Embarrassing?"

"Well, you know," he said, coyly. "Appearing in the papers like that. Some of us have even had journalists badgering *us*. Of course, we don't know what to say. We don't know whether it's true or . . ."

"It is."

We looked at each other and he said, "You're joking!"

"No."

"But how?"

"I don't know. I'm as confused by it as anyone."

"So what do we say to these people?"

"Nothing."

"But, they keep pestering us and . . ."

"*Nothing!*"

Charlie started fiddling with the Cartier cigarette case that Jorge gave him for his birthday. I could see how uneasy he was with the entire topic – after all, it had taken him five minutes to get round to discussing it – and I could easily imagine that he wasn't the only one.

"Don't worry," I said, a little bitterly. "I won't embarrass any of you. Not directly."

"Christian!" he protested, too vigorously to be sincere. "That's not what . . ."

"Sure it is, Charlie. I know you too well."

There was a lengthy pause before he looked up and said, "You do see it from our point of view, don't you?"

Jackson was suddenly standing at our table, casting an enormous shadow over us. "You all right?"

"Yes," I said.

He looked at Charlie and said, "Who's this?"

I rose from the table and looked back at Charlie. "So much for promises of amicable solidarity."

"What?"

We walked out of the hotel, so Charlie wouldn't think I was staying there, and came back in via the Flats Entrance. Jackson asked who Charlie was, and when I described him as a friend, he said it didn't look like it. I told him it didn't feel like it, either. We were silent until we were alone in the lift. Then I said, "Did you tell Gabriella that you thought she and I were involved?"

"I did. Why?"

"Just wondering."

"It was an easy mistake to make, you know. I mean, you look as though you're involved," he said, turning to me. Then he started to laugh and added, "And you'd *like* to be involved, right?"

"I didn't say that."

"You didn't have to."


On the morning of the interview, Gabriella received the things she'd requested. The parcel was wrapped in brown paper. It was delivered to her while I was still dozing on the sofa in the sitting-room. She opened the curtains and daylight charged in. I tried to fend off the brightness with a raised forearm across my eyes. She offered me the package.

"What's this?"

"A present. For you."

I struggled to sit up. Gabriella had excitement all over her face, as I started to peel the brown paper away. There were a selection of books and a collection of photo-copied essays. I picked up one which had been lifted from *Time* magazine. "Stigmata Leaves Its Mark" was the title of the article. I looked up at Gabriella.

"I thought it might help," she explained. "In place of talking to someone."

I flicked through a paperback called *Miraculous Evidence: An Investigation*. There was a slim hardback beneath it, entitled *The Blood Of Christ*, which claimed to give detailed accounts of alleged cases of stigmata. I rose from the sofa and stretched.

"That's very thoughtful of you," I said.

Her expression of anticipation mutated into relief. She smiled broadly. "It seemed like the obvious thing."

I took a shower. When I came out of the bathroom, Gabriella was making coffee with one hand and holding a book in the other.

"Listen to this," she told me. "Maria von Moerl of the Tyrol. She first had stigmata in 1834 and it lasted until 1868. According to J. J. von Gorres, who documented the case, there were thousands of people who witnessed it. He says he saw her in a normal condition, as well as during her ecstatic state, which happened during Holy Communion. Remember I said that?"

I nodded. "Intense prayer."

"Exactly. Here's another girl: Maria Dominica Lazzari of Capriana. Dr Leonard dei Cloche, who was the director of the Civil and Military Hospital at Trent, says he often saw her in a state of ecstasy between 1833 and 1834."

"More or less the same year," I pointed out.

"During these phases, a black spot appeared in the middle of her hand. It looked like a nail. There was often a similar mark on her right foot."

"Like St Francis of Assisi? The nails rising out of his body when he was dead?"

"That's right. The nails, the bleeding . . . it's all part of the same thing. According to Dr dei Cloche, she also had a wound in the side, but this was only seen by her family. Anyway, during the ecstasy, her body trembled and she told him that she had pain running through her . . . like you do."

Gabriella looked directly at me, but I didn't say a word. The kettle began to boil. She handed me the book and I flicked through several pages. Louise Lateau of Bois d'Haine in Belgium was, apparently, a girl of excellent character. The researcher said she wasn't especially emotional or imaginative. I assumed he'd made the point because it was relevant. In which case, he seemed to be suggesting that most of the subjects *were* emotional and imaginative. Perhaps they were encouraging the condition, either deliberately or subconsciously.

Louise Lateau, however, did not fit into this category. She was hard working, helpful and level-headed. All things being equal, she sounded boring. In 1868, she began to notice blood seeping from her hands, feet and side, after she'd been meditating on Christ's Passion. Dr Ferdinand Lefebvre, who was Professor of Pathology in Louvain, devoted six weeks to her case. More than a hundred medical colleagues examined her.

On one occasion, they turned up at her home unannounced, hoping to catch her out. Instead, they discovered Louise bleeding from her forehead and her right hand.

Lefebvre carried out an experiment on her. He caused an artificial blister, similar to the one which she claimed was a legitimate stigmata scar. The original blister bled, but Lefebvre's did not. Taking the test one stage further, he placed her hand in a heavy leather glove, so that it was impossible to get at the wound. The glove was securely sealed at the wrist and only removed on Good Friday, many days after it had been applied. Lefebvre saw a blister rise from the hand. It was a peculiar dark colour. Then it burst and bled profusely for several hours.

I shuddered at the account and felt both sympathy and empathy. The poor girl must have been terrified. The condition was bad enough, but having the doctors of her day conducting crude experiments on her must have made it worse. Their bafflement could only fuel her fear. Medicine might have progressed out of all proportion since 1868, but I had no desire to follow Louise Lateau's path. Being a scientific curiosity, the prime exhibit in a medical freak show, was a horror to avoid.

I snapped the book shut, as if that would close my mind to it. Gabriella handed me a cup of coffee.

"Are you all right?" she asked.

"Fine," I said, as we moved back to the sitting-room. "You know, all of this is very interesting, but so far, all I'm reading about is earnest young girls who bleed during prayer. No men and no healing."

"So far," she corrected me, pointing to the rest of the reading matter. "But it's all relevant. You have something in common with all of them."

"Most of them were believers. It happened during prayer, Gabriella. But me? I'm almost an atheist."

"Almost?"

I shrugged in frustration. "I believe in something . . . *abnormal*, something beyond rational explanation. But it's not a religious thing."

"Doesn't that make you question what's happened to you all the more? The bleeding makes no sense and yet here are accounts of similar phenomena. It's happened before."

"I know, but I just don't get it. I've seen the blood

coming out of me. I've *felt* it seeping through the wounds. I've seen what I can do, but I still don't believe in God the way all these people do."

"Do you have a better explanation?"

"No. But I haven't come up with a worse one, either. Besides, in the eyes of religion, these people seem to be good candidates. They're honest, toiling types who are down on their knees praying, when they're not too busy trying to eke out a miserable living. But that's not me. When I'm not working, I'm trying to spend all the money I make. I'm thoughtless and selfish. I drink, smoke and swear too much. Other people's problems don't concern me. The only time I'm down on my knees on a Sunday is when I'm in the bathroom after a rough Saturday night. So who could be less suitable than me?"

"That's not true," said Gabriella.

"Well, you know what I mean."

"Not every good man is good from conception."

"What?"

"People change."

I scoffed at the notion. "And you think I have?"

"I don't know. I never knew you before you saved my life."

I took a sip from my coffee cup and lit my debut cigarette of the morning. I always hated the first couple, but had to struggle through them to get to the satisfying ones which marked the rest of the day.

Gabriella said, "For what it's worth, I think you *are* good. You've got flaws – plenty of flaws – but who among us hasn't? The essence of you is good."

"I don't feel any different to before," I told her. "Apart from being thoroughly disorientated and scared witless, of course."

I sat on the sofa and sifted through the material on the coffee table. The information on healing was patchy. There was a Chinese woman from Nanking, who anaesthetized people with her hands, allowing them to undergo major surgery while still fully conscious. According to her patients, the areas she numbed felt hot, while she said her body felt cold. That struck a chord with me, but there were no further similarities.

The same article reported on a man living in the Tsinghai province of central China. He was famous in his district for healing fevers. His fingertips drew the illness out and then he plunged both hands into boiling water to neutralize the ailment. He never displayed pain and his hands never scarred. The article also said he was more than a hundred and twenty years old, which only serviced my lingering scepticism.

"Listen to this," said Gabriella, looking up from the pages of one of the paperbacks. "There's a man here called Lorenzo Sevilla. A Peruvian. His father was a teacher in Cuzco, up in the Andes. He was killed in a train accident while on a trip in Bolivia. He'd been on his way from La Paz to Arica, in the north of Chile, to visit a Catholic mission. An avalanche came down on the line and knocked the carriages off a mountain pass. At the time of the accident, Lorenzo was back in Cuzco and he experienced total vision. He saw the accident and started to bleed from his hands, feet, side and forehead.

"One of those who witnessed his bleeding was an old woman, who was struck with chronic arthritis. He relayed what he was seeing, while the bleeding continued, and, according to this, started to cry because he saw his father die. The crippled woman hobbled forward to comfort him. She hugged him and he laid his hands upon her, instantly healing her arthritis. He was only six years old."

Gabriella looked across the table at me. "Isn't that awful?"

"I suppose it is, yes."

"*You suppose?*"

"Is that yet another colourful account from another century?"

Anger flashed across Gabriella's face and she lobbed the book at me. "No! The year was 1976. There's even a colour photograph of Lorenzo Sevilla. Just to satisfy people like you, I guess!"

Lorenzo was wearing jeans and a plain white T-shirt. In the shot, he was smiling broadly, displaying teeth as dazzling as the overhead sun. The photo was dated April 1987. I read on. His aunt and uncle cared for him after his father's death, since his mother had died three years earlier. They lived in Juliaca, near Lake Titicaca, which was a place so remote that it made Cuzco seem like Manhattan. Lorenzo's talent was no secret and yet it wasn't widely acknowledged. For one thing, he rarely travelled away from the town. No reason was given. But those who travelled to Juliaca were gladly received and healed.

No one ever actually witnessed the healing process, other than his aunt or uncle, so there was some speculation as to how he did it. He refused to have an audience, which was suspicious. Except it wasn't because the results were clear. He healed. There were patients to prove it, although none of them seemed to be able to describe quite how he managed it.

I understood that brand of confusion.

But in December 1992, as his reputation was at last beginning to blossom, he made a serious mistake, when he publicly denounced the highly vicious Shining Path terrorist group that had become such a permanent feature of Peruvian life. They saw the danger immediately: a man of his astonishing capability could cause them all sorts of trouble, if he ever came to real public prominence. He could be just the type of man to lead a successful crusade against them. So they decided to make sure he didn't.

During a rare trip to nearby Puno, Lorenzo Sevilla was

murdered by Shining Path. His aunt and uncle were also gunned down in the attack, as the three of them left church after Mass.

I shook my head and muttered in disbelief, "They killed him."

"What?"

"Sevilla was murdered by Shining Path terrorists because they were frightened of what he could do."

I dropped the book on the table and walked over to the window. It was easy to understand their logic. What an enormous potential threat he must have seemed. Inevitably, my thoughts turned to Louis. Was that how he saw me? And again I wondered whether the attack at Gabriella's flat was intended as a warning or as something more permanent.

I felt her hand on my shoulder. "Are you okay?"

"I was just thinking about Louis and his Church."

"It's not the same thing, Christian. Shining Path are ruthless terrorists. Louis and his friends are misguided crackpots."

"How do you know that?"

"Because Shining Path blow people up with bombs and cut them down with assault rifles. They don't hit people with rubber truncheons, or fall downstairs, or allow someone like me to spray them in the eyes with an aerosol. That's how I know."

I was smiling and nodded. "You could have a point."

"Good. I'm glad you see that because I didn't go to the effort of getting this information just to scare you even more than you already have been. I got it because I hoped it would reassure you in some way. I'm sure if we read on, you'll find . . ."

Gabriella let the sentence hang in the air. The confidence in her assertion evaporated instantly. I turned around to face her. "Find what?"

She looked uncertain; hopeful, rather than sure. "That you're not the only one. That you're not alone."

# Chapter Twelve

"My final guest this evening is my mystery guest. Unless you've been living in outer space recently, or unless you're a high court judge, you'll know exactly who I'm talking about when I tell you that he's taking up more space in our newspapers than the Prime Minister . . . so he can't be all bad!"

There was a ripple of laughter from the dark.

"It's the greatest 'Hands of God' story since Diego Maradona punched the ball into England's goal during the 1986 World Cup!"

There was more laughter. I pictured Lorenzo Sevilla stepping out of a church with his aunt and uncle. The sun was shining overhead, spilling warmth on their shoulders. I envisaged the church on one side of a square. The three of them were chatting casually with other worshippers. And then out of the crowd came the gunmen.

The host of the show was still running through his introduction. "He is, of course, the individual at the centre of this amazing healing story. Tonight, on Night Talk, he goes public for the first time. Ladies and gentlemen, would you please welcome the man with the mission, the most anonymous celebrity in the country, the man and his hands . . . Mr Christian Floyd!"

An assistant nudged me in the back and I slipped out of the wings, onto the set. The meagre studio audience to my left were clapping, but I couldn't see them because they were behind a bank of lights which shone in my face. At the centre of the set, on a slightly raised platform, were three sofas and a coffee table. Night Talk was an informal late-night chat show. The guest sat on two sofas, which were divided by the host's armchair. The small audience was supposed to make up the fourth section of this cosy gathering, but they were isolated in the dark, behind the cameras. Smoking and drinking were permitted, in order to foster a relaxed atmosphere, as if it were any old social situation. It actually looked absurdly contrived.

This slightly off-beat approach was supposed to be conducive to conversation of a higher quality, thus ensuring there was no danger of the programme appearing anywhere near prime time. Channel Four chose to broadcast the show on which I appeared just after midnight. Since it followed a three-hour subtitled film, by Warsaw's most depressing director, I didn't expect many people to be watching.

Sean King, the host, was standing to greet me. He wore black, baggy trousers, an electric turquoise shirt and a hairy mustard jacket that needed shaving. King was carving out a reputation for himself as a slick host who knew precious little about interviewing, but who was quick with a quip.

I sat to his right, next door to Linda Tait, a biographer with a taste for chronicling the sexual and chemical pleasures of rock stars.

"So, in fact, you're a character assassin," King had concluded, earlier in the programme.

"Not at all," insisted Tait. "I'm an investigative journalist with a special interest in documenting the social pressures that exert themselves on those people who rise from cultural, intellectual and social backwaters, and who reach the rarefied atmosphere of superstardom. I'm fascinated by the psychological changes in behaviour that occur when this transformation takes place."

"What you're saying is, you like writing about poor kids

who make good in the music industry, and who then run around destroying hotel rooms, driving Ferraris into swimming pools, having orgies, drinking lakes of Jack Daniels and choking on vomit, right?"

Tait, to her credit, nodded, and said, "Absolutely," for which she won a round of applause. "It's also what sells and I consider my writing a business, so money's important."

On the sofa opposite me were two Americans. Cindy Buchausen made her name at twenty-one, when she accepted a film role which a score of other actresses had rejected, on account of the numerous explicit sex scenes. Buchausen had no such qualms and the picture was a huge success. She was a star and she traded on it shamelessly. The reputation she earned had less to do with her limited talents as an actress, and more to do with her talents in bed. She slept with anyone who would assist her career, or simply swell her bank account, both of which blossomed spectacularly over the years. These days, she was content to be an overpaid star in a glossy soap. She had graduated from being Hollywood's favourite nymphomaniac to Hollywood's favourite drunk. Carl Goldman knew Cindy well because she took her dogs to see him. He was the vet psychiatrist the stars sent their pets to.

"Well, good evening, Christian. Nice to have you on the show," said King.

My throat was dry. The set had looked so cramped when I saw it on the monitor in the minute hospitality suite. But as it turned out, the sofas and coffee table formed a little island in a vast ocean of darkness.

"Thanks," I said, looking away from him and towards the audience. I could just make them out in the gloom behind the lights and cameras. They seemed a mile away.

"Would you like a drink?"

It didn't feel right, but I said, "Thank you, yes."

"It's one of the advantages of coming on this show. In fact, it's the only advantage!" joked King.

Gabriella and Price had declined seats at the front of the audience. They stayed with me in the cramped, over-heated hospitality suite, where I'd had a few drinks to try and settle my nerves while watching the opening part of the show. Now they were somewhere in the wings. I could see dark silhouettes there, but didn't know if it was them. Linda Tait poured me a glass of red wine.

"Okay, Christian," said King, settling back and crossing one leg over the other. "You've kept us in the dark for long enough. There are a million things we all want to know, so let me start by asking this: how did you discover that you possessed the ability to heal people?"

I was on the verge of describing how I rescued and healed Gabriella. Luckily, I checked myself. That would have been quite a revelation. Instead, I turned my attention to Mr Leonard.

"Well, I wouldn't say I discovered it. I'd say it came to me, or I was afflicted by it."

"For no apparent reason?"

"None. I was with Mr Leonard and I . . ."

"He's the one you healed?"

"Yes. I found myself in a situation with him and suddenly . . . it took over. I was filled with this immensely powerful sensation and . . ."

As I sat there, my memory reminded me that at the time, that immensely powerful sensation had primarily been lust for Julia Graham. That was why I'd been there. I wondered whether she was watching the show.

"So I just went over to him," I continued, "and I let instinct take over. Before I really knew what was going on, I'd healed him."

The audience had been boisterous before my arrival, but they were amazingly quiet now. Even Sean King, who was prone to levity whenever possible, had begun to look a little serious.

"Just like that?" he asked.

"More or less. You see, I wasn't really conscious of what was happening during the actual healing phase."

"What did it feel like?" asked Carl Goldman.

Goldman was wearing an Armani suit and a bow-tie with silver thread. He was a little, neat man who was almost invisible in the company of Tait and Buchausen.

"Terrifying. At first, there was a sharp effervescent sensation, similar to the strange feeling you can get just before you pass out on some general anaesthetics. And then my body felt like ice, except at the bleeding points, where it was immensely hot."

Was that how Lorenzo Sevilla healed? Only his aunt and uncle had witnessed his healing, and they'd been murdered with him. None of those who'd been healed by him could remember. That made sense. Gabriella was confused about her moment too. She recalled events on either side of the healing quite clearly, but not the act itself. I'd read reports in the newspapers which said Mr Leonard was equally mystified by the process which had transformed his eyes.

"My memory is hazy about that," I said. "It was like I was sleep-walking outside of my body. I know it sounds odd but . . ."

"It certainly does!" chuckled King. "Like some sort of dozy astral projection."

The audience giggled.

"That's not a bad comparison," I told him.

Buchausen, who looked bored because she wasn't the centre of attention, picked up her glass from the table, took an unsteady sip from it and decided it was time to make her mark. "Perhaps you could cure me of my drinking problem?" she drawled, looking at me with eyes which were watery and slightly bloodshot but which still knew how to fix a steady stare.

"I don't know about that!" chipped in Sean King. "Healing a blind man's one thing, but getting you off the booze? That's another matter altogether, Cindy!"

Buchausen forced an insincere smile while Tait laughed loudly. Goldman looked acutely embarrassed and put his hands in his lap.

"Enough of that!" said King, milking the audience's laughter. "Before we go any further, there is one tiny point I'd like to clear up, and that's your name."

"What about it?"

"It's obvious, isn't it? I mean, there you are healing people with your hands, and your name is Christian."

I shrugged and said, "It's a coincidence."

"I'll say it is!" scoffed Tait, who was wearing a man's blue pinstripe suit and an open-necked, cream silk shirt.

"I can't help what I was named."

"What you were *christened*," she insisted. "Just like you can't help healing people and having stigmata?"

"Exactly."

Cindy Buchausen wore a rich red dress with a plunging neckline. Somebody in hospitality suggested she chose the colour so it wouldn't highlight spilt red wine. America's finest cosmetic surgeons had helped preserve the dramatic impact of her bust, much of which was on display.

"What's in a name? It's just a crock of shit!" she declared. "I mean, who goes by their proper name anyway? I know I don't."

King leaned forward to address Goldman and blocked her view of me. "What's your opinion about all of this, Carl?"

Goldman shifted uncomfortably in his seat. "As a psychiatrist, I would indeed relish the opportunity to speak with Christian in private, at length, but . . ."

"A psychiatrist?" intervened Tait. "You speak to people's dogs, Carl!"

"But he trained on humans, didn't you?" said Cindy Buchausen, coming to his rescue.

"I certainly did."

"Let him have his say," King asked Tait.

"Anyway, as I was saying, in my capacity as a psychiatrist, I think it's a very interesting case, but, as an ordinary member of the public, there are some things I can't reconcile."

"Like what?"

"Well, I'd expect something very different from someone who claims to be able to do what he says he does."

I frowned. "What do you want? Me in sackcloth and sandals, with a long beard, eating berries and speaking in riddles?"

There was laughter.

"You may find it funny, but the way you act doesn't lend any credibility to your claims, young man."

"It's not the way I act. It's the way *I am*. If I made a conscious effort to fit in with your stereotypical images, then I'd be acting."

"And acting's lying," said Cindy Buchausen. "Believe me, I should know, so give him a break, Carl!"

"But I understand the point he's making," said King. "It's hard to accept the stories when you know nothing about the man."

"That's right," confirmed Goldman.

King turned to me. "So, maybe we need to know a little more about you. At the very least, it would be easier to place everything in its proper context. And that might help some people to decide whether you're for real."

Louise Lateau had her doubters. They paid surprise visits to her home, to try and catch her out. They sealed her hand in a heavy leather glove and kept her under observation like an animal in a zoo. Lorenzo Sevilla didn't seem to have had that problem. His reputation had largely been local and those who knew what he could do were surrounded by proof of it, in the form of those he healed. There was no room for doubt in Juliaca.

"If that's what you're worried about, you should have had Mr Leonard on the show," I told King. "Maybe he would have helped you make up your mind."

"What's there to say?" said Tait. "Either he did it or he didn't. What he thinks, or where he comes from, makes no difference."

I nodded but King persisted. "I think it *does* make a difference. For instance, there are bound to be some people who view you in a religious light. The parallels are too blatant to ignore. And those people will be interested to know your views on, say, drink and drugs, or sex, or politics, or even religion itself."

King sat back and waited for me to tackle one of the subjects he'd offered. Sevilla had offered a political view, by denouncing Shining Path. It had proved to be a rather expensive opinion.

"So what do you want to know?"

"Let's start with religion," he suggested. "That seems the obvious one."

"I'm not particularly religious. I don't go to church or anything and as for belief . . . well, I *do* believe in a greater force, but it's got nothing to do with organized religion. I don't see a link between the super-rich Churches that rule by fear and a force of energy which is way beyond human comprehension."

"Which religion are you talking about?"

"Does it matter? It could be just about any of them, couldn't it? Do I need to be specific? When they're not too busy building magnificent churches and temples for themselves, they're at war. Do you think any god worthy of the title would want us to waste time, money and energy erecting extravagant monuments in its name? What sort of being would do that? The same entity as the miraculous force which accounts for the truly inexplicable? I don't think so."

"That opinion might upset a lot of people, don't you think?"

"Maybe, but I hope not. Like you've said, it's an opinion. It's simply what I think. It's not my intention to upset anyone."

"I'm sure it isn't, but if people are going to listen to what you say, shouldn't you be careful about the words you choose?"

"I'm not asking them to listen to what I say. I'm just answering the questions you're asking me. Nobody should be looking to me for advice or guidance, or for any sort of leadership at all."

"Well, you say that, but as I understand it, plenty of people *are* seeing you in a religious context. They *will* listen to what you say."

The prospect was not appealing. I didn't need people hanging on my word. For one thing, I didn't want the responsibility of other people's actions and attitudes put down to things I was supposed to have said.

"So, just for the sake of argument," said King, "what do you think of the current government?"

"I can only give you my view on that as an ordinary citizen. That question is completely irrelevant, so far as my ability to heal is concerned."

"Okay, but since I've asked it, what *do* you think?"

I shrugged and walked into it. "Most governments tend to be crap, don't they? I don't think there's been a good one in my lifetime and this one's no different. Politics bores me because the people in it are so . . . *small*."

"See?" exclaimed Linda Tait, suddenly. "He *is* normal. He thinks the same thoughts as the rest of us."

There were a few chuckles from the audience. I wondered whether Louis was watching. He was the principal reason for me being here. I was past the point of no return.

"Where do you stand on drugs?" said King. "Do you condone their use?"

"Not really, no."

"Not *really*?" he snapped, pouncing on the single word. "Does that mean, for instance, that while you'd stand against heroin and crack, you might favour the legalization of something like cannabis?"

King was beginning to irritate me.

"Listen," I said, "if it's against the law then I wouldn't recommend it to anyone. It's that easy. It's up to those people who are worried about it to get the lawmakers to change the rules."

"But what's your personal opinion?"

"That is my personal opinion. I couldn't care less whether it's legalized or not."

"Have you ever used it?"

I looked blankly at King. Cindy Buchausen spoke up.

"Well, honey, what about sex outside marriage?" she asked, before turning to address the audience. "If he can heal a blind man with those hands, I'd like to know what else he can do with them!"

Price had assured me about the integrity of the show, but I should have known better than to listen to him. Carl Goldman looked as embarrassed as I felt. We eyed each other cautiously. When the laughter died down, he spoke up.

"I haven't heard anything yet which would lead me to change my mind," he said. "I've seen all the stories in the papers and heard people arguing about it on the radio and TV, and now I've met you in the flesh. And I still don't believe it."

"That's unfair!" protested Linda Tait. "You can't dismiss him just like that."

"Of course I can," countered Goldman. "And until I

get offered some hard evidence, I'm going to continue to do so."

Sean King rose from his seat and a camera moved in on him. "And that, in fact, brings me neatly to the climax of tonight's programme, where we hope to establish the credibility of Christian Floyd's claim to heal."

I seized up as King stepped off the platform, leaving the four of us in dimmed light. A camera followed him as he moved to the back of the set. Silently, one of the screens parted and bright light spilled onto two new-comers. One was a woman dressed in a sober navy skirt and blouse. She looked to be in her mid-thirties. As the screen stopped sliding, she pushed forward a wheelchair, which was carrying the second newcomer. He was young, perhaps seven or eight, and I didn't need to get any closer to know he was desperately ill. He could hardly hold himself up in the chair and his hairless head hung limply to one side. His skin was deathly grey.

I looked into the wings and just saw Samuel Price's bulky silhouette. Little rays of light reflected off the lenses of his glasses. Sean King was addressing the roving camera and on the monitor in front of the set, we could see his face on the screen, playing back to us. His voice was as sincere and deep as a TV journalist covering a disaster on the news.

"Tonight we have two very courageous visitors. Would you please welcome Mrs Shirley Cooper and her son, Luke."

There was polite applause.

"Mrs Cooper," said King, moving closer to her, "I understand that Luke is extremely ill."

"That's right, Sean. He has cancer."

"Obviously we don't want you to go into all the details of his illness, but perhaps you could tell us what the doctors have told you?"

You heartless bastard, I thought. Shirley Cooper was

trembling. There were tears in her eyes and King was nodding sympathetically, gently encouraging her.

"They've tried all sorts of different treatments and none of them have been able to bring it under control. The doctors have been marvellous but it's just no good. We've even tried all the alternative treatments and none of them have . . ."

Mrs Cooper, Luke and Sean King were bathed in their own private cone of light. The dying boy seemed oblivious to everything around him. King was managing to manufacture an appropriate tear or two.

I thought of the simple girls, praying furiously before the bleeding started. Louise Lateau was contemplating Christ's suffering when she bled, and as I looked around the TV set, I felt humiliated. Sevilla had clearly been a decent, honest man. Even if he'd been living in Los Angeles, and not in the backwater of Juliaca, I couldn't imagine him doing what I was doing. I felt ashamed. It was too cheap. The combination of Price's slick assurances and my desire to stick it to Louis had brought me down to this. The next thing I knew, I was on my feet.

"Where are you going, honey?" whispered Cindy Buchausen.

"Anywhere away from here."

The lights had been dimmed over our part of the set, while King moved to the back with Mrs Cooper and Luke, so it was a few moments before anyone noticed I was leaving. A cameraman hissed at me to sit down, but I was already on automatic. Several members of the audience started to murmur. I was off the set and striding towards the wings when King came bounding towards me, followed by a camera.

"Where do you think you're going?" he called out.

"Away from this circus."

"But you've got to help," he replied, indignantly. "You have to!"

"No, I don't. I don't *have* to do anything. I make the decision."

I stopped in my tracks and turned round to face him. The area we occupied wasn't prepared for sound, so the majority of our conversation was inaudible to the audience.

"What do you think I am?" I asked him. "I thought it had been made quite clear that this was just to be a simple interview. What the hell's wrong with you people?"

"You can't leave!"

"Watch me. And don't blame me. I'm not the heartless one. No one's going to make me heal just so they can boost their show's ratings."

King sneered at me. "You're running away because you can't cut it. You're a fraud!"

I smiled bitterly. "Nice try, but it won't work."

"It's the truth, isn't it? You can't do it!"

"Consult Mr Leonard's doctors and specialists. They'll tell you whether I can do it or not."

I stormed into the wings, leaving King to sort through the wreckage of the show. Price's corpulent figure blocked my path. His hands were on his hips. There was perspiration across his brow.

"Do you hear that?" he asked, pointing behind me, towards the disgruntled, booing audience. "Now get out there and do something about it."

Gabriella was at his shoulder, in tandem with the producer of the show, who was fiddling with his pony-tail.

"You knew what the conditions were," I reminded Price. "Nobody gets to exploit me like that."

"Sure I knew what the rules were," he conceded. "And they broke them. That isn't my fault."

"*They* broke them? And you had nothing to do with it?"

"Please," implored the producer, who was now altering

the position of his pink-rimmed glasses, "you're destroying the continuity of the programme."

I said to Price, "I just don't believe you."

"Christian," sighed Gabriella, looking desperate.

"Don't you call me a liar!" shouted Price. "Now get back out there and try to salvage some dignity, will you?"

"Fuck you!" I replied, barging past him.

Price clattered into a pile of packing boxes. Gabriella grabbed me by the arm. "You've got to go back!" she urged me.

"What?"

"You've got to go back on! Please! For the child!"

"You disappoint me, Gabriella. I'd never have expected you to side with Price."

I shook her hand off my arm.

"Oh Christian, please!" she cried, but I went past her into the labyrinth of gloomy corridors behind the set.

When I reached the street, it was just beginning to rain.

# Chapter Thirteen

"Vodka, please."

"You want anything else in that?"

"Yes. Vodka. And some lime."

The barman gave me a guarded glance which seemed like a warning. I shifted uneasily on my barstool and looked around. Vientiane was full, as usual. The air was thick with choking cigarette smoke. Anonymous faces drifted through dim beams of light which spilled from the ceiling. Nothing had changed in the months since my last visit.

They shut the doors at two o'clock. I actually arrived a little late, after stalking the damp streets, but the doorman let me in anyway because he recognized me from an era when I drank there regularly. Both Vientiane and the restaurant upstairs were owned by a Laotian called Claude, whose French mother appeared in large black and white photographs on the walls.

The bar top was a large slab of polished pink marble. I tapped my fingernails on it while waiting for my drink. I was furious with myself. I should have known better than to trust Samuel Price. I'd heard the warning bells from the first moment he opened his mouth and I'd ignored them.

He was full of sincere gestures and solemn assurances. And none of them were worth spit. The fact that he had one of his baboons break into my flat should have told me something. When confronted, he would doubtless point to our expensive accommodation and our minders as proof of his concern for our well-being. But that was window-dressing. As for the cost of those things, I expect he could have paid for that out of small change from the money he was making on the publicity.

The reality was that Price had done nothing of consequence for me and I doubted he would. The fiasco of Night Talk was a curiously appropriate affair; cheap and nasty, just as he promised it wouldn't be.

Once the management closed the doors of Vientiane, those on the inside were usually permitted to carry on drinking as long as their livers and wallets could stand it. The bartender placed my drink in front of me and I took a long sip. It was just what I needed. When I was halfway through my second, I ordered a third.

"Do you want to pay for the first two?"

"You think I'm going to do a runner?"

"I'm sure you wouldn't."

But he still wanted money up front. Normally, I ran a tab, but I wasn't going to argue with him. An unfriendly bartender could only compound my problems. I took out my wallet, put it on the bar and dug my fingers into it, searching for a banknote.

"Hi!" said a chirpy voice, just behind my right shoulder.

I turned around and there was a stocky girl standing there, with spiky blonde hair. I'd noticed her before, sitting at the table closest to my barstool, with three other girls and a lot of empty glasses. I looked over to the table and the rest of them were watching us, giggling in the half-light behind the veils of their hands.

"I'm Diane," she announced, in an American accent.

"Really?"

"Yeah. Listen, I hope you don't mind my asking, but are you famous? We were just talking about it and we couldn't decide who you . . ."

"I can't be that famous then, can I?"

Diane thought about this. "I guess not," she admitted,

"but you look awful familiar. Nancy – she's the one with the red hair – she says she's seen you somewhere, real recently. She's sure of it."

I peered into the gloom to see which one was Nancy. Red hair was hard to spot in that light, but I guessed she was the one in the middle, the one staring unashamedly at me. Not the shy type, I thought.

"I'm not famous," I told Diane, who looked disappointed.

"Are you sure?"

I smiled and said, "I think I'd know, don't you? She must have confused me with someone else."

Just as Diane turned to go back to her table, which was now groaning under the weight of a fresh round of huge cocktails in monstrous glass basins, Nancy's eyes bulged in the dark and she pointed directly at me.

"Oh my God! It's him!" she squealed. "It's the healer! You know the one – he healed that blind man. I'm sure it's him!"

For a moment, my blood froze, despite the generous ration of vodka in it. I steadied my grip on the brass bar rail. Diane was facing me again.

"What's his name?" asked the girl to Nancy's right.

"Oh . . . I've got it . . . I've got it . . . oh, what is it? I'm sure it's him! But his name . . . I can't quite . . ."

"Is it true?" asked Diane.

I wondered how Nancy could be so sure. Maybe she'd seen the show earlier, except there wasn't a television in Vientiane and it looked as though they'd been at their table all night. Or perhaps she'd seen me in the papers, except the photographs they'd printed were so poor I didn't see how anyone could make a match.

"Like I said, she must be thinking about someone else."

"I wish I could remember his name!" screeched Nancy, her hands clutched together just beneath her chin.

I felt the edge of the wallet slip from my fingers. I

looked around and saw my sulky bartender holding it. He plucked a Parke Millen business card out of it and said, "Christian Floyd's the name on the card."

"That's it! That's it!" she cried, ecstatically.

The bartender took a twenty-pound note and handed me back the wallet with a sour smile. Diane looked confused.

"But you said you weren't!" she protested.

I shrugged. Nancy was looking at me with glazed eyes, like I was a film star. The attention made me uneasy.

"Why deny it?" persisted Diane.

"I don't know. I . . . I just came in here for a quiet drink and . . ."

"Because the bastard's a fraud!" cried a small, fat man in a blue blazer. He was sweating in the bitter heat of Vientiane.

"How would you know?" asked Diane, suddenly protective.

"I saw it on the TV."

"When?"

"This evening. He was on Night Talk. Weren't you?" he asked, looking at me, aggressively.

I didn't answer.

"They brought on this child who had cancer. His doctors had told his mother he only had a few days to live. And you know what this guy did? He got up and walked off the show! Just like that!"

"Is that true?" asked Nancy, in a voice which clearly hoped it wasn't.

I looked my squat, sweating accuser in the eye and said, quietly, "Yes, it's true."

I felt hostility growing around me, but I didn't feel any fear myself. Bitterness and anger were the things I could taste.

"Why?" asked Diane.

The truth was so ridiculous. I could see that. "They broke an agreement," I murmured.

"Did you hear that? They broke an agreement!" cried the fat man, playing to the gallery, before turning back to me. "If you can do what you're supposed to do, you should have healed the child anyway. How could you let an agreement prevent you from treating him? That's so . . ."

"And what the hell would you know about it?"

The menace in my voice shut him up. He looked at me with eyes so wide I might have just punched him on the jaw. I heard grunts of disapproval coming from the gloom. Somebody lit a cigarette to my right, the lighter flame illuminating his lined face.

"I can heal," I told him, "but I'm not a fucking circus act! You got that?"

"If you're in a position to do something like that, you do it, no matter what!" continued the fat man, wiping his forehead with the sleeve of his blazer. "I reckon the real reason you bottled out was because you couldn't do it."

"I made a mistake," I said, dryly. "I know that now and I regret it. But that doesn't make me a fake."

"Until you prove otherwise," he said, "you're a fake in my book. A fake and an arsehole!"

The fat man was standing too close to me. I took the lapel of his jacket in my right hand and dragged him closer. "You shouldn't be so quick to judge, little man!" I growled. "Otherwise, you might just . . ."

But I stopped. What threat could I make that would serve a purpose? I let go of his blazer and turned my back on him, casually dismissing him.

"You might what?" he retorted, like a little lapdog snapping at the heels of something sensible.

He reached for me with his arm but I shrugged it off and moved ahead, as though I'd never seen him in the first place.

"Get lost, you bastard!" he shouted after me.

I was jostled on the way out of Vientiane. Those who'd heard the exchange barged into me from one side and then the other, grumbling slurred insults and half-threats. Alcohol diluted their menace.

The rain was drilling the street when I reached the pavement. I stepped into the downpour and heard the door to Vientiane opening behind me. A woman in an ankle-length overcoat emerged. As she passed me, she spat at me, hitting me on the arm.

"You disgust me!" she muttered.

I didn't bother to react to it. We walked in different directions. The city was dormant. Occasionally a car sailed past, sending up a wall of spray in its wake. Traffic lights changed colours for no one. Electric billboards clicked as they rotated. Tramps pressed themselves into shop doorways to escape the wet and cold. It didn't bother me. I didn't even pull my collar up. I let the rain beat down on me.

I stalked the empty streets and ended up calling Julia Graham because there was no one else I could speak to. I felt alienated from Gabriella. Katy was gone. Jorge was away and no one else appealed. A solitary lorry cruised by, throwing spray against the side of the phone-box. My view through the glass was chequered by a multitude of credit-card-sized stickers advertising call-girls. Some had crude ink sketches on them. The women were in suspenders and stilettos, or dressed as schoolgirls or nurses, all making claims as absurd as their outfits. The names were foreign and the promises seedy: Olga liked it with whips, Heidi needed instruction, Manuela and Sylvia were twins who were willing to satisfy any grim perversion. The traffic lights turned red.

"Julia?" I asked, cupping my hand around the mouthpiece when I heard the click of connection.

There was a pause and I could hear her shifting position, before she eventually said, "Christian?"

She was alert now. "I'm sorry," I said. "Did I wake you?"

"Where are you?"

I looked through the rain-streaked glass. "I'm not sure."

"What do you want?"

I wasn't sure of that, either. The hostility at Vientiane lingered, souring my thoughts. I wondered where Luke Cooper was. I ran a finger down the dirty glass in front of me and shook my head in silence.

Julia said, "Do you want to talk? You want to meet up?"

"Yes."

"Come over here. You know where I am."

"What about the journalists?"

"They're gone. It's safe."

Safe. The word was a slap across the face. Now I knew the answer to her earlier question: I wanted to feel safe.

I took a cab and paid off the driver a hundred yards from her apartment. The pavements glistened beneath the street lamps, puddles shivering as the rain fell. Just being in the same street again brought on a sense of panic. I approached her building with trepidation, feeling the urge to flee grow stronger with every step I took towards it. She buzzed me in over the intercom.

The hall was quiet. Mr Leonard's door was closed. Uncollected mail lay on the table. The blood had been cleaned from the walls. The stifling odour of industrial shampoo stained the air. The strip of blue carpet which ran between the front door and the elevator bore the tell-tale sweeps of a carpet-cleaner, the small hard wheels leaving imprints on the material. I looked up at the guilty device, the small, interior security camera which had frozen me in crucifixion. Its gaze covered the hall. A ghostly shiver ran through me. I passed by Mr Leonard's door, hardly daring to look at it. Ahead of me stood the lift, ready and receptive, like Julia had been when she stood in it and removed her underwear. Then, taking the sweetest option would have been taking the easy option and, from where I now stood, the best option. But I hadn't done that and now there was no way back. I ignored the empty lift and chose the stairs.

Julia stood in the doorway to her apartment. She wore jeans and a baggy chocolate-coloured jersey.

"Hi, Christian," she said, flatly.

"Did I get you out of bed?"

"No," she lied. Her tousled hair and sleepy eyes betrayed her. "Come in. You look like . . . like I imagined you would."

I frowned and followed her into the apartment, closing the door behind me. "What do you mean?"

"I saw you on the TV."

She turned round to gauge me reaction and my surprise showed. I said, "I wouldn't have thought it was your sort of thing."

"It isn't. I was just flicking through the channels. Drink?"

"Sure."

She led the way to the kitchen, past her bedroom. I peered in. The double bed had been slept in, the duvet thrown back and the sheets creased. That had been my destination once. Her bedside lamp cast a pool of warm light over the squashed pillow. The other one lay untouched on the far side of the bed. My pillow, perhaps? The prospect flickered fraily, like a candle in a draught. I tried to envisage how the night might have evolved, but I found I could no longer picture anything which deviated from the gritty reality. All I saw was blood trickling down Mr Leonard's parched skin, Julia screaming, my sodden clothes, unknown faces with mouths agape.

Julia took a bottle of white wine from the fridge and

poured two tumblersworth. She handed one to me and said, "How come you called me?"

I shrugged uselessly and said, "There wasn't anyone else. Not really."

She smiled wryly. "Last name on your list, huh?"

"I didn't mean . . ."

"I'm joking, Christian. Relax. Take off your coat."

I took off the dripping article and draped it over the back of a chair. "Did you see what they tried to get me to do on the show?"

"Yes. I saw. It was unfair."

There was doubt in her voice, so I said, "But?"

"But you were wrong."

The faces from Vientiane rose up again, like flames from a momentarily rekindled fire. I nodded sheepishly. "I know."

"And it made you look like a fraud. If I'd been Joe Public watching that . . . well, there's no doubt what I'd be thinking now."

"But you know differently."

"True," she admitted, sitting on the edge of the kitchen table. "But quite *what* I know is another matter. All I saw was you looking as though you were crushing his skull and digging your thumbs into his eyes. And then there was blood everywhere and suddenly he could see."

I glanced at her, wondering how to interpret her flat tone. "You do believe I did it, don't you?"

She didn't respond immediately. When she did, she averted her gaze. "I know Mr Leonard can see now, so yes, I believe it. I believe it, despite myself. Every other instinct tells me not to. I know what I saw but I don't understand how it happened."

"For God's sake, Julia! Do you think I do? If I could give you a neat explanation, I would. But there isn't one. There's no method in this madness."

She cocked her head to one side. "I guess not. If there

was, it'd be some monk in a plain robe, not a banker in a hand-tailored pin-stripe, right?"

I smiled weakly. "That's right. I'm the most unlikely choice, but that doesn't alter the fact, does it? It's me. I can do it. End of story."

Julia looked me in the eye and said, "What about what's-her-name?"

"Gabriella?" I replied, instinctively.

She let her surprise show and I blushed. When I allowed my eye to be caught by hers, she said, "What a complicated life you're leading, Christian."

There was no hostility in her voice. Indeed, I thought I detected amusement somewhere in there. "You mean Katy."

Julia nodded. "Yes. How's she taking all of this?"

"Why?"

"I wouldn't imagine she'd cope with this very well."

I felt a flush of indignation. "What do you mean?"

Julia displayed no signs of abandoning her customary bluntness. "I thought she might be rather inflexible. Brittle, even. This entire episode, after all, does require some latitude of imagination, some suspension of disbelief. She didn't seem to me like the kind of person who would make that effort." And just as she was letting this sink in, she added, "Actually, I thought she might not even be capable of it."

The fact that Julia was right didn't make her incisions any less wounding. Quite the contrary. I simply said, "I haven't spoken to her recently."

I sat down on a chair by the kitchen table. Julia leaned across the scrubbed wooden top and filled my glass. Wine splashed across the back of her hand. She put down the bottle and licked the chilly alcohol off her skin.

"I don't even know her," she said, "but you two were obviously a mismatch, right down to the core. You may seem similar, but you're at different poles to each other."

"You don't know *either* of us," I pointed out, curtly.

"Exactly. And since it's that obvious to a virtual stranger, I'm surprised someone as bright as you never saw it. Maybe you never looked."

Feeling progressively less comfortable, I said, "I didn't come here to talk about Katy."

Julia raised a mischievous eyebrow. "So what exactly did you come here to talk about?"

I couldn't answer that so I shrugged.

"Maybe you felt you had unfinished business here?" she suggested, standing up and moving across the kitchen floor towards the fridge.

"You mean . . .?"

When she turned round, she was smiling. She said, "Why not? After all, it wasn't mutual loathing which brought us together in the first place, was it?"

"No. Of course not! But that's just . . . that's not . . ."

I was flustered by her casual composure. She appeared to enjoy that. This was how she'd been when I first met her. I could easily imagine that the hysteria she'd displayed in the entrance hall when I healed Mr Leonard had been a very rare occurrence indeed.

"Casual encounters like that, Christian, ride on the crests of infrequent waves for people like us. I don't make a habit of it and I'm sure you don't. So when that opportunity comes, you've got to seize it there and then, otherwise it's gone. For good. Our moment came and went."

I thought of Gabriella waiting in the wings, pleading with me to go back in front of the Night Talk cameras. And I thought of Julia and the thrill she sent through me at the hotel as we left the ball. I said, "That's right. I came and went."

She opened the fridge and took out a jar of olives. She unscrewed the lid and offered me one, which I declined. "The papers were prepared to pay good money for my side of the story."

I shuddered at the prospect of further erratic coverage. "How much?"

She scoffed at my question. "I never got round to that, but a lot. Or so they said. There were three of them, all competing against each other, yapping into the intercom and ringing me on their portable phones all day long. They'd obviously never come across the word 'no' before."

"I'm sorry."

"Not as sorry as they were."

"Why? What did you do?"

"I lost my temper. I threw a pan of boiling water over them and told them to fuck off."

I was momentarily speechless. There was no doubt in my mind that Julia was capable of it. But all the same . . .

"You did what?"

"I was cooking pasta. It was about eight-thirty and they just wouldn't go away, no matter what I told them. So I snapped. I took the pan over to the ledge, opened the window and tossed the contents out. And while they were brushing the scalding spaghetti off their coats and out of their hair, and while they were swearing among themselves, I told them to get lost or they could expect more of the same."

"You're joking!"

"Not at all. And they haven't been back since, or even lodged a complaint against me."

I laughed through incredulity as much as amusement. Julia just smiled, as if to say, "Would you expect anything less from me?" She ate a couple of olives and put the jar back in the fridge.

I looked at my watch. "I should get going."

"You don't have to on my account."

"Thanks, but I think I'll go all the same."

"Where to?"

"We're staying in a hotel."

"*We?* You and the other one?"

"Gabriella, yes," I said, awkwardly, bowing my head and acknowledging the slip. "She's . . ."

But before I could offer a feeble explanation, Julia said, "Don't bother, Christian. It's easier not to. Besides, it makes no difference to me."

I looked up from my shoes. "I don't understand you."

"Then don't try to."

"But I'm curious. You're taking this so well. It's not natural."

"You're a fine one to lecture on what's natural and what isn't! Look, you and I were thrown together by circumstance. Our paths crossed at the right time, that's all. Normally, we would have had one of those flings that lasts a night, maybe two, and then stops. Who can say? One thing's for sure: nothing permanent would have come of it. You and I wouldn't work well together. Maybe for a night or a weekend, but long-term? No chance. And since we missed our window of opportunity, there's no need to dwell on it. As for what happened downstairs . . .

"That was like seeing a ghost, or a UFO, or having a wild hallucination. It was something real and yet so unreal that to try and deal with it logically is quite pointless. You just have to accept it, and if other people reject it, then you have to accept that too. Because unless you were there, you'd be crazy to believe it.

"It was a spectacular moment in my life. And when I'm seventy, I'll look back and that's still what it'll be. You and I will go our separate ways and I'll be left with the memory, nothing more nothing less."

"So it's thanks for the memory?" I quipped.

She grinned. "I guess it is."

I found her calculated reasoning hard to accept. "You really mean that? You can be that practical about it?"

"Yes, I can. It's the way I am. I know I went berserk when it happened, but . . . well, that was in the heat of the moment. Since then, I've had plenty of time to analyse it."

"And these are your conclusions, are they?"

"They're not conclusions. They're my current thoughts on the matter. I dare say that with another fifty years of contemplation I might feel differently. But for now, this is how I feel, yes."

I rose from the chair and reached for my coat. "Did you know that I wasn't sure what I was doing when I went over to touch him?"

Julia frowned. "No. No, I didn't."

"It was only the second time I've ever done it. The first time, I didn't even know it was happening."

She seemed genuinely shocked. "But you appeared so calm when you were doing it. Your face was . . . well, you had this look on it. Peaceful, relaxed, almost serene. I just assumed you knew what you were doing because you'd done it plenty of times before. That's what it looked like."

I shook my head. "I'm afraid not."

"And I thought I had it all figured out," she murmured.

I put on my coat. The damp collar felt clammy against the back of my neck. She walked me to the front door.

"Are you okay?" she asked. "You sounded so anxious when you called."

"I was, but I'm fine now," I told her. "Thanks for everything, Julia."

"I didn't do anything."

"*Plus ça change.*"

She faked a coy look and said, "Don't blame me. I was waiting for you in the lift. Remember?"

"How could I forget?" I replied, as I kissed her on the cheek and then turned away. "In case I don't see you again, look after yourself."

As I reached the top of the stairs, she said, "Hey, Christian, are you going to do it again?"

It was just after four when I arrived at Grosvenor House, drenched from head to toe. A desk clerk tried to prevent me from entering. It wasn't easy persuading him I was resident there. I took the lift to the fourth floor. Nigel and Steve were on duty. I caught them both on the border of sleep. As they struggled to their feet, I put out a hand to stop them. They looked shocked by my grizzly condition.

"Don't say anything, please," I said.

I let myself into the flat as quickly as I could and tiptoed into the living-room. I ached from a blend of tension and cold. I was mixing a drink when she spoke.

"That'll definitely make things worse."

She stood in the doorway wearing a pair of underpants and a crumpled blue T-shirt. She ran a hand through her hair.

"I didn't want to wake you up," I said, apologetically.

"How could you? I wasn't asleep," she replied, before opening the flat door and disappearing for a moment.

"What are you doing?" I asked, when she returned.

"Price told Nigel and Steve to call him as soon as you reappeared. I was telling them not to."

"Why not? I thought you and Price were . . ."

I stopped.

"What?" she prompted. "Working together, or something like that? Don't be pathetic, Christian!"

That was exactly what I felt. I lit a cigarette and surveyed the cascade of rain falling from my clothes. Gabriella watched me with pity and annoyance.

"I'm sorry," I said, slumping into a chair with a squelch.

"You need to rest before you do anything else. A confrontation isn't going to help anyone right now."

I rubbed my temples and said, "I can't believe what I did."

"You're under pressure."

"That's not an excuse."

"No, but it's part of the reason."

I wiped rain out of my eyes. "Nobody wins and Luke Cooper loses. I really screwed up, didn't I?"

"Yes, you did," she replied, offering me a hand and pulling my weary body out of the chair. She guided me towards the bathroom.

"What am I going to do?"

"Right now, you're going to take a hot shower and get some sleep. You're not in a frame of mind to be making decisions at the moment."

I stopped in the doorway and looked back at her with an exhausted smile. "God, you can be sensible sometimes."

I made it sound like a crime. She said, "Not always, I can promise you. Only when it's absolutely vital. Now get in the shower."

She was right about the need to recuperate. The morning was when clear-headed decisions should be made. *Would* be made. After ten minutes in the shower, I strolled out of the bathroom with a towel wrapped around my waist. Gabriella took me by the hand and led me into the bedroom. Before I could protest, she silenced me with her fingers on my lips.

"You must sleep properly tonight, Christian," she insisted. "Besides, I'm still not sure why you were so adamant about sleeping next door in the first place. I wasn't asking you to marry me, you know. And that sofa doesn't look too comfortable."

I was far too tired to protest. As soon as I reached the edge of the bed, I fell among the sheets. She disappeared into the bathroom and, a couple of minutes later, I felt her sliding into the other side of the bed.

"Don't worry," she said, in the dark. "We'll figure something out."

"I hope so," I murmured.

Her leg brushed mine and one of her hands slid slowly over my shoulder. I could feel the cotton of the blue T-shirt against my ribs. Her fingers played with my hair before she let them glide over the side of my face and down my neck. Her lips brushed my cheek softly.

"Whatever happens, I'll be beside you," she whispered into my ear, before kissing me once on the lips. "Now go to sleep."

I awoke with her arm across me, her fingers just touching my collar-bone. Pale light spilled through the crack in the curtains. I gradually extricated myself from Gabriella and the bed, pulled on a pair of jeans and a shirt, and crept out of the bedroom. I opened the main apartment door. Brian Bradfield and Jackson had already replaced Nigel and Steve.

"What time is it?" I asked them.

Bradfield checked his watch. "Eight-fifteen."

I put a hand to my aching head and mumbled, "Jesus! What a night!"

"I know," said Bradfield, flatly. "I saw it on TV."

I looked at him and then at Jackson. Neither could have looked less animated if they'd been dead.

Jackson said, "Can you *really* do it?"

I nodded. "Yes, I can."

"So why didn't you?"

"Because I got it wrong. All right? I let the situation cloud my judgement. I was angry and nervous and I let my own feelings get in the way of the real priority. Is that good enough for you?"

I turned to go back inside.

"Hey, Christian," said Jackson. "You made a mistake. That's all it was."

I looked at both of them. "Yeah, but it was a pretty large one, wasn't it?"

"Sure, but it's still only a mistake. That can happen to anyone in a moment like that."

I smiled wearily. "Thanks."

Brian Bradfield said, "He's right, Christian. What's more, you're lucky."

"How's that?"

"Because you're in a position to do something about it."

I went back inside and made myself a cup of coffee, before settling down with the books and essays.

It was difficult to find any cross-over between healing and stigmata. There was plenty of material on each subject, but the only point where the two seemed to meet was me.

Of all the documented cases of stigmata, the vast majority were experienced by religious devotees of one brand or another. So far as I could tell, there were three generally acceptable possibilities.

Firstly, there was divine manifestation, the choice for true believers. It was a miraculous process which needed no further debate because the converted needed no rational explanation, and those who didn't have faith dismissed this possibility out of hand anyway. The second option was for true cynics and suggested that the wounds were self-inflicted. It didn't necessarily mean they were done consciously, but that the subject might be driven to self-mutilation by some ecstatic desire to be crucified with Christ. The third possibility seemed to fill the middle ground. It proposed that stigmata were psychosomatic, that sheer force of will could bring on the condition. Such influence of the mind over the body would certainly be extraordinary, but not necessarily miraculous.

Assuming these three options more or less covered the ground, I could discount two immediately. Self-mutilation was out and so was the third possibility. There couldn't be anything psychosomatic about my condition because nothing could ever have been further from my thoughts when I first came across Gabriella in the car park. My mind just wasn't conditioned to stigmata. I had no cognizance of it at all, so how could I encourage it?

This left me with the first option: a first-class, *bona fide* miracle. But it was worse than that because there was also the healing to consider. With me, you got two miracles for the price of one. I was in a highly exclusive club. So far, Lorenzo Sevilla was the only other member I'd discovered, but I figured there had to be more.

"Couldn't you sleep?"

The sound of her voice made me jump. I turned round and she was standing in the doorway. She yawned. When she stretched her arms above her head, the blue T-shirt rose, to expose her stomach.

"I had too much on my mind," I told her. But now that I found myself looking at her lissom figure edging out of the partial shadow, none of it seemed quite so important any more. My eyes fell upon her slender legs. When she moved, her hips swayed elegantly. I thought of the moment when the threat of the kiss had come and gone. She'd been standing in exactly the same place and I'd been just inches away. I looked up from her legs and asked, "Did you sleep all right?"

"It was fine, until I woke up. And then I saw you were gone. I thought you might have done something stupid."

"I think I've already used up my quota of that."

I wondered how long it was since I started reading. Total immersion in the material had obscured any notion of passing time. What I'd discovered had been utterly engrossing. And deeply worrying.

I said to her, "What do Lorenzo Sevilla, Mercedes Batista, Rosa Fleischer, Yukio Tanaka, Clarence Ebute and Virginia Calloway have in common with me?"

Gabriella shrugged. "You tell me."

"They all healed and they all experienced some type of stigmata. We are the people where the two phenomena meet."

"Well, that's good. I told you we'd find other people, that you wouldn't be alone."

I nodded and smiled bitterly. "But there's something else."

"What?"

"What do you suppose they have in common with each other, but *not* with me?"

"I have no idea."

"They're all dead."

Gabriella was searching for some reasonable reply, but couldn't find one. I'd scoured page after page, looking for one example to break the rule, but I hadn't succeeded.

"Everyone dies, eventually," was all she managed to say.

"Gabriella, none of them even got close to middle age. And it wasn't bad luck, either. Sevilla, Batista and Ebute were all gunned down. Tanaka and Calloway were knifed to death. Fleischer was burned, for Christ's sake! Sounds medieval, doesn't it? But it's not. All of them lived and died in this century."

She bit her lip and asked, tentatively, "Is that all of them?"

"I don't know. It's all the ones I've managed to find."

"Well, maybe there are others that didn't ..."

"Gabriella!"

She looked hurt and I closed my eyes. I imagined Sevilla squinting in the sun, outside the church in Puno, catching the first glint of gun metal as the assassins split from the crowd, primed for the kill.

Rosa Fleischer had been killed by the folk who lived in her German village, not far from the town of Bayreuth, by the German-Czech border. Scared to distraction by her amazing ability to heal the sick, and by the multiple wounds which appeared when she did it, they succumbed to some sort of collective hysteria. So they dragged her into the main square, stoned her until she was unconscious, before drenching her in petrol and setting her on fire. She was twenty-seven years old. The year was 1962.

Virginia Calloway was knifed to death in a motel room in Lincoln, Nebraska, in 1971. She actually came from Morgan City, Louisiana, and was on her way back there, after a visit to Aberdeen in South Dakota, to heal a cousin who'd contracted multiple sclerosis. Her killer was a religious nut named Charles Hudson. He'd been following her like a secret disciple ever since he saw her restore hearing to a deaf man eighteen months earlier, in Oklahoma City. The police found him sitting cross-legged on the motel room floor in a lake of blood, with Calloway's heart in his lap. He was praying out loud. They never found out why he did it because he committed suicide in his cell before they could question him in any detail.

The others died similarly unpleasant and unnatural deaths. But these two had shocked me the most because their murders occurred in modern countries, during modern times. And yet the driving mentality of the killers belonged in the Middle Ages.

I said to Gabriella, "I'm sorry. I didn't mean to raise my voice."

"I understand," she replied, before coming over to the sofa and sitting down beside me. She pushed her hair back and looked at the open books spread out across the coffee table. "Show me everything."

So I did. I guided her from book to book, from article to article, showing her where I'd gathered my information. She soaked it up like a sponge. When I'd finished, she said, "There's no reason for you to follow them," she said.

"Believe me, it's not my intention. I have no desire to . . ."

"I know what you're thinking, though. Louis and the Church of the Divine Science, right?"

I nodded. "Of course."

"Well, we'll have to make sure it's a rule you break."

Her sympathetic smile wasn't convincing. I could see it in her eyes and she knew it. There wasn't a thing she could say to deflect the truth. So she silently crossed the space between us and kissed me.

# Chapter Fourteen

"Floyd! Where the hell are you?"

Price threw open the door to the sitting-room and stood in the frame, legs astride. Gabriella and I were tangled up in each other. We broke our kiss, as he exclaimed, "Jesus! I don't believe it!"

As I rose from the sofa, she clutched my arm. "Christian, don't do anything stupid," she said, firmly.

"Whatever it'll be, it won't be stupid."

Price looked more tacky than ever. His chocolate-brown shirt was undone to the chest, revealing a thick coat of hair.

"So where's the gold medallion?" I asked.

This passed him by. "Huh?"

His little eyes were ludicrously magnified by the tinted lenses in his glasses. As he walked into the sitting-room, his bulging belly quivered through his shirt.

"You might have knocked," I suggested.

He looked furiously at Gabriella and then back at me. "By the look of it, you were about to do enough knocking for both of us."

I forced a bitter smile. "Very amusing."

"Can you imagine what the papers will be lining up for tomorrow morning?"

I shook my head. "I hadn't given it a moment's thought."

He snorted in disgust. "I'll bet you hadn't! They're going to butcher me because *you* made a mockery out of me."

"You made a mockery out of yourself," I retorted, pointing an accusatory finger at him. "I never asked you to appear on the front page of the *Daily Mirror* and proclaim yourself as some sort of charity-working messiah."

Perhaps he expected me to automatically assume a defensive position because he looked genuinely surprised by my tone. I retreated into the cupboard-sized kitchen and flicked on the kettle. "A cup of coffee?"

"Shove your bloody coffee! I want answers!"

"You want answers? I want an apology."

"You what?"

"You made a string of promises to me and didn't keep a single one of them."

"That wasn't my fault," he whined. "They let me down."

"I thought that was the whole point of going on Night Talk. It was a small show, so you'd be able to control the format and circumstances. That's what you said, while you were boasting about how good you were."

I poured boiling water into the mug and moved past him, back into the sitting-room.

"You cocky bastard!" he grumbled.

My temper was rising. "Remember this: you pushed me into that programme. You said you were the best in the business, but from what I've seen, you're nothing."

Price pointed fiercely at me. "You'll regret this!" he hissed.

"No, I won't. The only thing I'll regret – that I *do* regret – is the way I treated Luke Cooper. And frankly, I lay a good portion of the blame for that at your feet."

"What?"

"I wasn't thinking straight when I stormed off the set, otherwise I'd have done something about the child. But I was so distracted – *so fucking incensed!* – that I walked past him like he wasn't even there. What I did was inexcusable, but my motives were entirely justified."

Price shook his head in open-mouthed amazement.

"Well, what about my reputation?" he complained. "What you did was bad for business, you know? It was unprofessional! You made *me* look second-rate!"

"Fuck your reputation. And fuck you."

"Stop it!" shouted Gabriella. "Both of you!"

She was standing between us, but Price and I were staring with hate at each other and barely saw her.

"You're despicable!" she said to him, before turning to me. "And you're not helping, either. What's the point of you two screaming at each other?"

"Despicable? *Me?*" choked Price, his expression clouding over. "You bitch! You're just a bloody interference. If he wasn't so busy screwing you, perhaps he'd be able to think straight."

I put down my coffee cup. Before she could prevent me, I'd pushed past her and had him by the throat. Both hands squeezed together, bringing colour to his flabby cheeks. His piggy little eyes bubbled in their sockets, behind the tinted glass. I drew his face close to mine.

"What did you say?" I whispered.

His amorphous lips tried to form words and failed. My knuckles went white from the pressure. He gurgled. Gabriella grabbed my arms and tried to loosen my grip, but couldn't. His breathing was staccato.

I looked into his terrified eyes and hissed, "Speak up, fat man, I can't hear you."

"Christian, let go!" Gabriella implored me.

I held on for a couple more seconds before giving one final, crunching squeeze. Then I released him with a shove and he staggered backwards, hitting the arm of the sofa and tumbling to the carpet. The glasses fell from his face. He was gasping for breath and massaging his jowly throat. I was still in two minds. Gabriella sensed this and tightened her hold on me.

He put on his glasses and looked up into my steel gaze. I may not have been digging into his foul flesh any more, but the intent was still there and he could see it. He averted his eyes.

Eventually, I broke free of her grasp and moved over to the window. I looked down onto the Park Street entrance to the hotel. A line of black cabs waited for fares in the drizzle. I lit a cigarette and tried to gather myself.

I heard Price say quietly, "Listen, I'm sorry." The sincerity in his voice surprised me. I glanced over my shoulder and, shock aside, he appeared genuinely remorseful. It didn't suit him, but there it was. I looked back out of the window.

There were people going to work. Some carried umbrellas whose spokes threatened the eyes of those that didn't. Normally, I would have been safely ensconced behind my desk by now. Danny and I would resort to our ritual banter, most of which would bypass Chantal. And I would snatch glimpses of her, when her attention was diverted, allowing my imagination to dwell on unlikely scenarios. The long day would pass quickly and I would be in no rush to leave when the evening came. Danny could never understand that. He said my reluctance to go home at the first opportunity was evidence of a flawed character. I took another drag on my cigarette and watched the grey people trudging through the early morning gloom. And I was jealous of them.

When I turned round, Price was back on his feet. He looked as desperate as Gabriella looked concerned. I was confused, mustering both anger and sympathy for him. But neither was as strong as my own sense of disappointment.

I headed for the door and Price's anxiety got the better of him. He reached out and took hold of my arm. Gabriella intercepted and restrained him.

"Let him go," she told him.

"I mean it, Christian," he said. "I really am sorry."

I nodded. "I know. So am I."

*

It was good to be a faceless face in a crowd. Even the cold, damp air felt good. The drizzle was invigorating. Shed of reminders of my recent past, it seemed I could step right back into normality. No Gabriella, no Price, no minders, no bleeding, no healing, no unwelcome recognition. How long could it last? Shelving reality was never going to be more than a momentary pleasure. Sooner or later, I'd have to return. But for now . . .

I watched a businessman in a flower shop selecting bunches at random by pointing with his folded umbrella. The collection grew unreasonably large, leading me to the conclusion that they were either for his mistress or formed part of a monumental apology to his wife . . . probably for having a mistress. A grey Bentley oozed past me, driven by a liveried chauffeur. There was a small boy lost in the back seat, in a charcoal-coloured school uniform with a matching cap on his head. One of the staff from an Italian restaurant was scrubbing the pavement with a broom, working soapy water over the stones, driving filth into the receptive gutter.

It was hard not to submit to stereotyping. The secretarial-looking types wore too much make-up and fussed with every step they took. Would the rain upset their hair? Would spray from a car mark their tights? Would pressing the pedestrian button at the traffic lights chip a scarlet fingernail? Would a smile crack their make-up?

The plodders and the flyers walked side by side. The pavement was the only place where they could be equal, but they weren't. The balding, middle-aged men with round shoulders, dead eyes, bad suits and terrible shuffles were so obvious next to the upright, well-shod, fresh-skinned, youthful executives. It was survival of the "acumenically" fittest, where the men of half the age and twice the pay took the decisions to end or extend the miserable employment of their elderly underlings, the corporate foot-soldiers. That was one of the things which had always driven me: the fervent desire never to be one of the spirit-broken journeymen, sitting in obscurity, year after year, getting greyer and frailer, waiting for some young turk to deliver the final cut.

This was reality and it was where I belonged. I watched them filing into their expensive Mayfair offices, some jaunty, some crushed, some moving as though they were still asleep, going through the tedium of the day on autopilot. Again, I was jealous.

My life had been dedicated to the pursuit and achievement of ease. I wanted a job that I could be good at without killing myself and I found it at Parke Millen. I wanted enough money to never worry about bills and that's what I got. I wanted friends around me who'd be relaxed and uncomplicated; pleasure-seekers, not drama-hunters. By and large, that's what I thought I'd managed and I was happy. Katy was supposed to be another part of my simple jigsaw.

It was no time at all since I'd believed I had everything right, and that all I had to do was maintain the status quo. I'd reached my designated altitude and all there was left to do was cruise. Then the engines fell off.

My feelings towards Price, were muddled. Hostility had been uppermost in the aftermath of the Night Talk fiasco, but now I wasn't so sure. His remorse and concern seemed genuine. I'd already learned one lesson about taking Price at face value and yet I couldn't help nudging the benefit of the doubt towards him.

"You shouldn't have left without me."

Jackson was standing at my side.

"You weren't there," I said.

"I was taking something down to Brian, who was in the car. You should have waited for me."

"I needed to be alone."

"I know. But that's not a good idea."

I looked around at the rush-hour. "Jackson, this is Mayfair in the middle of the day. I'm not a rich white boy lost in the Bronx at two in the morning."

"It's my job," he sighed.

The drizzle matured into proper rain. I said to him, "Let's get some coffee."

We found a café. At least that's what it described itself as, but it had nothing in common with the greasy-spoons I knew. It was really a tea-room. Fragile circular tables were covered in heavy white tablecloths. Gilt-framed paintings hung on the wall between gilt-framed mirrors. The silverware sparkled beneath the heavy chandelier which threatened to bring down the ceiling. We took a table near the window. Most of the customers were business types, enjoying an over-priced croissant and a pot of tea while they scanned the salmon-coloured pages of the *Financial Times*. Jackson, who looked like some warlord out of *Escape From New York*, drew more than his usual quota of unguarded glances. I was getting as used to that as he was.

He said, "Can I ask you something?"

"Of course."

"When you told Brian and I that you could do this thing, did you really mean it?"

"Did you think I was lying?"

"No, it's not that. It's just you seemed . . . I don't know. You don't behave like someone who could do that. Neither of us could picture you."

I sighed wistfully. "Yeah, I know what that's like."

"I mean, we've read the papers and Price's told us plenty, but it's just hard to believe. The more we know you, the less likely it seems."

"I can understand that. Sometimes I don't believe it myself. In fact, until I healed Mr Leonard, I *didn't* really believe it. Gabriella knew, of course, but I couldn't conquer my own doubt. I came to accept that I'd bled – that I'd experienced stigmata – but healing? That was too much. That was why I took the chance with him. If I hadn't, maybe none of this would have happened. Perhaps Gabriella would have given up on me, I would have returned to my normal routine and no one would be any the wiser."

Our coffee arrived. I lit a cigarette. Jackson looked absurd, handling delicate china cups with fingers the size of baseball bats. He smiled to himself and said, "I'm not sure Gabriella would have let it drop that easily."

"Well, we'll never know now, will we?"

"She's got it bad for you, Christian."

"I wonder."

"You that blind?"

"It's not that. It's the reason I'm worried about. Maybe it's because of what I did and that wouldn't be right. I keep thinking how . . ."

"That's your trouble, man. Too much thinking and not enough *doing*."

"Oh yeah? Look where action before thought has got me so far."

By the time we were back on the pavement, both the rain and the congestion had subsided. We ambled down South Street. The drizzle drifted waywardly on the breeze. A delivery van partially blocked the pavement. Clouds of fat pigeons fluttered overhead. We moved into Farm Street. We passed an oncoming couple, who were strolling arm in arm. Over the quiet of the street, I heard the murmur of a car's engine behind us.

"You want to go back, yet?" Jackson asked.

"No," I replied. "But you're welcome to."

"Sorry," he said, turning up his collar to the wind. "I've got to go wherever you go and . . ."

It was a hot tingling feeling and it was accompanied by the sound of a soft rip, which would have been inaudible on a busy street, but which was quite clear where we were. The heat blossomed at the base of my back and then

212

climbed my spine. As I started to turn, something hit me on the nape of the neck. There was a harsh pop, followed by a halo of splintering glass around my head.

Everything seemed to move at a glacial speed. Jackson's eyes registered pain and shock as something smacked him so hard his entire body shuddered. But like a champion, he was countering before the blow had even been fully absorbed. He spun on his heel, deflecting another blow from an attacker who was thrown off-balance by the rapidity of the reaction.

The purring engine was screeching now. Out of the corner of my eye, I saw a Volvo mounting the kerb.

Somebody was yelling. My back was a criss-cross of burning lines. Jackson was moving towards me as I felt my legs dissolve. He grabbed me by the lapels and shoved me backwards with all his strength. The Volvo hit Jackson's attacker full on. The body rose over the bonnet and smacked the windscreen. Jackson was clipped by the left corner of the bumper. I saw him spinning off the edge of the car, as I crashed to the pavement.

My back was hot and my ears were ringing. I looked up and saw an indistinct figure standing over me. In his left hand was the dripping blade. I was too dazed to follow his diatribe, but it really had him going. His jaw was pumping up and down like an over-active piston, the sinews working like well-oiled cables.

Somebody cried, "Get him in the back!"

They were hauling the motionless form off the bonnet of the Volvo. The windscreen looked like a colossal spider's web. The man with the knife was babbling incoherently at me.

"... You were warned ... Day of Judgment is at hand ... the whore with no shame ... bleed for your sins ... the devil must die ... purge the horror ..."

He raised his knife and leaned down towards me. The arm came in a broad arc, sweeping the tip of the steel dagger towards my face. I got my left arm up just in time, feeling the cutting edge slice through my jacket, shirt and skin. A diabolical fury blazed in his eyes. The swipes came one after the other and I did my best to fend them off with both arms. Suddenly it stopped.

I looked up and saw Jackson take him by the arm and snap his wrist in a single fluid movement. The assailant's eyes bulged with horror as his knife clattered onto the wet pavement.

Awesome is a word generally used too often and too lightly, especially by Americans. But what followed, fully deserved the adjective.

By the time Jackson had recovered from his close encounter with the Volvo, a second vehicle, a van, had arrived. I couldn't tell how many weekend warriors there were in total, but it didn't make much difference. Brian Bradfield had been right. Jackson was a slaughterhouse once he got going. He was outnumbered and they were outclassed.

It was incredible. He was a blur which tore through them like a tornado, administering invisible, crippling blows. Looking out for individual strikes was like trying to single out one beat of a hummingbird's wing with the naked eye. It amazed me that a man of his size could be so supple, so lightning quick.

Down they went, clutching their injuries and succumbing to instant shock. They were too slow to blink, let alone defend themselves. The crack of breaking bones competed with their agonized cries.

"We're going!" someone screamed. "Come on!"

I shifted myself and felt my hand slide on something wet. I looked down to see blood pooling around me. A searing heat raced up my back.

Once they were in retreat, Jackson spared them further punishment, allowing them to shovel their wounded into the two vehicles, as he reached for the portable in his pocket.

The van was grinding into reverse, one door still open. The Volvo backed off the pavement. I just caught a glimpse of a woman in the back seat, with a hand cupped over her nose and mouth, blood streaming down the front of her shirt.

Jackson stuffed the portable back in his pocket and watched both vehicles, until they disappeared. Then he scoured the scene for further trouble. There were two astonished bystanders on the other side of Farm Street and a further three up by the corner of Chesterfield Hill. He came back to me. I was shivering.

"I think I'm cut," I said, feebly.

We were in front of the Church of the Immaculate Conception. There was broken glass across the pavement, in addition to two home-made truncheons, several stains of spilled blood and one Volvo wing-mirror. Jackson sat me up and said, "Brian's on his way. It's only going to take him a minute to get here. Just as long as the police ain't first . . ."

"I'm cut," I groaned.

"I know. Take it easy. We'll get you to a doctor."

The pedestrians didn't come close. A small gathering began to grow at the end of the street. I felt blood on my back. And just as a distant police siren cut through to our frayed nerves, Brian Bradfield drove into Farm Street.

Dr Fisher said, "You're lucky."

"I don't feel very lucky," I replied.

He smiled sympathetically and went over to the small sink by the far wall. The last of the stitches were in. "Take it from me," he said, "you are. How long was the blade?"

"I don't know. Six inches. Maybe more. I only saw it for a second."

"Those cuts on your lower back are in a dangerous

215

area. It could have been extremely serious. As it is, your tailor will probably be broken-hearted, but that's about it. There shouldn't be any complications."

The sense of relief made a sweet contrast to the fear I'd felt in the back of the Mercedes, as Brian Bradfield carved through London's traffic. I'd broken into a cold sweat and been largely oblivious to Jackson's assurances that I would be fine. I supposed that was shock; I still felt jittery.

Bradfield had called ahead to Fisher's practice in Cavendish Street. When we arrived, an assistant was waiting and hurried us through an alternative entrance. I never saw another patient.

Fisher was a small, fat man, who may have been a medical expert on many things, but not, presumably, on diet. His belly hung over his trousers, concealing the belt which held them up. His balding pate gleamed beneath the fluorescent overhead lightning. He squinted at me through thick-framed glasses.

"If you'd just been wearing a shirt, he might have also made much deeper cuts on your arms. That kind of hacking motion often results in nerve and sinew damage. That can mean permanently limited movement. Just as well it was cold and damp, otherwise you might not have been wearing your jacket."

"You're full of good news, aren't you?"

He finished drying his hands on a small hand-towel. I could feel the collection of stitches tugging my skin at the base of the spine. Fisher dumped the towel on his desk and said, "Here, let me help you," as he manoeuvred my aching arm into my sleeve.

"You haven't got concussion from the blow you received," he said, "but I'd take it easy for a day or two anyway. Apart from the cuts, you've obviously been badly shocked."

I smiled ruefully. "Not for the first time. Just recently, life has been one shock after another."

Fisher lowered his voice. "Mr Price told me to be quick and ask no questions, but I've got to know. Is it true?"

"Yes."

"Extraordinary," he muttered. "How do you do it?"

"I wish I knew."

"You'd make a fascinating case study."

"I know. I've worried about that."

He nodded seriously. "I'll bet you have. Probably with very good reason, too."

"You think so?"

"Somebody somewhere would want to put you under a microscope, so to speak. Are you the only one?"

"So far as I know."

"Just as well," he said, with a smile, "otherwise I'd be out of a job."

He helped me to my feet. I felt a little unsteady and reached out. He took my arm until I recovered my precarious balance.

"Don't worry about the stitches," he told me. "They'll take care of themselves."

Price and Gabriella had joined Bradfield and Jackson in the corridor. Gabriella looked aghast and Fisher hadn't time to utter a word before Price said, "How is he? Is he going to be okay?"

"He'll live. He's got some stitches, but all the cuts were superficial. Grazes, really."

I wanted to say they hadn't felt like grazes. I looked over at Jackson. "Are you okay?"

"Just a bit of a bruise on the leg. Wouldn't stop me from doing it again."

Price said to me, "We'll get these bastards, I promise you. Meanwhile, I think you should go back to the hotel."

"And get some rest," added Fisher.

A driver I didn't recognize drove Price away in the

blood-stained Mercedes. The rest of us climbed into an identical vehicle and headed back towards Grosvenor House. I kept reliving the first flush of heat at the base of my back, accompanied by the soft tear. It was hard to tell what was making the noise. Material or flesh? Then the cloud of glass exploded around my face.

I slumped in the leather seat and looked out of the window, submitting to a sense of gloom. Gabriella held my hand, said nothing and looked anxious. Jackson could easily have missed me. Although I'd only left the hotel a few moments before he followed, it would have been no surprise if he'd taken one wrong turn and never located me. Then what?

I was still watching the wet tarmac glide by when I asked him, "How many do you think there were?"

"Eight or nine. Maybe ten. I think there were three or four women among them. Two for sure, and perhaps one driving the van, and maybe one other."

I felt Gabriella shift beside me. "Women?"

"I popped at lest two," said Jackson.

"Did you see how many were armed?" I asked.

"Five, I think. Possibly six. There was the guy who knifed you, who also had the bottle. Then there was the fool who tried to truncheon me. He was the one who got hit by the car and bust the windscreen. And there was also another one with a truncheon. I did his knee. A couple more, maybe. I can't be sure."

Gabriella asked, with undisguised incredulity, "You fought all of them by yourself?"

"I didn't have to," said Jackson, modestly. "Two of them were driving and a couple of the others chickened out."

"Chickened out?" I said. "More like sensibly opted out, I'd say."

Gabriella looked to me for confirmation. I smiled wearily and said to him, "They must know where I'm staying, otherwise how could they have picked us up?"

He nodded. "Yeah. They'll know. And I guess they'll be watching when we get to the hotel. Don't worry about it, though. They won't try anything there."

"How can you be so sure?"

"It'll be too risky for them, especially now Price's got extra guys hanging around."

"He has?"

"Yeah. On our floor, down by the flats entrance and also in the main hotel lobby. And even if they got past them, they'd still have to get past us."

That was the most comforting part. I looked at Gabriella. She said, "Price organized it all while you were with the doctor. He's worried about you."

I didn't want an argument. "I see."

Brian Bradfield said, "We've got to be extra vigilant from now on. I know it's boring, but you shouldn't leave the flat unless it's vital. And if you have to, give us plenty of warning so we can sort out some proper protection for you."

Once Gabriella and I were alone in the flat, there was an unwelcome tension. I felt jumpy and she seemed unsure of how to treat me, or how to behave herself. We eyed each other cautiously and forced unconvincing smiles designed to reassure us but which actually had the opposite effect. Our small-talk was similarly subversive.

It was Gabriella who broke the spell. I was pacing when she took hold of both arms to stop me. She didn't say anything, but just looked at me with eyes that seemed to deliver the message which words couldn't. I didn't break away and we hugged in silence, drawing comfort from each other. The anxiety dispersed and evaporated.

Gabriella rolled up the sleeve of my left arm. Only the first slice had required stitches. There were four of them holding the skin together. The rest had been cleansed and covered with Band-Aids.

"I can't spend the rest of my life with these people hanging around," I told her.

She looked up into my eyes and said, "I know."

"They would have killed me if he hadn't been there. Maybe we were luckier than we knew, when we escaped from your flat."

"Maybe," she agreed.

She took me by the hand and led me into the bedroom. I sat at the foot of the bed. When she said, "Lie down," I did, and then she asked me, "Does that hurt?"

"Not much, no."

"Good."

She climbed onto the bed beside me, leaned down and kissed me slowly, and then asked, "Does *that* hurt?"

"Not much, no."

"Good."

# Chapter Fifteen

We were cautious creatures and made love slowly. At times, it hurt, the gentle pressure still being enough to test the doctor's needlework. But the pleasure was too sweet, and even if the stitches ripped, I wouldn't have wanted it to cease. We rolled gradually and she snaked her long limbs around me, her smooth skin sweeping over my body like a warm breeze. We kissed until our lips felt bruised. When it was over, we lay with our arms and legs inter-woven, like some single multi-limbed creature.

I was sublimely content to have her in my arms and to drift on the border of sleep. She drew patterns on my chest. Later, she made me roll onto my front so she could examine the cuts on my back. A forefinger delicately traced each laceration.

"Can you feel anything?" she asked.

"It's a little tender, that's all. What does it look like?"

"The lower half looks like a terrible map. Major roads and railways. The planner should be fired."

"Well, he ran into Jackson, which is probably worse."

"You've got five stitched cuts. I didn't realize there were so many."

I half turned to her and gingerly propped myself up on one elbow. "When he hit me with the bottle, I was dazed. I remember staggering forward and reaching for the nearby railings for support. And while I was doing that, he was slashing away with the knife. I couldn't tell you how many times he cut me or how deep each one was."

Only one arm wound had been stitched. The other cuts

weren't too bad. They stung a little, but that was no hardship when I considered the possible alternative.

We made love again. Afterwards, we fell asleep in each other's arms. When she woke me, I noticed the sky was darkening. I felt jaded, like I always did when I slept during the day. Several hours had passed. Gabriella was sitting cross-legged on the bed, wearing jeans and a long-sleeved shirt. Her face was radiant.

"What is it?" I asked.

"I found him."

"Who?"

"Paul Julien."

The name meant nothing to me. "Who is he?"

"The one we've been looking for. An American. He heals, he experiences stigmata when he does it and – wait for it! – he's alive."

"He's alive?"

"Alive and kicking and living in the USA."

I tried to sit up too quickly and felt the lacerated flesh straining. I winced and Gabriella told me to be careful.

"Where did you discover him?"

"Among the material I got for you. I've been reading through some of the papers you hadn't yet got round to."

"You're sure he's still alive?"

"Unless he's come to some misfortune since the article was written. It's only two months old, Christian. He's been healing for over twenty years."

"So how come he's not a household name?"

"That's his choice. Apparently, he's something of a recluse."

I got up from the bed and dressed awkwardly, before joining Gabriella in the sitting-room. She had the information spread out across the coffee table. There were three photo-copied articles and two book references to Paul Julien.

The most recent article, lifted from the *New York Times*,

was part of a larger feature on "miracle-healers". More interestingly, a 1982 article in *Time* magazine carried an interview with him. I scanned the text, hungry for familiarity. I wasn't disappointed.

**Interviewer:** How did your first experience come about?
**Paul Julien:** That was when I was living in Los Angeles. Me and Mary (*Messinger – Julien's girlfriend at the time*) were coming out of this restaurant when this drunk driver lost control of his car – a big blue Buick – and it hit her full on. She landed about thirty feet away. Those that saw it will tell you how badly injured she was. Both legs were broken and she was horribly cut. I just got down on the ground and held her, like any guy in my situation would have.
**Interviewer:** No one tried to stop you, no one thought you should leave her until the medics arrived?
**Paul Julien:** I can't tell you. I guess there were some who were saying that, but I wasn't hearing them, you know. And then it happened. I couldn't tell what was going on around me. I was ice on the inside. Then the blood began to flow, burning my hands, going all over Mary. People started screaming. It was coming out of my forehead like sweat. They tried to peel me off her, but couldn't. My grip was steel.
**Interviewer:** How long did it last?
**Paul Julien:** A couple of minutes, I've been told. I got no recollection of passing time myself.
**Interviewer:** Did you know right away what you'd done?
**Paul Julien:** (*laughs a little*) Not really, no. I mean, I knew it was something crazy! I was covered in blood and felt weirder than I thought was possible. And when I looked down and saw her . . . I tell you, I was very confused. I could see the evidence right in front of my eyes, but I just couldn't believe it. Not at that time. It was just too much, you know?

**Interviewer:** So, when did you finally accept it?
**Paul Julien:** The second time I did it.

I looked up at Gabriella, almost breathless with shock. "It's just the same. I could be reading about myself."

"I know. That's what I thought."

"It's identical, right down to losing track of time and the burning points where the blood flows."

I couldn't soak up the transcript quickly enough. My eyes darted back and forth, seeking anything which provided new information for me, or which simply bore some similarity to my own experience.

**Paul Julien:** I never figured it was something I was supposed to promote.
**Interviewer:** How do you mean?
**Paul Julien:** Well, I learned very early on that my condition has limitations. It might seem to an onlooker that this talent doesn't have any restrictions – that it crosses all conventional boundaries of reality – and in a sense it does. On the other hand, it has its own set of limits, its own rules that can't be broken.
**Interviewer:** Such as?
**Paul Julien:** The numbers, my recovery time, that sort of thing.
**Interviewer:** Could you be more specific?
**Paul Julien:** About a year after I got it, I went to the Carlsson Institute, just outside Lafayette, Indiana. It was a place which specialized in treating children with chronic physical disabilities. I tried to heal a whole bunch of them – I forget how many, exactly – and ended up helping none of them.
**Interviewer:** Why?
**Paul Julien:** I over-extended myself. That was something new to me. I had no idea. I mean, all my intentions

were good, but I just didn't know enough about what I could or couldn't do.

**Interviewer:** What happened to the children you tried to help?

**Paul Julien:** (*a long pause*) Two of them died. (*Another lengthy pause*) And I worsened the condition of two more. Mercifully, the others were fine. They were in pain during the attempt, but they didn't suffer any lasting side-effects.

(*Paul Julien served two years and four months in a federal penitentiary for involuntary manslaughter. He was released on parole in 1975. His sentence was reduced after the parents of the two dead children testified on his behalf.*)

I was inconsolable. It really carved me up. Prison didn't seem a harsh enough punishment at the time and, on several occasions, I seriously contemplated suicide.

**Interviewer:** But the parents of the two children who died never criticized you, did they? In fact, they acted on your behalf.

**Paul Julien:** They'd met me before I visited the Carlsson Institute. They'd seen what I could do. It was just grossly unfortunate that no one at that time knew what I *couldn't* do.

**Interviewer:** And what is that?

**Paul Julien:** I can't heal *too much*. Don't ask me why. I don't know the answer. I just know it's a reality. The bleeding taxes the body very heavily. I have to have time to recuperate between healings.

**Interviewer:** So you can only do one at a time?

**Paul Julien:** Well . . . not necessarily. I reckon two at once is a safe maximum. I have actually managed to heal three people simultaneously on two separate occasions, but I made myself extremely ill in the process. Ultimately, it's how you feel at the time.

**Interviewer:** Could you explain that?

**Paul Julien:** (*another pause*) I guess it's like if you're into jogging. You might do it three times a week, say, and perhaps you usually go for five miles without any trouble. But every now and then you just don't feel good – you're tired, you don't have any energy – and you'll find a mile a real struggle. It's sort of like that.

**Interviewer:** So two's the limit?

**Paul Julien:** The *safe* limit. I've never had a problem with two.

**Interviewer:** You're on record as saying that prison changed you profoundly. Could you expand on this?

**Paul Julien:** Certainly. From the moment I accepted my ability, up to the incident at the Carlsson Institute, I'd revelled in the condition. I envisaged fame and fortune and . . . God knows what else. Adulation, I guess. But the Carlsson thing followed by twenty-eight months' incarceration radically altered me. The whole disaster taught me one crucial lesson: because of my own physical limitations, I was never going to be able to become a prolific healer. For one thing, it takes several days to recuperate after each healing. And so I realized I was always going to disappoint more people than I could ever help.

**Interviewer:** How, exactly?

**Paul Julien:** It seemed to me that the more I healed, the more my reputation would spread and, therefore, the more hopes I'd raise. It didn't take a genius to work out that in no time at all, I'd be swamped by sheer force of numbers. For each one I could help, there'd be the misery of disappointment for many more.

Gabriella noticed I wasn't turning the page any longer and guessed what had stopped me. She said, "Food for thought, isn't it?"

I looked up and felt brutally sobered. "Yes, it is. The

whole Carlsson thing and imprisonment . . . no wonder he changed his thinking. Poor bastard."

"It could have happened to you."

"Don't remind me."

"That's assuming you and he are the same," she pointed out. "You think you could do two?"

I shrugged and said, "Maybe. I certainly felt stronger after healing Mr Leonard. I mean, I was shattered, but I think I could have given more. I don't know. It's something to consider."

I returned to the article.

**Paul Julien:** So when I got out of jail, I decided it was something to keep quiet. It was better that way.

**Interviewer:** You returned to the Carlsson Institute, didn't you?

**Paul Julien:** I was asked back. Some of the parents came to visit me when I was inside. By this stage, I'd figured out what went wrong. I told them what I thought and when I was released, they asked me back.

**Interviewer:** That seems incredible, after what happened the first time.

**Paul Julien:** I know. But you have to remember they'd all seen me do it before.

**Interviewer:** Where?

**Paul Julien:** I healed a blind boy in Indianapolis, about two months before they asked me to heal their children. They'd heard about me and came to check me out, to see if it was true.

**Interviewer:** And what happened when you returned to the Carlsson Institute?

**Paul Julien:** I healed them all.

**Interviewer:** *All?* How many were there?

**Paul Julien:** Forty-two. It took me five months. I lived at the Institute, taking a room in the staff quarters.

**Interviewer:** You healed forty-two physically disabled children?

**Paul Julien:** Yes.

**Interviewer:** And yet no one seems to know anything about it? That's hard to believe. A story like that would make headline news around the world. But this one didn't. How come?

**Paul Julien:** That was part of the deal. I gave them the same reasons that I've already given you; the kind of publicity you're talking about is just the sort of thing I had to avoid. Not for my sake, but for the sake of all those who'd have their hopes raised, just so they could be crushed. I explained this and they accepted it. They agreed not to utter a word about what was going to happen.

**Interviewer:** What about the staff at the Carlsson Institute?

**Paul Julien:** (*smiles*) Who do you suppose set it up?

**Interviewer:** They sanctioned this?

**Paul Julien:** Naturally. I couldn't have done it without their full and willing cooperation. You have to understand the kind of place it was. It wasn't some high-security hospital. It was very friendly and homely. Everything was low-key to make it as little like an institution as possible. The parents of the children helped run the place. They subsidized it with their own money. *They hired the staff.*

**Interviewer:** But presumably, if you healed everyone, there was no point in the facility continuing to exist?

**Paul Julien:** Right. If you look at the records, they'll show you that the Carlsson Institute closed down six months after my release. Officially, that was because it was costing too much to run. They'll probably tell you that the patients got transferred to other institutions in the state and that the staff got laid off. But they weren't laid off . . . they were *paid off.* Handsomely.

\*

The article stated that several journalists had made a concerted attempt to find one person – one shred of evidence – to back Julien's claims and had failed. The tone of the report was designed to discredit him. If I hadn't known better, I would have dismissed him as a crank.

After he'd healed the last patient at the Carlsson Institute, it seemed Paul Julien had vanished, opting for a nomadic life. There were reports of him over the following years, popping up in New Mexico, Montana, Oregon, Wisconsin. Generally, he kept away from metropolitan centres, preferring isolated rural communities, where the chance of trouble was least.

I looked at Gabriella and said, "No wonder he's still alive. No one can find him."

The *Time* journalist had spent several months tracking him down and persuading him to give the interview, which took place in Denver, Colorado, in 1982. I wondered how he'd filled the intervening years. The recent *New York Times* article simply stated the Julien had last been seen in Odessa, Texas, at the same time as the alleged healing of Stacey Cavanagh, a thirteen-year-old who'd contracted terminal leukaemia. The story grabbed a lot of space in the local press.

Stacey had passed the point of no return. There was nothing further medicine could offer her. So the parents took her home to die. The very next morning, when they were downstairs preparing breakfast, Stacey called out to them. Fearing the worst, they rushed up to her bedroom, only to find her wrapped in sheets sopping with blood.

The blood was tested and proved not to be hers. And when she was tested, she proved not to be ill. It made headlines for a half a week over the south-west, but the story soon died, with most people believing it to be a hoax. Subsequently, there had been just one possible sighting of Julien. Someone matching his description had spent one night at a motel in Amarillo, Texas. He'd told the manager

229

he was heading for Canada and that was where the trail died.

Gabriella said, "It's quite something, isn't it?"

I nodded. "It's amazing."

"I knew you wouldn't be alone."

It was just after four in the morning when I got up. On the few occasions I'd managed to doze, it hadn't lasted long. Typically, I awoke as soon as I moved. A quarter roll or the slightest shift in position would aggravate the cuts on my back and test the stitches.

Paul Julien. What an intriguing prospect he was. If the facts were correct, he'd had more than twenty years to figure it out. I'd had less than twenty days. Every time I thought of what happened at the Carlsson Institute, I felt a horrible lurch in the pit of my stomach. *There but for the grace of God go I.* His conclusion was such an obvious one. I knew I would have come to it soon enough. In fact, I was halfway there, but for slightly different reasons.

I was coming to believe my power was a burden not because of those I'd risk disappointing, but because of what it was doing to *me*. It marked me out for attack, it made it impossible for me to conduct my life normally, it plunged me into darkness. My reasons for questioning the gift were selfish and Julien's were the opposite.

He'd had two years and four months in a cell to chew over what his tremendous talent had done for him, for the two dead, disabled children and for their loving parents.

And despite losing their children, the parents had never criticized him. In a country where you can sue for millions for the most trivial offence, where financing intolerance is a national industry, they'd shown unparalleled compassion. They'd even testified on his behalf, helping reduce his manslaughter sentence. Who did they think he was when they saw him restore sight to the blind child in Indianapolis?

Perhaps that was another reason Paul Julien faded into obscurity once he'd finished his work at the Carlsson Institute. He didn't want to live under the pressure of expectation and false belief.

I looked down at another part of the interview.

**Interviewer:** So have you refrained from healing altogether?

**Paul Julien:** (*pauses and then smiles*) No. Not exactly. Here and there, from time to time . . . I've done it since then. But I've never looked for it.

**Interviewer:** I would have thought a gift such as yours might be a rewarding thing. Don't you get to see people overflowing with joy?

**Paul Julien:** Yes.

**Interviewer:** For many people, that kind of spontaneous adulation might be quite addictive.

**Paul Julien:** I don't understand what you're suggesting.

**Interviewer:** That you might achieve some fulfilment from what you can do. That it could be a pleasurable experience.

**Paul Julien:** After what I did? Are you crazy? No amount of weeping gratitude will wipe away that memory. The guilt never diminishes and I never want it to. I could never heal for fun, which is what you seem to be suggesting. When I do it, I'm reminded of what I did before, so it's a painful experience. Always. Which is how it should be.

**Interviewer:** Isn't that rather a self-pitying line to take?

**Paul Julien:** You mean in contrast to the rather self-serving line you're advocating?

My thoughts turned to Luke Cooper, sitting lifelessly in his wheelchair, while egos flared around him in an incandescent display of vanity. He hadn't even been able to hold up his head; it hung limply to one side. He was probably the only person not to be offended by what happened on Night Talk, but only because he was too ill to comprehend what was going on. If he died, would I be scarred with the same guilt that marked Paul Julien? At least he'd been trying to help when he made his ghastly error.

I went to make myself a cup of coffee. While the kettle boiled, I stood in the doorway to the bedroom and watched Gabriella sleeping. She was a leap in the dark for me. I was used to the security of guarantees. I felt naked without them. But if ever there was a risk worth taking . . .

I returned to the sitting-room with the cup of coffee and turned on the TV, reducing the volume to a whisper. It was the early morning news, full of good cheer, as usual: a new flood in Bangladesh, an escalation of civil war in Chad, a new corruption scandal in France, fifteen shot dead by a maniac in a McDonald's in San Antonio, a strike by car-workers on Merseyside, another royal marriage running aground on tabloid rocks.

My thoughts strayed from the litany of depression radiating off the screen. An idea began to crystallize into intent.

It was just after eight when I went back to the bedroom. Gabriella was still asleep, lying on her left side with her hair fanning out across the pillow. I padded round to her side of the bed and placed the cup and saucer on the bedside table. I kissed her forehead. She shifted a little and half-murmured something. The eyelids started to flicker and she gradually changed position. Her nose twitched and she mumbled, "What time is it?"

"Time for me to ask you a question."

"What?"

"If I left here, would you come with me?"

Her voice croaked with sleep. "If you left the hotel?"

"No. The country."

Her eyes widened and she looked awake. "Where are you going?"

"I'm not sure yet. America, perhaps," I said, presenting her with the cup and saucer.

She eyed me warily. "How long have you been up?"

"A few hours."

"A few *busy* hours, by the sound of it."

"I've kept myself occupied," I agreed. "So, would you come?"

"I don't know. Would you want me to?"

"Of course," I said.

"*Of course?*"

"Yes. I want you to come, but . . ."

Gabriella took a sip of coffee and said, "But what?"

I bowed my head. "Nothing. It's stupid."

"I expect it is," she said, "but tell me anyway."

I took a deep breath. "Ever since you walked into Parke Millen, you've been fighting my corner and you've been invaluable. I don't know what might have happened to me if you hadn't been there."

"So?"

"If you come with me, I want it to be because you really want to, and not because of what happened."

"I see," said Gabriella flatly, almost sighing as she did so. "You thought everything I've done so far was out of gratitude, I suppose?"

"Something like that."

"Including making love with you?"

I shrugged uselessly. "Well . . . it wouldn't be unheard of."

She smiled. "If it was a matter of gratitude, Christian, I'd give you a present. I wouldn't sleep with you."

"I'm sorry."

She reached up and put a hand around my neck, pulling me into a long, luxurious kiss. She ran her fingers over

233

my lower back, picking up the stitches through the shirt's cotton. I instinctively froze.

"Still painful?" she asked.

"I couldn't sleep because of them. Every time I moved, they seemed to be tearing."

"So you got up?"

"Yes. I was reading all the stuff on Paul Julien. The more I looked at it, the more it struck a chord. This thing about those he can help and those he can't . . . it really makes sense. Horrible sense, but sense nevertheless. If I allow myself publicity, I will always disappoint far more than I'll ever help. I'm not sure I can shoulder that responsibility."

"It's a real Catch–22. You have an extraordinary ability and the more people you heal, the more people you'll hurt. What have you decided to do?"

"Well, for one thing, I'm going to heal Luke Cooper."

I collected the phone from the other bedside table and rang Price's home number. His private secretary transferred me to his car-phone.

"Morning, Christian. What's up?"

Traffic competed with some radio station for dominance of the background noise.

"I want out," I said.

"You what?"

"I've had enough and I want out."

All I heard was the rumble of trucks and the twitter of some feather-brained DJ. Gabriella looked up at me with questioning eyes.

"Out?" coughed Price.

I reached for the cigarettes in my pocket but they weren't there. My mind's eye could see them on the coffee table in the sitting-room.

"That's right."

"But . . ."

"I've got a non-negotiable deal for you," I said, cutting

him off before he could start moaning. "I want to help Luke Cooper and prove to the doubters that I'm not a fraud. You want to restore your reputation. We can do everything in one blow."

"How?"

"You arrange some event where I perform like a show-monkey and then you help me to get out . . . permanently. Everyone ends up happy. How does that sound?"

"What do you mean by get out?"

"Abroad. Somewhere safe."

When he finally spoke, there was obvious caution in his voice. "Are you serious?"

"Naturally. But there are conditions. Luke Cooper *must* be one of them. Without him, there's nothing."

"One of them?"

"Yes. I'll heal two people."

"I see. And where do you want to go afterwards?"

"I'll let you know. But for now, do you accept?"

"Yes," he replied, briskly. "Definitely. Incidentally, have you had a chance to see today's papers?"

"No."

"You're on the front page again, Christian, and none of it's good. I've got one tabloid in front of me right now. Ever since the story first broke they've been calling you St Freak. You know what they're calling you now?"

"They were calling me St Freak?"

"Sure. They had the video-shot of you just after you'd healed Mr Leonard, bleeding in the crucifixion stance. Don't you get it? You're a saint for healing him and a freak for bleeding on him!"

Price was laughing heartily. I shook my head. Which moron had languished behind his desk in a drunken stupor and come up with that?

"So what are they calling me now?" I asked.

"What else but St Fraud!"

"St Fraud?"

235

"That's their headline, for Christ's sake. *St Fraud!* Big four-inch letters, no less. But you know what the tackiest part is?"

"What?"

"On the bottom of page two they've got a telephone number and they want readers to call in and give their verdict. *St Freak or St Fraud? You decide!* A free call to their phone-line to pass judgement on you, Christian. They're going to publish the results tomorrow."

"I can hardly wait."

# Chapter Sixteen

"I hope you don't mind, but I had to see you in person and I didn't want to do it when there were too many other people around."

"Well, you'd better come in. Coffee?"

"As long as it's not decaffeinated."

Gordon Rowdy ushered me into his office. The light was tastefully dim considering it was six in the morning. Moorgate had been virtually deserted as I was driven up it.

"I've seen the stories," he said, "but I still find them hard to believe."

"So do I, sometimes."

He handed me a cup and saucer and sat down behind his desk. "I imagine you've come to hand in your resignation."

"Yes."

"You'll be missed."

"By some, perhaps."

"More than you might think. You have quite a reputation. Only the day before yesterday, I met a lady called Maria Kohler, who was very upset that she wasn't going to meet you."

"Maria Kohler? The slave-driver?"

"She's a slave-driver?"

"Ask Daniel Peck."

"She sure as hell didn't come across like one."

He put his hands behind his head and leaned back, crossing one leg over the other. One of his computers came alive without any apparent provocation. The screen filled with green numbers, which flickered in a frenzy before dying and leaving a simple code in the top left corner. Rowdy glanced at it, but did nothing.

"What are you going to do?" he asked.

"I'm not sure yet. But the reason I'm leaving Parke Millen is because I'm leaving the country."

"So? One call from me and you could be installed in the office of your choice."

"I appreciate that, but the fact is, I don't know where I'll end up, or when I'll end up there, or what I'll end up doing."

Rowdy lit a cigarette and pushed a hand over the thinning hair on his head.

"Whatever it is," he said, "I can't really see you as a full-time healer."

"Neither can I. It's not my style."

"No, it's not. Well, all I can say is we'll be sorry to lose you. We had high hopes for you. You could have been a star, but just so long as you're not jumping ship to join a competitor . . ."

"Nothing could be further from my mind."

"Then I wish you all the best. If there's anything I can do, or if there's something Parke Millen can do, you know the numbers."

I was surprised and it must have shown.

"I'm misunderstood," he said, smiling through a face of theatrical self-pity. "You of all people should appreciate that."

I nodded. "I do now. Thank you, Mr Rowdy."

"You've earned it. Before you go," he said, reaching for his coffee cup, "allow me to offer you one piece of good advice: follow your instinct. I still don't really know what's happened to you, but I can see the resulting chaos. Sometimes it's hard to know what to do when everything's turning to shit. But you're lucky. Your instinct is good. I've seen it myself. So use it."

More digits appeared on the computer screen. He gazed at them lazily, punched a button and they all vanished.

"I'll bear that in mind," I said, leaning forward and placing my cup and saucer on his desk. "As a return favour, would you allow me to be cocky enough to offer you a parting piece of advice?"

"Sure."

I took a deep breath and said, "Fire Robert Poulsen."

Rowdy grinned slyly, leaned back in his chair and said, "This wouldn't be personal, would it?"

"It certainly would be," I conceded. "But it's also professional. He's dead weight."

"Oh?"

"Chantal Loursain and Danny Peck are doing all his work. Not only that, but he's a disruptive influence on everyone around him."

"He's always said the same about you."

"I'm sure he has. But if you want to find the truth, conduct a survey."

Gordon Rowdy was pensive for a few seconds and then seemed to relax. "Since you're leaving us, I'll tell you this: Poulsen's position is already under scrutiny because of this newspaper business. I'll make your views known, though. It'll help paint a fuller picture . . . and to point us in the right direction."

Danny and Chantal were already at their desks by the time I went to clear mine. I didn't keep much personal stuff at Parke Millen. There were a couple of address books, a smart pen here, a good lighter there. I never wanted a photograph on my desk.

"The prodigal son returns," said Danny.

"Morning, Mr Peck."

"Rejoining the physical working world after your extra-curricular spiritual activities?"

"Nope. Resigning."

This caught them both flat-footed. Danny looked

unusually serious and it didn't suit him at all. He ran a hand through the wreckage of his hair.

"You're kidding!"

"No."

"Is it all true, Christian?" asked Chantal.

"That depends on what you read."

"Did you do it?"

"Heal the blind man? Yes, I did."

Danny and Chantal glanced at each other. Danny was pale. Chantal swallowed and said, "It doesn't seem to have made you very happy."

I nodded appreciatively. "You're the first person to say that."

"What about all the other stuff that's been in the papers?" asked Danny.

"I made a mistake, but I'm not a cheat. I'm going to put it right and make them eat their words. And after that . . . well, we'll see."

There was an awkward silence. I lent over and kissed Chantal on the cheek. "I better be on my way. So much for the illegitimate love child we were supposed to have."

She smiled frailly and said, "Oh, I don't know. We could still produce interesting offspring, I'm sure."

"A healer in Chanel?" said Danny. "I don't think so."

"That's what I'm going to miss most about you, Danny. Your taste and tact. How will I live without it?"

"If you keep in touch, you won't have to worry about that."

I collected Jackson from the reception area. As we left Parke Millen, the office was beginning to fill. Maintenance staff were polishing glass, scrubbing floors and spraying luminous green polish onto the plants in the atrium, as I strode across the stone for the final time. By a beautiful coincidence, Robert Poulsen was coming through the large glass doors as we were on our way out.

"Already finished your work for the day?" he asked, snidely.

"I've resigned."

"What a pity!" he said, before checking out Jackson. "By the way, I didn't appreciate your telephone call. Your insult was beyond the mark."

"It was right *on* the mark," I corrected him.

He frowned. "I'm sorry?"

"You certainly will be."

His confusion embarrassed him, so he simply said, "Goodbye, Floyd. I can't say I'm sorry to see you go. And I don't suppose Parke Millen shall mourn your departure, either."

"Nor yours," I replied.


"Look at this! Bloody marvellous, eh?"

Price was at his happiest. His fat arms were outstretched in my patented crucifixion pose. Gabriella and I looked around.

"I'm happy you could come here," he told us.

Brian Bradfield and Jackson were standing by the window. Price had brought us to his head office in Percy Street. There was undiluted pride in his voice, as he described how the builders had gutted the entire edifice so he could have his dream headquarters. Rather like his home, it was impressive only in so far as it was obvious that no expense had been spared.

"I've got conference rooms, the latest computers, the whole bloody bit!"

The way he said it made them sound like social niceties, not professional necessities. He liked the look of things; he loved the way the stretched Mercedes had slid to a halt outside the entrance, and how Jackson and Bradfield had cleared the pavement before we were allowed out of the car and across three yards of paving stone to the glass door with SZP painted on it. In gold, naturally.

In the entrance hall, a receptionist sat behind a desk of stone with Samuel Z. Price Management engraved into it. Now we were on the third floor, in his own office. He walked over to one corner and pulled open a fridge, stocked with cans of Coke, bottles of Perrier and Evian, and a variety of fruit juices.

"Drink?" he asked, extending a hand towards the contents, like some game-show host showing off a prize.

"I can't see anything in there I'd describe as a drink."

"Ah yes! The Dipso Dream Doctor."

I looked at him quizzically. "The Dipso Dream Doctor?"

"I know, I know. The names they conjure up. But who's complaining?"

"I thought you were."

"Not any more. All that publicity could have burned me badly. It could have been disastrous. But now? I've turned it all around."

"How did you manage that?"

"Double exposure. They printed all the bad stuff anyway, so then I announced you were going to prove your legitimacy beyond all doubt. Naturally, they printed that too. Like I said, double exposure. There's no such thing as too much publicity in my business. Neat, don't you think?"

"Distinctive, certainly. I'll give you credit for that."

He said, "I don't think I've generated this much press coverage since . . . since . . ."

He moved over to one wall and took a large photo off its hook. It showed two giants slugging it out in a boxing ring with a bloodthirsty crowd urging them on.

". . . since this," he said, proudly showing us the photo. "Larry 'The Light' Deloitte versus Clarence Clubber Carpenter, for the WBC and WBA world heavy-weight titles at Wembley Stadium."

"I remember the fight. Carpenter took Deloitte in the eighth."

"It was the tenth, actually. What a glorious night! It would have been perfect if those midget-dicks at the IBF hadn't refused to join the unifying process, but that's another story. Anyway, now *you* are cooking up a storm, and when the time comes for you to do your thing, I'm going to make sure everyone gets value for . . ."

He stopped.

"For money?" I prompted him.

"It's just a phrase," he said, defensively. "You know what I mean."

The truth was that I no longer really cared whether Price profited from this or not. It would all be over soon anyway. My high and mighty declarations about not being exploited were worth nothing any more, so what did it matter?

"I've used all the bad press to my advantage," he continued. "It's going to get better, too. You want to know how things are shaping up?"

"Isn't that why you brought us here? Apart from being able to admire your new offices, of course."

"You like them?"

"Very good for your business, I should think."

Price returned the shot to its hanging place. He plucked a small carton of orange from the fridge and pierced its foil top with a straw. He slurped loudly when he sucked.

"Let's hope you can still strut your stuff, eh?" he said, moving behind his desk. "Otherwise, we're all buggered."

He finished the drink and tossed the crumpled carton into a tall wastepaper bin, with the ubiquitous SZP emblem printed on it.

"Where do you suppose you're going to do the healing?" he asked, with a cheeky glint in his eye.

Knowing Price, and judging by the evident delight he

was taking in this, it would have to be somewhere on the border between bad taste and something worse.

"A church?" I suggested.

He frowned. "How did you know?"

"You're not serious?"

"Never more so," he insisted. "In a church! Isn't that bloody brilliant?"

I was speechless.

"Actually, it's not a proper church," he said. "It's been deconsecrated, or whatever they call it. You know what I mean . . . it's gone out of business."

"Out of business?"

"That's right. And I've bought it. I'm turning it into a small rock venue. It fits in perfectly with my musical interests. It'll be a breeding ground for new talent and . . ."

I was still trying to cope with the concept. "In a church?"

"That's right. It's a wonderful place. It's not open yet, but it's in a good enough state to stage the healing. It's called the Electric Church. Good name, don't you think?"

"If you say so."

"I don't know why I didn't think of it earlier. And then I had another brainstorm. I'm getting Hand-To-Mouth Productions to stage it for us. It'll be the same crew that did Night Talk."

"Including that prick Sean King?"

"Yes. I hope you won't cause a problem there, Christian. He'll be given strict orders this time, I promise you."

I was too weary to wage this battle again. "Go on."

"I mean, the publicity value of King hosting the show is just too good to pass over. After the conflict last time around . . ."

"I get the idea."

"As for your departure, that'll be no problem. We call it The Getaway – an escape procedure perfected for getting rock stars out of arenas before the groupies rip them to shreds. I know you don't quite fit into that category, but The Getaway will be useful. As soon as you're finished, we get you to the back of the building, where there's a coach waiting. We'll have clear access to the Marylebone Road – the Electric Church is just off it – and then we can take you out to Heathrow. You'll be able to wash on the coach. I imagine you'll be rather . . . well, rather . . ."

"Bloody? I should think so."

"Also on the coach, there'll be some clean clothes, your passports and the First Class tickets to New York."

"New York?"

"You didn't specify where in America, so it seemed like a good guess. Once you're there, that'll be my part of the bargain fulfilled. The rest is up to you."

"And who shall I be treating?"

"That's not finalized yet."

"Remember that Luke Cooper must be one of them."

Price removed his glasses and started to wipe the tinted lenses with a lime handkerchief. I could hear Jackson laughing outside, in the waiting-room. Denise, Price's secretary, was giggling.

"We do have a *little* problem there," said Price, timidly.

"How little?"

"Well, Mrs Cooper is rather reluctant to put Luke through the same experience."

"I call that considerably more than little. Have you explained that it won't be the same experience? I *guarantee* to heal her son. Have you told her that?"

Price refitted the glasses. "Indeed, but she was very upset by what happened on Night Talk. So was Luke."

I shuddered at the memory and said, "I'm not surprised. When you say she's reluctant, what exactly do you mean?"

"She told me to piss off. She said she wasn't interested."

"I stand by what I said. No Luke Cooper for me, no extravaganza for you."

This was not what he wanted to hear. "What if she won't come round?"

"You're a slick, silver-tongued cavalier. I'm sure you'll persuade her that it's the best thing for her son."

"Supposing she's adamant?"

"Then it's off."

"It doesn't have to be. I could find a replacement. I could find someone *iller*," he declared, triumphantly. "I could find someone who's not weeks from death or days from death, but *hours* from death, perhaps less. Imagine it! *Minutes* from death ... a desperate ambulance races across London at high speed with a baby who ..."

I strangled a bitter laugh. "You're a law unto yourself, aren't you? You'd fillet your mother for a profit."

"My mother's dead, so please don't take her name in ..."

"It's Luke Cooper or no one. That's final. This way, I can ensure you really make the effort with Mrs Cooper."

Price sighed like an exasperated parent with a stubborn child. "Okay, okay, I'll do my best. It was just an idea."

"A grotesque one."

Price changed the subject. "It's a shame you've decided to retire so soon. There's a future for you here, you know."

"Don't bother trying," I warned him, politely.

"I'm not trying. I know you too well, but I thought you might be interested to hear what's happening. I've had to hire two extra telephonists to deal with sick people from all over the country, all desperate to see you. Every disease you've ever heard of has been mentioned over our phones in the past few days."

"That's why I'm getting out. I can't help them so it's unfair to raise their hopes. If my heart was really in the right place, I wouldn't even be doing this. It's just that it's the easiest way to sort things out."

"At least you're honest. That's quite rare, in my line of work. I might add that it's not just the sick who want you.

246

There are people calling us because they want you for commercials and interviews and supermarket openings. Politicians want you to make statements on their behalf and appear in their tacky political broadcasts. Providing you come good on the night, of course."

"Of course."

"You're absolutely sure you don't fancy any of that?"

"Absolutely sure."

Price shook his head and smiled. "What a pity! It's such a waste!"

"You'll get over it."


I wanted to see Katy once more. Price and Gabriella both thought this was a bad idea. Price didn't like it because he considered it an unnecessary excursion. He only felt safe when we were cooped up inside the flat. Gabriella didn't have to say why she didn't want me to go; had our positions been reversed, I would have felt the same. Nevertheless, I needed to see Katy, in case I never saw her again. At the very least, I thought we could perhaps purge the bitterness.

"You must be out of your mind," muttered Jackson, darkly, as we sat in the back of the sinister Mercedes. "If I was with Gabriella, I wouldn't go to see my *wife*, let alone my ex-girlfriend."

The car came to a halt in Walton Street, where Polly de Blanche had her Interior Design shop. The driver parked it on the pavement. I spotted Polly de Blanche looking out into the street. She couldn't see me because of the tinted windows, so I was sure she was thinking big money was about to walk through her door. When I stepped inside the shop, disappointment dominated her face, so the trip was already a qualified success.

I gave her a cursory nod. She was perfectly made up, as always, looking as sexless as a mannequin, in a formal navy skirt and jacket. Her face was a mask of white plaster. Katy was in the far corner, sorting through half a dozen rolls of fabric. She turned to see me and was shocked.

"Christian!" she choked. "What are you doing here?"

"I have to talk to you."

She didn't know what to say and looked at Polly de Blanche, who said, "I don't think your coming here was at all advisable."

"Well, I came here to see Katy and I'm sure she can make up her own mind. And I'm sure if she wants to speak to me, you'll allow her a few minutes."

"If it's what Katy wants ... otherwise, you must leave."

We ended up round the corner in a café with prints of Toulouse Lautrec's Moulin Rouge posters on its walls. The waiters hung idly around one end of the bar, muttering between themselves and occasionally buffing the top of the counter with their tea-towels. It was the middle of the morning and only two of the twenty or so tables were occupied.

Katy's conversation had been as dry as toast between Polly de Blanche's shop and the café. She said, "Where did you pick up the big black car and the big black minder?"

"I'm being loaned the car," I half-lied, "and Jackson is here to protect me."

Jackson was actually standing outside, on the pavement. His lurking presence prompted speculative whispering among the waiters, who eyed us suspiciously.

"To protect you?" she said, acidly. "From whom? Me?"

"I wish I really knew."

"I can think of a few possibilities," she murmured, looking down at the table.

Our coffees arrived. I lit a cigarette and said, "I understand you're seeing Justin."

It sounded ridiculous, like a criminal charge, and Katy responded to it with a suitable look of disdain.

"If you brought me here just to have a go at me, I might as well get back to the shop."

She spooned sugar into her coffee and began to stir it. She was silent for a moment. When she next spoke, she seemed less thorny than before. "I'm sorry for the way things have worked out, Christian. But the truth is, it's better this way."

I rolled the lit cigarette between my fingers with a certain nonchalance but it didn't look good and I knew it. I nodded casually. "Yeah, well, whatever. I suppose it's all for the best. Or something."

An embarrassing silence followed. Who was I kidding? Given half a chance, I would have gone to bed with Julia Graham and that would have been no less an example of infidelity than anything Katy had done. As for Gabriella . . . that was a hard one to call.

I said, "I'm going away. That's why I wanted to see you."

"Going away? Where to?"

I didn't want to be specific, so I said, "I'm not sure yet. But I don't think I'm coming back."

She tapped her spoon on the lip of her cup and dropped it onto the saucer.

"Ever?"

"I don't think so. The more I consider it, the less I can see it."

At last, she was really listening to me. "But your job and your friends and . . ."

"I've quit my job, and as for my friends . . ."

I thought about my chance meeting with Charlie and how he reported their ludicrous version of concern.

". . . well, they can come and visit me when I find somewhere to live," I said, without enthusiasm.

Katy looked anxious. "Are you going to be all right? I mean, you can't just stroll off into the sunset by yourself."

"I won't. I've got company."

Katy's look asked a silent question which I didn't answer. So she smiled and said, "Maybe we'll both end up better off than when we started."

"You've seen and heard the reasons for this, Katy. But the main reason I'm leaving hasn't happened yet."

She frowned. I ordered two more coffees.

"I'm going to heal on television, to prove I'm for real. After that, I don't want to be around."

"If it's forcing you into such drastic action, why do it?"

"Because it'd be even worse to remain here and walk around the streets with total strangers coming up to me and telling me that I was a liar and a cheat. And believe me, that's exactly what would happen. It's already happening. That's why I wanted to see you before I went. I reckoned you deserved an explanation from me. Face to face."

Katy patted me on the hand. "Thanks."

"There's something else."

"What?"

"I want you to come to the healing. I want you to see it so you really know I'm telling the truth."

She tensed. "I'm not so sure."

"I understand your reservations, but I'd really appreciate it. You don't have to come alone. Come with Justin. Or Charlie. Any of them. *All* of them. Just promise me you'll consider it."

She smiled. "Okay, I'll think about it."

# Chapter Seventeen

The significance of what I had decided to do was brought into brutal focus in one moment. Bradfield and Jackson were sent to each of our apartments to gather essential items for our flight to America. And when I was refused permission to go with them, the finality of my decision was stunningly clear. As I described every item for collection, I attempted to direct them to the correct locations in each room. This process served as some sort of guided tour through a familiar museum, a nostalgic trip through a place I'd never see again. It highlighted the sobering fact that I was abandoning everything; my friends, the apartment, my job, the city I considered my own. And although the prospect of an unshackled future in a new country was exhilarating, I found the clinical way I was condemning all I knew to history depressing. Incarcerated in our hotel apartment, my nerves frayed and I slipped down the sharp, scree-covered slope towards total decline.

"Nervous?" asked Gabriella, appearing in the doorway.

"Yes."

"In a few hours, it'll all be over. You'll be free."

"I know. I keep trying to focus on that, but it's not easy."

Brian Bradfield and Jackson arrived. Bradfield was wearing a dark blue double-breasted suit. His shirt was plain white. Jackson wore jeans, a white T-shirt and a navy jacket. This was formal wear for him and he looked uncomfortable in it.

"Are you ready?" asked Bradfield.

I nodded and he signalled to two men who had been

waiting outside. They came in and took away everything that was bound for the bus to Heathrow.

"There's a bit of a crowd outside," said Jackson. "But don't worry. It's nothing to get excited about."

Bradfield said, "We'll wait for you out here."

They stepped into the corridor and closed the door behind them. Gabriella and I were alone again. She looked at me and asked, "What's wrong, Christian?"

"I was just thinking about how I treated Luke Cooper last time."

"Well, don't. You've got a chance to change that."

"On television."

"You agreed to it. You *suggested* it."

"I know. But I wish I hadn't. I should have just tracked the child down, done the deed and disappeared. Letting Price shower glitter over everything can't be a good idea."

"What you're really worried about is the lunatics, not the boy, right?"

I imagined Lorenzo Sevilla squinting in the bright Peruvian sun. A flash of light caught his eye; a sunbeam on gun metal. They were breaking from the crowd. I nodded halfheartedly.

"He'll have security everywhere," she explained.

"But they've already found us. They tracked us down here. They did this to me," I said, gesticulating over my shoulder.

"Only because you ignored what you were told. You wandered off and made yourself vulnerable. That won't happen today. You'll be protected and then we'll be gone."

I tried to muster a smile. "You're right. Let's go."

When we reached the ground floor, Gabriella and I were steered away from the Flats Entrance.

"The car's on the other side. It's quicker to pull away into Park Lane," explained Brian Bradfield.

I was conscious of the stares we drew as four extra men joined the guard, forming a circle of six around us.

Jackson's eyes were alert, picking up every sharp movement from anywhere in the lobby. When he caught me watching him, he tried to pretend he was relaxed. Ahead of us, through the glass entrance, I spied the crowd.

I was expecting a gathering of about a dozen, but there were far more than that. They blocked the pavement and pressed against the men who had been instructed to keep a path clear between the hotel and the car. Some had placards and banners. As we reached the entrance, they saw us and started to raise their voices to fever pitch. They were wrestling with those who were restraining them. I tensed.

"Don't worry," murmured Jackson. "It's not a problem."

But the way he and Bradfield exchanged glances betrayed the truth. Gabriella bit her lip. The colour drained from her face. The protesters were clawing at the beleaguered human security cordon. I spotted police officers struggling to enforce any kind of order. We paused by the door and Bradfield took a firm grip on Gabriella. He nodded vigorously and I saw somebody step off the kerb and open the back door of the Mercedes.

Lorenzo Sevilla returned to my thoughts, accompanied by Virginia Calloway and Rosa Fleischer. Or any of the others. I was searching for anything distinct as it broke from the crowd, but everything was a blur. To my right, I noticed a bright light dancing over the heads of the throng. Cameras. There was a young woman on the left screaming something inaudible at us. The baby she was holding was crying. The door to the hotel was yanked open and we surged forward. Rain hit my face and abuse filled my ears.

The crowd started to break down the protection. They pressed forward as a tide. I glanced left and right. I saw a banner declaring "Lucifer Lives!", while another simply said, "Burn! Burn! Burn!" over my name.

Brian Bradfield and Gabriella were ahead of us. As the

restraining pocket began to collapse, I saw him place his arm around her shoulders and yell at her to bow her head. Jackson was trying to push me forward but the crowd were now barging into us. A stray hand grabbed Gabriella by the hair, jerking her head back. She yelped. In an instant, Bradfield dropped his shoulder and lashed out with his right arm. The attacker let go and reeled backwards. The last I saw of him was as he melted into the crowd, clutching his remodelled nose. Bradfield virtually carried Gabriella the rest of the way to the vehicle. I saw him bending her into a crouch as they approached the back door. Then my view was blocked.

Three protesters cut through the security chain, before the rupture was healed by Price's human sealant. There were two men and a woman. She had steel grey hair scraped into a tight bun. Her eyes were fanatically wild as she lunged at me, while her two companions fended off any attempts to prevent her from reaching me. She grabbed me by the shirt before I could get out of the way.

"Don't do it!" she screamed. "Don't do it!"

To my left, someone had broken a placard in two and was hitting someone else with the lower half. The crazy woman was pawing at my shirt.

"Give it up!" she yelled. "Repent and you can still be saved! *It's not too late!*"

Someone clutched her olive sweatshirt and tried to tug her backwards, but her hysteria gave her extra strength. Jackson started to swing me round so he could get closer to her. He grabbed her shoulder and started to drive her down to the pavement with one muscular arm.

"Turn to the Church of the Divine Science!" she screamed, as her knees buckled under the pressure. "Pray to the Lord for mercy!"

Jackson forced her to the ground, but she wouldn't relinquish her grip. The name of the church chilled me. I scanned the rabble. She wrapped her arms around my legs so I couldn't move. There were tears on her face and her chin quivered as she babbled.

Jackson held his hand over her head and commanded, with volcanic menace, "Let go of him."

Two bodyguards came to peel her off me. As they started to wrench her arms away, she changed her style, suddenly looking angrier and crazier. She began to kick at them, her arms flailing wildly. One stray blow caught me in the back, just above the stitches. It was close enough to be agonizing. The shot fried my nerves. My legs turned to dust and I cried out in pain.

"You're going to die!" she howled, spit streaking her chin. "You're going to die today and then you're going to burn! *You'll burn for ever!*"

Jackson prevented me from falling to the ground. I was trying to catch my breath. I spotted TV cameras out of the corner of my eye. Scuffles were now brawls. Bradfield was calling from the back of the car, imploring us to hurry.

"You'll burn in hell for this!" screeched the woman, who then bit one of her suppressors on the hand.

He let go and she wriggled free, throwing herself at me once again. But she didn't make it this time. Jackson unleashed a fearsome backhand swipe which caught her fully on the left cheek. She seemed to disintegrate under the force of the strike, bouncing against the boiling crowd before crumpling limply to the pavement. Jackson was driving me through the madness towards the car.

Fists and insults were traded. I kept my head low and forged forward. As we approached the Mercedes, the back door opened fully and I tumbled into safety. Bradfield and Gabriella moved out of the way. Jackson followed me in and shouted, "Go!"

The car lurched forward. Hands hammered the roof and maniacal faces twisted into the tortured screams which were directed at me from the other side of the tinted, reinforced glass. The driver swung away from the kerb, nudging a couple of protesters. Then he kicked the accelerator and I sank into the quicksand of the smooth, leather back seat. I turned round and looked through the rear window. The chaos on the pavement was spilling into Park Lane and the police were halting all oncoming traffic.

The architects had retained many of the building's features. The room which I had been assigned was once the vestry. The stage was where the altar had been and since the church's design was cruciform, the transepts had conveniently become wings. Acoustic improvers were suspended from the original buttresses. Fluted columns now provided the vertical axis onto which complex lighting rigs were attached. A surprising amount of the original building had been incorporated into the design of Price's plan. The Electric Church was an impressive marriage of two utterly alien ideas.

When we arrived, Price was standing ankle deep in a thick undergrowth of cables and wiring. People flocked to him with problems and he dispatched them with solutions. As soon as he saw us, he deserted them. He dragged me to one side, clutching my arm tightly, and waved away everyone else as though they were flies.

"Are you all right?"

I was badly shaken by what had happened, which only served to strengthen my anxiety about what lay ahead. "I'm fine," I said, unconvincingly.

"I don't want you to worry, Christian. No one's going to get close to you. Security will be tighter than a duck's arse. No client of mine ever came to grief while I was looking after them."

On the other side of the stage, I saw Sean King, the presenter of Night Talk. Price looked at me earnestly. "Everything will be fine," he assured me.

King rolled over to us, exuding self-confidence.

"Sammy, mate! Good to see you again," he said, extending a hand which Price shook. "And you too, Mr Floyd."

He put a filterless Gitanes between his lips. "I heard what happened. You all right?"

"More or less."

"About the other night," he said to me, as he tried to work his lighter. "I hope you understand it was just business."

I offered him my lighter.

"Thanks," he said. "I wouldn't want you to think it was personal. No hard feelings, eh?"

"No feelings at all," I said.

King frowned in confusion, but managed a face-saving, crooked smile. "Right. Well, I'm going off to my dressing-room. I'm breaking in a new assistant. Says she's nineteen."

He gave us a wink and strode away. I turned to Price. "A class act. He says it was just business. You wouldn't know anything about that, of course."

Price was cautious and, as far as I was concerned, that was an admission of guilt. I lit a cigarette of my own. My hands were shaking. I saw her rabid face again, beseeching me to plead for forgiveness, oblivious to those who were manhandling her. Then came the blow. She must have been unconscious the moment Jackson's knuckles left her face. The crack had been as loud as a breaking branch.

"You said it wouldn't make any difference."

"It doesn't," I said. "I never believed you in the first place."

He frowned. "So why didn't you walk out?"

"I figured you'd still be the best person to help me out, providing I took certain precautions."

"Like?"

"Like not trusting you."

Price looked genuinely hurt. "After all I've done for you, and it turns out that it's *you* who's exploiting *me*."

"We're exploiting each other," I said. "But that's okay. We're both getting what we want, after all."

Price smiled slowly and slyly. "I recall how proud and pure you were when we first met. You remember that?"

"As Gabriella will testify, I was very naive."

"You know, you and I are not so different. We both believe the same thing: everything has a price. You made a career out of trading too. In your case it was European securities. From what my sources tell me, you were very good at it. Me? I've always been buying and selling, ever since I was a kid. In those days it was grubby snaps of naked women, or stolen watches, or whatever. These days, it's talented people. It's just one form of merchandise over another. And that's the only real difference between you and me."

I shook my head. "We're not that similar. For one thing, this experience has taught me something which I didn't appreciate before."

"And what's that?"

"You're just about right when you say everything has its price. There's virtually nothing you can't buy or sell. But this is true too: some things *shouldn't* be bought or sold. There are some things at the mercy of the market which should be protected from it. But nothing exists to save them from those forces, so they're traded like cocoa, or cars, or CDs. I should know, I've been there. And until now, I've always judged the quality of my life by the figure in the profit margin. But not any more. What's happened has changed all that. I guess that won't impress many people because they were probably never dumb enough to live their lives in such a blinkered fashion, in the first place. But for me, it's a revelation. Just because you can make a profit out of something, that's no reason to do it."

"Are you having a go at me?"

"I'm just explaining to you how tonight, after the show, I'm going to be a happy man. I'm going to step into the

future, free of the past. The very fact that you don't
understand any of this just goes to prove my point."

"I'm lost. What point would that be?"

"That you and I are *not* the same."

Price shrugged. "Listen, so long as you do your bit and
everything goes as slick as curry through the colon, I'll be
a happy man."

I shook my head, patted him on the shoulder and smiled
sadly. "I rest my case. All those millions of years of evolu-
tion and here we are. Was it really worth it?"

The vestry, which now served as my dressing-room, was
peculiar. It looked as though the original architect had
decided to make it octagonal and then changed his mind
halfway through construction. It now had six white walls
where eight would have looked neater, and none of them
was the same size. The widest wall supported four large
mirrors, with a dressing table beneath each. In one corner,
there was a well-stocked fridge. On a circular table there
was food; small pastry discs with cream cheese and something green on them; little biscuits with shrimps; the inevitable cocktail sausages, speared by thin wooden needles.
A bowl carrying carrot sticks, cucumber chunks and rods
of celery sat in a dish full of ice, next to a selection of
multi-coloured dips.

I didn't recognize her at first. She strolled into the
dressing-room without knocking. She looked younger
than I remembered her – more like late-twenties, not mid-
thirties – wearing a dark jacket and skirt, with a cream
silk blouse. She wore an expression of undiluted severity.
I was pacing nervously, drawing on my cigarette. She
startled me and I instinctively drew away. She gave me a
disapproving look when I extinguished the cigarette.

"I assume, Mr Floyd, you're aware of how reluctant I
am to put my son through this again."

I swallowed anxiously and motioned for her to take a seat, but she ignored the gesture.

"Yes, and I can understand that," I answered.

She looked at me contemptuously. "I very much doubt whether you can. You have no idea how much suffering you've caused."

"No," I said, humbly, "of course not."

"But everyone tells me this will be different."

"That's right."

Shirley Cooper's face mellowed slightly. "You can honestly heal him?"

"I believe so. I healed Mr Leonard."

"The blind man?"

"Yes."

She sized me up and then nodded. "I hope for Luke's sake you're telling the truth."

"I am. And I'd like to apologize for . . ."

"I don't want your apologies!" she snapped. "If you want to make amends, heal my son. That's all I have to say to you."

She walked out of the dressing-room before I could respond, passing Gabriella on her way out. Gabriella watched her disappear down the corridor and then closed the door.

"Wasn't that . . .?"

"Shirley Cooper? Yes."

"What did she want?"

"Reasonable assurances."

Later, while Gabriella was somewhere talking to Price, there was a knock at the door. It was Jorge Sanchez. I had to double-take. He was about the least likely person I expected to see. When last I'd heard, he was still in Madrid.

Once I'd recovered sufficient composure for speech, I said, "Jorge, what the hell are you doing here?"

"You didn't think I'd miss the hottest show in town, did you?"

"Come on in," I said.

"The security out there is ridiculous, Christian. It's more fun trying to run heroin through Bangkok Airport. They did everything but stick a torch up my backside. And all this to see you . . ."

The good humour receded. I shrugged in a useless fashion and said, "I know. How was Madrid?"

"Forget Madrid. What about you? Everything I've heard sounds so crazy, but I understand it's all true."

"Yes, it is."

"I've been out of touch, so my first knowledge of it was this morning, at the airport. You made the Spanish press. I couldn't believe it was you in the papers. When I got back, no one knew where you were, so . . ."

"I've had to hide."

"From what?"

I turned around and lifted my shirt so he could see the stitches. "From the people who did this."

"Jesus Christ, Christian! Katy never mentioned this."

"You spoke to her?"

"I rang her. She said you saw her, and she told me everything. She asked me if I wanted to come."

"She's here?"

"Sure. Apparently you made her promise to come."

"I asked her to. But I didn't tell her about the cuts. There didn't seem much point."

He nodded sympathetically and asked, "Do you want to see her?"

"I don't think so."

"Well, she kept her word. There are a few of them out there in the audience."

"I wasn't sure," I said. "She promised to think about it, but . . . you know."

Jorge looked unusually earnest. "They're saying some

silly things about you, Christian, but it's only because they're confused."

"Sure."

"Like me."

"Me too."

He shook his head and half-smiled. "This is so stupid. I mean, first of all, I can't believe it's you. How could it be? How could *you* do this? You're no saint! I should know, right? So then I start thinking to myself, 'Okay, let's say he can do it ... what's he going to be like?' and naturally I imagine you're going to be a completely changed person."

I flicked through our mutual memory album: arguments about the superiority of Lineker over Butragueno; the pavement waltz at three in the morning; the two of us nursing Charlie through the aftermath of another amorous rejection; slurred debates over our fuzzy futures; the Grand Prix at Jerez where we stayed with Jorge's cousins; the time I spent all night waiting outside the operating theatre, while the surgeons put him back together after his car wreck on the Embankment.

It was a precious collection. He looked as exasperated as I felt and said, "I thought you'd be nothing like the Christian Floyd I've got to know so well. I expected you to be so different, but it seems to me you're not."

"Yes, I am."

The authority of my reply gave way to an awkward pause. Jorge smiled nervously and then asked, "After this is over, will we see each other again?"

"I'd like to think so."

"But?"

"But that's the best I can do for now."

He looked uneasy and said, "I better get back to the others."

I nodded and said, as he reached for the door, "Jorge,

thanks for coming. Tell Katy I appreciate it. I won't forget any of you, I promise."

I was still feeling low when Gabriella led Price into the dressing-room. He was bubbling with adrenalin as the moment approached. He hoped it would be infectious, but it wasn't. Brian Bradfield and Jackson escorted Gabriella to the bus, to check everything was in order for The Getaway.

"Don't look so downcast, Christian," said Price, plucking at something creamy and puffy on a shining plate. "You'll be fine."

"It's just nerves," I said.

"Of course it is. But they'll pass. They always do. I have absolute faith in you. In fact, my only doubt is over your judgement."

"Don't rake that up again, please."

"I'm not talking about what you could do for my business, Christian. I'm not talking about what you could do for yourself, either. I'm talking about God."

I looked up to see if Price was serious. Since he wasn't grinning, I assumed he was. He picked up a miniature biscuit with a couple of shrimps on it.

"Let's leave Him out of it," I suggested. "He tends to complicate the issue."

"Maybe, but it's relevant."

"Only if you're a believer."

"What other possible – *reasonable* – explanations can there be?"

"I have no idea."

"Exactly. And since He's decided to bless you with this talent, don't you think you should use it as best you can? Let's face it, nobody else can do what you do. Now, if you're lucky enough to have been given . . ."

"Lucky?" I interrupted. "You did say *lucky*, didn't you?"

Price lapsed into silence.

"Okay," I said, acutely aware of my rising temperature, "let's suppose God does exist and that He *did* actually give me this ability. Does that make me lucky? Did I ask for someone to come along and fuck up my life? No, I didn't. Did I ask to be made a target for persecution? Not as far as I can recall. My life may not have been perfect as it was – indeed, it may have been deeply flawed – but I was happy with it. I never asked to change. This healing thing just happened. I wasn't given a choice! Now, if God is responsible for it, then He's also responsible for all the chaos it's caused. So don't give me any bullshit about being lucky, or how I should be grateful and waste my time repaying Him for his generosity."

"Take it easy, for Christ's sake!" said Price, backing away.

I thrust an accusatory finger close to his face. "If anybody owes anyone anything, He owes me. So don't you ever – *ever* – try to tell me how lucky I am! Now get the fuck out of here!"

Price knew a lost cause when he saw one, so he bit his tongue and retreated. He slid out of the dressing-room, meekly promising not to disturb me until I was needed. I slammed the door shut behind him and cursed loudly several times. There was a click from the other side of the room, followed by the hiss of the swinging fire-exit door.

"Well, well, that was most revealing."

It was the voice. I spun round. He was standing by the fire exit, as it slowly clicked shut behind him. I couldn't see how he had manipulated the push-bar system. Somebody must have tampered with it earlier. What I could see, though, was the gun in his hand.

"Louis!" I gasped, knowing I was right.

He smiled viciously and nodded, milking pleasure from my fear. "You look shocked. Is it the gun that unsettles you? Or perhaps it's simply the fact that I'm here?"

The voice was even more hideous when there was no

telephone to distort it. He narrowed his eyes and spoke slowly, in a crackling whisper.

"Or is it my physical appearance which shocks you?"

# Chapter Eighteen

"Didn't your mother tell you it was rude to stare?"

Indeed she had, but it was hard not to. Louis was a small man with skin that looked as though it ought to smell. Some patches appeared deeply tanned and weather-worn, like a mariner's. Other blotches seemed to have been caused by a pigmentation disorder; some were pale nd pinkish, others were a dull grey, as though dead flesh had been carelessly grafted onto the living. It made him look as though he was decaying and I waited for the first hint of a rotting odour. His shoulders were rounded like an archer's bow and his head sloped forward on a scrawny neck. As he edged away from the fire exit, he shuffled unevenly, trying to disguise a pronounced limp.

Louis was a pitiful physical specimen. The joints on his spindly fingers were horribly swollen. His face had cheekbones which threatened to tear the dying tissue that covered them. His eyes had retreated so far into his skull they were almost invisible. Occasionally, when he raised his head to the light, I saw them escaping from the shadows; stained jelly shrouded in a milky mist. He was more than simply damaged goods. He was an abomination.

"Aren't I what you expected?" he asked, twisting his mouth into a crooked smile, revealing a full set of discoloured teeth.

He leaned against the dressing table furthest from me and raised the gun slightly, pointing it in my direction without any real aim.

267

"I've never fired a gun before," he admitted, "but if you force me to, I'll submit to beginner's luck."

The metal was bright silver and sparkled brilliantly under the dressing-room light. The handle looked like carved ivory.

I swallowed anxiously. "What do you want?"

"To see you. In the flesh, so to speak. Just once."

The wish wasn't mutual. The skin around his eyes was dark grey. He slowly surveyed the dressing-room. I said, "I need a cigarette. Can I get one?"

I indicated the packet on the dressing table and he nodded. I started to edge slowly around the perimeter of the room, never breaking eye contact.

"I don't suppose you ever thought we'd actually meet," he said.

"I wasn't sure."

"So you thought it was a risk worth taking?"

I collected my cigarettes and started to shift back to the other side of the room. The gun's chunky nose slowly followed me, as though we were two parts of a wheel; me as a section of the tyre and the gun as the hub, with a straight, invisible spoke running between us.

"Why are you here?" I asked.

"Because you made it necessary."

Fear created a little courage. "You want me to repent? You want me to drop to my knees and plead for forgiveness, or something like that?"

He smiled thinly at my cheap bravado and said, "No, I had something else in mind. Something a little more radical."

"Like what?"

"Can't you guess?"

"You want me to cancel the healing?"

"It's too late for that."

"Then what?"

He pushed a few strands of greasy hair out of his eyes,

smearing them back over his scalp. "You could have denied everything and gently slipped back into the tranquil waters of anonymity. I've granted you more chances than I need have. But it didn't make any difference, did it?"

I lit a Marlboro. "Who are you to grant me anything?"

"I don't need to justify myself to you, Mr Floyd."

"Well, there's got to be some justification for this. There has to be a reason."

"There is."

My frightened courage was leaning towards resentment. "I see. Perhaps you *still* think I'm a fraud? Is that it? Would you like me to show you?"

Louis edged backwards and leaned against a table, clutching the gun with both hands. He looked at me and cleared his throat again. Whatever he was trying to shift must have been as thick as treacle, judging by the effort he put into it. He sounded like a coffee percolator.

"If you were a fraud," he said, "the Church of the Divine Science wouldn't be concerned with you. It would only be a matter of time before you brought yourself down. All frauds do, eventually."

I hadn't expected this line at all. "That's a bit of a change, isn't it?"

"All that's changed is the way you understand the message. My position has been constant. The problem arises because I know that you *can* heal."

"I don't understand."

"No, I don't expect you do. But I understand fully. I know you. I know what you are. I know what you can do. I've seen through the eyes of another what you've done and I know how poisonous it really is."

"The eyes of another? What are you talking about?"

He ignored my questions and stared at me in silence for a few moments, before saying, "I really believe in good and evil."

"So do I," I replied, a little too quickly.

He shook his head. "No. Not in the same way. You see, I believe in God, in Heaven and Hell, in sin and redemption. I had faith long before I had proof."

"Proof?"

He nodded, smiling slyly. "That's right. I never needed it, but now I have it anyway. I saw what you did and it looked good, but I knew it wasn't. Your heart is corrupt. You're a slave to greed, a trader of dishonesty and dishonour. You're a prince in a godless world. And that's why such a gift could never be good in someone like you."

"You've lost me."

"The Devil can heal a mortal just as easily as the Lord."

I considered this. "You mean because I was successful and selfish it couldn't have happened to me? Is that it? Well, let me tell you something: it did. I didn't ask for it and I certainly never wanted it, but it happened to me anyway. That's just the way it is."

"No. That is *not* the way it is. That is the way it *looks*. But I know what you really are."

"What do you want from me? You keep saying you know what I can do, but you won't accept it. What would convince you? You want me to grow a beard and preach universal love? You want me to wander around in sackcloth and sandals, turning water into wine?"

Anger flashed across his distorted face. He jabbed the gun in my direction and I jumped, as though I'd been hit. The cigarette slipped from between my fingers. I felt beads of sweat erupting over my skin. As I tried to catch my fleeing breath, I raised a hand. "Please!" I whispered. "Don't do that!"

I retrieved my cigarette from the carpet where it had begun to burn a small hole. An acrid whiff rose up from the singed material. Louis was watching me with undisguised fascination, never blinking.

"You cannot corrupt me," he said.

"What?"

"My faith has given me strength. I can resist you."

We reached a stalemate. I couldn't discern anything from the expression on his face. He was looking at me as though I should be the one to speak, but I couldn't think of a thing to say. Such thoughts as I could individually identify were all to do with saving my own skin. The rest were fried and mixed.

Finally, he asked me, "Do you know why the Church of the Divine Science exists?"

"No, not really. One of your people did try to explain it to me, while he was attempting to beat me senseless with a truncheon."

Louis leaned back slightly. "Ah yes! The three stooges. Miss Fiorini was rather more resourceful than they anticipated. Not cerebral types, you understand."

"That's an understatement."

Louis suddenly pointed the gun directly at my chest. For one endless instant, I thought he was going to fire. My heart stopped. I braced myself for the thundering impact. Instead, he motioned with the gun, directing me into a chair, close to the fridge. I exhaled audibly. Louis didn't seem to take any pleasure from my terror.

He said, "The Church of the Divine Science is preparing for the second coming of the Lord."

"You and all the rest," I quipped.

Louis ignored the remark. He looked fanatically serious; intense bordering insane. I felt sick with nerves. I didn't know how much longer I could sit and talk with him while he brandished the gun. Why wouldn't someone interrupt us? Every thought of safety was neutralized by the knowledge of how the others ended up. Paul Julien's survival was no comfort at all.

"It's imminent," he said.

"What is?"

"The second coming of the Lord."

I might have laughed if he hadn't been holding the silver weapon. But he was, and he looked dangerously earnest. I took a drag from the cigarette; the obvious comparison with the condemned man's final wish hadn't eluded me.

"And you have a role to play in that, do you?"

"Yes."

I shook my head and it irritated him. I said, "I'm sorry, but I just can't buy that."

"I'm not surprised. Not in the least."

"What authority do you have to make . . .?"

"I have the highest authority of all," he insisted. "God is my authority."

I tilted back on my chair. A sinew was quivering in his neck.

"I'm not sure I understand what you're saying."

"I knew you would come before Him. That is what I was told."

"Wait a minute. Are you trying to tell me you spoke with God?"

"He commanded me in a dream," said Louis.

My disbelief was complete. "In a dream?"

"Yes."

"How do you know it was God's voice?"

He fixed me with a scornful stare. "The world into which He will be born is a dangerous place, filled with enemies. The Messiah requires people prepared to sacrifice themselves for his protection. I was chosen.

"At first, I protested. I asked Him how could I possibly perform such an enormous task, especially considering my fragile health. He told me that my strength of spirit would overcome all physical barriers.

"He said that dark forces would know the Messiah was coming and that they would do all they could to prevent it. They would try to discredit and destroy the truth. It was my mission to ensure they didn't succeed. I wanted to know how I would recognize these forces. Surely their disguises would be too clever for a fool like me? God told me I would see when it was necessary to see. Nevertheless, my doubt persisted, as it does in all of us, so God said a sign would be sent to me."

"A sign?"

"Yes. An angel."

My eyebrows arched. "*An angel?*"

Louis carried on without regard to my scepticism. "Yes. I saw an angel standing at the foot of my bed."

My incredulity achieved new limits of elasticity. "You saw an angel in your dream?"

"No. When I awoke."

"There was an angel standing there in your bedroom?"

"Yes."

All I could picture was a man with a pair of theatrical white wings. I shook my head and forced a weary smile. "So then what? He drew the curtains? He asked you what you wanted for breakfast? This is ridiculous! I suppose he . . ."

"*Silence!*" cried Louis, extending his arm and pointing the gun at my head.

I stiffened and raised my hands into the surrender salute, before mumbling a humble apology. Louis was shaking. His nostrils flared with each deep breath. I waited for him to calm down before gradually lowering my hands.

He continued. "The angel instructed me to enlist help. I was to make all necessary preparations because the next time he came to me, it would be to send us into action. I said I didn't know how I would be able to persuade others to accept my word and follow my instructions. The angel said I should have more faith."

Louis was in a fantastic orbit, far beyond the gravitational pull of balanced minds. I didn't know whether to feel sorry for him or not. He waved the gun around like a conductor with a baton and it terrified me. He was just as likely to fire it accidentally as deliberately.

"Look at me!" he commanded me. "I'm deformed, ugly, perhaps even repellent. Weak and worthless. Since birth, I've lived in the slime. I've been persecuted for my frailty, my ill health, my appearance, my very existence. I don't seek pity when I say this; I've long since grown accustomed to my lot. I know what I am: a freak, an outcast, *nothing*.

"But the angel was right. I succeeded. I recruited people and they became believers and followers. Disciples. Despite what I am, they do exactly as I say, enacting any order, no matter how apparently absurd. They would give up their lives if I commanded them to. They would never question the instruction. Their devotion is unwavering. How do you explain that?"

"I don't know. But I don't believe it's got much to do with angels standing at the foot of your bed."

"Well, you don't *believe* in anything. You don't *believe* that God gave you your extraordinary ability, do you?"

"No."

"Well, you're right about that. He didn't."

There was an ominous pause, during which I resisted the obvious temptation to ask who the donor *had* been. I heard the continuous background noise of preparation outside the dressing-room. All it would take was one person to come in and ask a question. I wondered how long we'd been alone together. It felt like for ever and a bit longer.

"Christian Floyd," sighed Louis, allowing himself a rueful smile. "Your pedigree is . . . *questionable*."

"My pedigree?"

"Take your father, for instance: a vile man, a confirmed sinner. Hardly a role model."

I was about to protest but Louis showed renewed interest in the gun, so I remained quiet.

"But he was not alone in his behaviour, was he? Your mother was a whore, committing adultery with any man who ever paid her attention. Your parents had a marriage built on infidelity and dishonesty. And you were the result-ant offspring of that ungodly union, so I suppose it cannot be considered a surprise that you have led your life in a similar style. You are the inevitable result. You have no faith, no morals, no goodness. You made a successful career in a godless trade where greed is life itself. Your private life is no less disgusting; Miss Katy Donaldson is a woman whose notions of fidelity appear to be as redun-dant as your mother's were. You wallow in your sin-infested existence, ignorant and contemptuous of the rest of the world and those of us who suffer in it. And now you and your latest whore are . . . *here!*"

His evangelical rant was reflected in the fires which burned in his eyes. The flames danced and he looked more unstable than ever. He gripped the gun tightly with a hand that trembled. I found myself wondering whether the safety-catch was on.

"It was such a clever choice," he said, grudgingly. "After all, what you can do is essentially so good."

"So what's the problem?" I asked, cautiously.

"*You.* You are the problem. By giving you the gift, the power to heal is debased. You make a mockery of it. Once you and your gift are exposed by the mass medium of television, you shall infect all who see you. As an example to others, you'd be a disaster beyond compare, but your influence would be strengthened by what you can do and by the millions who'd watch you. You poison the power to heal and that's why the world must not see you. I have to confess, the scheme is not without its brilliance."

"*The scheme?* What do you mean? There was no plan. It just happened."

Louis rocked back and forth gently. "Samuel Price and Miss Fiorini and you," he muttered, gloomily. "What an unholy trinity you make. You form a collective antithesis to hope and goodness."

I didn't know which I feared most: the hysterical tirade of before, or the calm composure he was currently displaying.

"Your imagination needs reins, Louis."

He shrugged in a way that almost suggested my words had been taken as a compliment. But then his brow creased again and his face darkened. "Satan wears a coat of many colours, all brilliant, but we see through his disguises."

That was what he said. In the silence that followed I watched him watching me.

"Are you suggesting I'm the Devil?" I asked him, eventually.

He just smiled.

"You really are crazy," I told him.

"How do you think I found you?" he asked.

"I don't know. You tell me."

"The angel."

"The angel who was hanging around at the end of your bed?"

"The same angel, but on a different occasion. The angel told me about you, while Miss Fiorini was being assaulted in the back of the light blue Toyota. It was like a live radio broadcast. He described everything as it happened. It was a rainy Thursday night, wasn't it? He told me how you entered the car park, how the hideous man yelled at you to go away, how you dragged her free and kicked the car door shut, breaking the wrists of . . ."

"This is bullshit!" I snapped. "You know what I think? It sounds to me like your crew were the ones that did it. I mean, the detail and . . ."

"You're wrong."

"That kind of behaviour certainly isn't beyond them, is it?"

"You're being illogical. What would be the purpose of constructing such a scenario? None that I can think of. To stage an assault so that you could chance across her and then rescue her? For what? Really, that is too ridiculous."

"*Too ridiculous?* You talk to me about being illogical, and in the next breath you're trying to convince me you talk to angels!"

He dismissed me with an arrogant wave of a bony hand. "You're still avoiding the issue. And that is, we wouldn't benefit from such an assault. No, that was just an unfortunate occurrence which you chanced across. A coincidence. You and I would have encountered each other whether you'd gone to her rescue or not. It was inevitable. *Unavoidable.*"

"Did the angel tell you that?"

"He didn't have to. It was obvious."

"Nothing is obvious any more."

"The angel told me everything about you. Your history. Your character. Your situation, as it was. Your name and address."

I put out my cigarette. "Not only an enrolling officer for the spiritually misguided, but also a living Directory Enquiries with wings and a halo. Not bad."

Louis didn't rise to the bait. He said, "Haven't you wondered how I first found you? Haven't you wondered how I knew what you'd done? I expect I'm still the only one to know that the girl was the first one to fall under your healing spell, right?"

I wasn't going to submit to him. "Yeah, I've thought about it. I've thought about it a lot and I still haven't come up with an answer. But given time, I'll dream up a thousand better explanations than the one you're offering."

"No, you won't and you know it. And you'd better know this, too: you won't be permitted to pollute the minds of the innocent. If you defy me, there'll be an almighty price to pay. You shall be judged by a higher authority but . . ."

There was a knock at the door. We both looked at it. The patchy skin tightened over his skull as he grew more intense. He stopped leaning against the dressing table, straightening himself into the standing position. There was another knock at the door, followed by a voice.

"Christian, are you in there? Christian?"

It was Price. I looked at Louis. His eyes were commuting between me and the door, but the gun stayed still. I thought I could feel a cold tingling in my chest at the point where I imagined the bullet would hit me.

"Are you going to shoot me?" I asked.

Another knock. "Christian, are you okay?"

Louis started to retreat towards the fire exit, apparently confused. He kept the gun trained on me. Price's hand was rapping the door again. Louis reached for the push-bar and said, "Go out there and make your confession."

"What confession?"

But he was gone. He'd disappeared through the fire exit which had provided him with an entrance.

# Chapter Nineteen

The fire-exit door clunked shut. It felt as though someone had cut me open and every life-sustaining force was flooding out of me. I gripped the edge of the table for support. Price was still hammering on the door, the volume of the voice rising in tandem with the urgency of the tone. I tried to control my wretched breathing. *What confession?*

Seeing angels at the end of the bed? That was usually the prerogative of drunks waking up in the night. But he was still the only one who knew Gabriella had been the first. And although I'd made the charge, I didn't believe he or his cohorts had been responsible for attacking her. All of which, as usual, left me with more questions than answers.

I moved over to the dressing-room door and opened it. Price looked relieved to see me. "Jesus! What's going on? You deaf or something? I was beginning to think . . ."

"Louis was here," I said.

He creased his brow. "Louis?"

"As in the Church of the Divine Science."

Price looked perplexed and peered over my shoulder, perhaps expecting to see Louis in the dressing-room.

"He went out by the fire exit," I explained.

"How did he get in?"

"The fire exit."

"How?"

"I don't bloody know. Somebody fiddled with it, I guess."

"But our security people . . ."

"... aren't worth shit! He had a gun, for Christ's sake!"

Price's jaw slackened into a gormless gape. I saw Gabriella standing further down the corridor, between Brian Bradfield and Jackson. They were cast in partial darkness. I could hear the muffled sound of someone addressing the audience through the booming amplification of the sound system. The metallic voice echoed in the wings.

Price rubbed his chin. "What did he want? I mean, he can't have been here to hurt you, or else he would have used the gun, right?"

"He wanted me to make a confession in front of the cameras."

"What kind of confession?"

"He didn't say. Presumably, he thinks I already know."

"But you don't?"

"After the jumbled bullshit I've just been subjected to, it could be any one of a dozen things."

Price frowned. "You all right?"

I felt numb. Not frightened or angry, just numb. "I'm okay."

"Do you want to cancel? I mean, if you think . . ."

Yes, I wanted to cancel. There was nothing I wanted more. But I couldn't. Luke Cooper awaited. I'd given my word to his mother and I couldn't let either of them down again. Louis could froth at the mouth all he wanted, but my mind was made up. His fanaticism was, I'd just discovered, one of the few things which could inspire a semblance of fortitude in me.

"No. I'm not going to cancel."

"Are you sure?"

"For once, I'm positive."

I could have healed Luke Cooper in private and slipped out of the back of the Electric Church. That was one possible course of action. As I saw the problem, there were many ways to get round it, but only one way to take it on.

"I'm not the Devil," I said to Price.

He looked lost. "Sorry?"

"I've got nothing to be ashamed of."

Price still didn't get it, but he'd heard what he needed to hear. He called out to Brian Bradfield. "I want all the doors shut. *Now!* Nobody else gets in. And check all the fire exits to make sure no one's tampered with them."

Bradfield disappeared and Price put his hand on my shoulder.

"You'd recognize him if you saw him again?"

"Certainly."

"You sure?"

"Believe me, if you'd seen him, you'd remember him."

"In that case, I'm going to stick extra people in the wings, and down by the front of the stage. If you see him, at any time, you point him out and we'll deal with him. We won't let anything happen to you."

"He's outside, though."

"It doesn't matter. Anything you don't like, we'll deal with. And if he really is outside, he won't be coming back in."

"From what he said," I continued, "I get the feeling he may already have some of his lunatics in the crowd."

"It's unlikely. We've been vigilant about searching everyone who's come in. But even if a few have slipped through, they can't get to you. There'll be too many of my men in the way."

Price led me away from my dressing-room. The sound of the audience grew louder. The corridor smelt of fresh paint. I looked up into the darkness and saw the dim web of the lighting rig, suspended over the stage. A few shadowy bodies moved along an overhead gantry.

"Lighting technicians," Price assured me.

"They better be."

"They are. Now stop worrying. You concentrate on your job and let me do mine."

We moved into a wing, just feet from the stage. We were in virtual darkness, but the stage itself was brightly illuminated. I reached for my cigarettes and pulled one out.

"Sorry, sir," said an assistant, with a clip-board. "No smoking."

Gabriella appeared. I felt uncannily calm. I kept thinking I should be quaking with fear. Maybe that moment had gone for good, a milestone I'd reached and passed. I'd looked into the black hollow of the gun barrel – a small but shocking abyss – and I was still here. Gabriella put an arm around my neck and kissed me on the cheek. We looked into the light from our tunnel of gloom. Sean King strolled onto the stage to crackling applause. His emerald jacket and chocolate cotton trousers looked especially vivid under the powerful overhead lamps. He held his hands open and twirled around, like a fashion model.

"What do you think of the threads? Not bad, eh?"

The audience gave their murmured approval and King started his opening monologue. His slick phrasing brought titters from his admirers as he outlined the format of the programme, inserting little jests wherever he could. Anything for a laugh.

"You'll be okay," whispered Gabriella.

I looked at Price. Neither of us mentioned Louis. I wondered where he was? Loitering outside the Electric Church ... with his big silver handgun? Unlikely. There were too many police circling the area to make it safe for him. The crucial thing was that he wasn't here.

And once I'd done my sworn duty, I'd disappear just as slickly as he had.

Sean King brought his speech to an abrupt halt and then introduced Shirley Cooper and Luke. They made their entrance from the opposite side of the stage, the mother pushing her son in his wheelchair. The second "patient" was a young girl from Newcastle. I didn't know how Price had come to select her over all the other candidates. Lorna Robson was a thirteen-year-old who'd been deaf for nine years. Her parents accompanied her and the three of them joined the Coopers, next to Sean King. Lorna was seated on a chair, which was placed next to Luke Cooper's wheelchair. Two male assistants stood on either side. King introduced everyone to the audience.

"Any moment now," Price said to me.

"You just keep your eyes peeled," I said.

The assistant with the clip-board patted me on the arm and asked, "Are you ready?"

"Absolutely not."

"Well, you'll be on in just a second, and once you're out there, you'll be fine."

Gabriella squeezed my arm. "Good luck."

"And now," announced Sean King, "let's go to the man himself. You all know why he's here and you all know who he is, so without further ado, let me introduce you to Christian Floyd."

King turned towards me and the assistant nodded for me to go on. I glanced once at Gabriella and stepped into the sharp, hot light. Polite applause bubbled on my right. My eyes were dazzled. King shook my hand and turned me towards the audience and the cameras.

"Welcome, Christian. Now tonight you're going to attempt to heal two young people, both of whom have terrible illnesses, and you'll be doing it in front of a live audience, with cameras to record and broadcast the event. Perhaps you'd explain why you've agreed to this."

This was where Louis would doubtless expect me to make my confession. What was I supposed to say? I looked down briefly at Luke Cooper's fragile frame. Louis could rot. I would heal, no matter what it cost me.

I said, "As you know, there has been some speculation as to whether I can really heal or not. This doubt has been fuelled by a number of things and . . ."

"Such as your appearance on Night Talk?" said King.

"That's right. And now I want to set the record straight."

If Louis was watching, he would consider this the point of no return. I took a very deep breath.

"And so I have agreed to this, in order to do what is right and, at the same time, to prove that I am not a fraud."

Where was the outrage, the protest? Nowhere. I half expected a repetition of the scenes outside Grosvenor House. There was nothing. Just silent anticipation from the audience. My eyes were getting accustomed to the light, but I still couldn't pick out much detail beyond the edge of the stage.

"Thanks, Christian," said Sean King, pointing me towards the others. "So let's go and meet the Coopers and the Robsons."

He made it sound like an introduction to contestants on a game-show. I shook hands with the parents. Shirley Cooper fixed me with a stare that promised retribution if I didn't succeed. I looked into the wings, hoping to catch a momentary glance of Gabriella, but it was totally black. I heard people coughing in the audience.

King took a couple of minutes outlining the illnesses of Luke Cooper and Lorna Robson, even bringing on specialists to testify to the severity of their respective conditions. Luke Cooper did look desperately ill. He had visibly deteriorated, even since Night Talk. Each pathetic breath seemed to take more than it gave. His bony mouth was permanently half open as he fought for air. Lorna Robson sat still on her chair, clearly bewildered by the fuss generated around her. The doctor who examined her confirmed she was absolutely deaf. Mrs Robson communicated with her daughter in sign language, trying to keep pace with King's rapid patter. When King had earlier spoken to Lorna, she had replied with speech that was slurred to the point of being unintelligible. It was painful to watch because she invested so much effort in trying to make herself understood.

I waited patiently while King did his best to build up the drama of the event, manufacturing an artificial atmosphere for television's tasteless demands. Finally, he turned back to me, moving to my side and sticking a microphone under my nose.

"Okay, Christian, you've heard what our specialists have said. Lorna's been completely deaf for nine years and Luke's condition is pretty serious, isn't it?"

"It is," I agreed.

"And you're confident you can help?"

"I am."

"All right. Before you start, perhaps you could give us some indication of what to expect?"

I didn't know what to expect myself. "To be honest, I'm not sure how it happens," I said. "I find it hard to recall the process, so you'll just have to wait and see."

"Should we expect to see blood?" he asked.

He wasn't expecting blood; he was *demanding* it. I nodded.

"But this shouldn't give undue cause for alarm?"

"No."

"Right, in that case, I think the time has come to let you make your final preparations."

He encouraged a round of applause from the audience. I moved in front of Lorna and Luke. I wanted to say something reassuring. Mrs Robson was at my side, ready to sign for her daughter.

In my mind, I had an image of Gabriella and me lying on a deserted beach with white sands beneath us, an azure sky above us meeting a turquoise sea in front of us. And not a worry between us.

"I don't want either of you to be frightened," I said, suddenly aware of how dry my mouth felt. "This is going to feel very strange to you. It may even hurt. But remember this: if it *does* hurt, then it *is* working. And don't be afraid of the blood. It's not going to be yours. It'll be mine. Be brave and we'll do this together."

I tried to force a smile and couldn't. The muscles in my face just weren't prepared to lie any more. Luke Cooper looked so ill that I didn't feel I had time to waste. He could barely focus his eyes.

"Don't interfere, please," I told the two assistants. "Even if it looks as though they're in pain. Don't do anything until I release them."

They nodded and took a step back. Sean King was at my side.

"Are you ready?" he asked.

"Yes."

"Ladies and gentlemen, would you kindly remain silent."

I turned my back to the audience. The stage lights dimmed, except for a small circle in which Luke, Lorna and I were incarcerated. A respectful hush descended over the Electric Church. For a moment, I could really believe I was with nobody but the children. I banished all thoughts of untimely interference from my mind and focused on the three of us.

What now? Would the power desert me? Who should go first? I took Luke's right hand and Lorna's left. They both felt cold. Luke's eyes were blank; they looked through me, not at me. His paw was lifeless in my grip. Lorna was more alert. She began to look anxious, her fingers strengthening their grasp on my hand. Nothing happened.

For me, the atonement of sin could only come through

healing. As Shirley Cooper had indicated, apologies were nothing. If I wanted to make good the bad, then I had to succeed. I wanted it – *needed it* – more than anything else. Luke was breathing in painful gasps. I let go of his hand and stroked his forehead.

It seemed to take for ever to start, but I recognized it, as soon as the first sign came. The cool core, growing, freezing. The tingling working along each finger and into the hot heart of the palm. The crystallizing of my heart. The emotional tide swelling inside. I pulled both children towards me, as if some other storm might try to tear them away.

I closed my eyes and felt the scalding wetness seeping through my skin.

# Chapter Twenty

All my senses were frozen, so it was only when the thaw began that I gradually became aware of what was happening around me. I felt the cold burn of winter in my veins and the hot burn of blood leaking from my wounds. Lorna and Luke were tight in my grasp, my hands around their skulls. They clung to me like I was a life-raft in a maelstrom sea. A crimson pool of blood was billowing beneath me, spreading across the stage.

Sean King was standing only feet away. Shock had him by the throat. His skin was pale and lifeless, almost as though it was his blood draining onto the floor, not mine. As a scarlet stream meandered towards him, he stepped out of the way so it wouldn't tarnish his Gucci slip-ons. He looked at the three of us with a mixture of astonishment and disgust.

"I don't believe it," I heard him mutter, softly. "I just don't believe it."

In rather the same way that the passing of numbness can be painful, so the recession of the ice-flow stung. My aching muscles protested and I slipped back, dragging both children with me. Lorna slid off her chair, unwilling to let go of me. Luke toppled forward, stumbling from his wheelchair. He held onto me with a determination and strength that had not been there before.

"Lorna!" cried Mrs Robson.

Her maternal instinct for protection was too powerful and she lurched forward to help her blood-soaked daughter. But Mr Robson restrained her, gathering her in his arms. He was trying to reassure her, but really needed someone to reassure him.

When it was over, I released both children. I unfurled my bloody hands and dropped my head back, gulping in deep breaths of stale studio air. It took the children a few seconds to feel confident about letting go. Their small hands relaxed and they edged away tentatively. I was exhausted, drained to the verge of drought.

Lorna Robson slowly crawled away from me, inching through the purple puddles. Blood dribbled from her ears, as though both eardrums had ruptured. It matted her hair. Her face was streaked red. She was in shock, unable to fix her stare onto anything for more than a fraction of a second. A cameraman started to circle her, like a vulture targeting a corpse. One of the assistants dropped to her side and put a comforting arm around her. The programme director was urging Sean King to follow the cameraman, but his stunning disbelief left him disorientated. He knew he'd seen it, but his mind refused to accept it. I'd seen that look before.

Luke Cooper was kneeling in blood next to me. He looked up and managed an expression that came close to a smile. I looked back at Lorna. Her evident bewilderment approached terror and I could understand that. The volume and clarity of the commotion must have been stunning to her, after nearly a decade of silent isolation.

"Lorna, can you ... are you ... can you hear what I'm saying? Can you hear me?"

Sean King was bending over her, microphone in hand. His customary confidence had been butchered. The cameraman stood behind him, aiming the machine just over his shoulder. Lorna wanted to say "Yes" but the instinct to cry was greater. She began to nod forcefully, vainly attempting to look happy through the tears. Her parents looked even more astounded than she did. Their faces were pictures of incredulity; sober and strained, drawn in disbelief.

Lorna's speech was still slurred, but her message was clear. She couldn't concentrate on King's questions; the brilliant, vital, brand new sounds which surrounded her completely hijacked her attention. Luke was gamely struggling to his feet. The effort was magnificent. Weeks consigned to bed or wheelchair had robbed him of what little strength he ever possessed. Even the will to live had been eroded to the very point of extinction. But now, the difference was absolute. There was gritty determination in his face. It would take time to rebuild his atrophied body, but the success of the healing could be measured in the eyes alone. The dullness was gone, replaced by sparkle and focus. The cancer was killed. Spirit returned.

Shirley Cooper didn't want apologies from me, she just wanted her son back. And now that I'd done that, I didn't want thanks from her. I watched Luke gingerly raise himself from the floor with the staggering uncertainty of a foal learning to stand. He shook off the helping hand offered by an assistant. Then he walked to his mother with a fractured stride, like a drunk trying to find his way home. Shirley Cooper caught my eye for a second.

What is understood need not be discussed. She nodded and I reciprocated. Then her attention turned to her son, as he wrapped his arms around her waist.

I wanted to lie down and go to sleep. Paul Julien had said two was never a problem. He'd been right. Were we the same, then?

Sean King was waffling. "... Are you okay ... congratulations, Christian ... incredible sight ... how does it feel ...?"

The audience sounded restless. King was standing close to me, thrusting his microphone under my nose. The bright overhead lighting made me flinch. I raised a hand to shield my eyes. My bloody eyes.

"Could you explain what you felt during the healing?" asked King, when I failed to answer any of the first batch of questions.

I could feel the individual trickles carving uneven passages down the side of my face. They'd sprouted across my forehead like beads of perspiration. Dew drops of blood. The final missing mark of my complete stigmata. I looked up and King was waiting for an answer.

I said, "What?"

Gabriella and Price were together, waiting in the gloomy wings with Jackson and Brian Bradfield. Somebody was shouting instructions at Sean King but he couldn't hear them because of the cries rising up from the audience. I saw faces near the front, most of which were trained on me. Some were revolted by my bloody condition, visibly angry. Others looked inconsolably upset. A few were even crying. My own eyes were damp and bloody. Whatever their individual emotions, they all stared at me with the same unshakable intensity.

I peered deeper into the audience. Where were the black and silver baseball caps? The Church of the Divine Science had been supposed to prevent me from healing Luke and Lorna – or at least, that's what I had understood Louis to mean – but their threat had turned out to be impotent. Was that the truth of it, then? Were they nothing more than a group of toothless misfits?

It shouldn't have been a surprise to learn that their quasi-religious rhetoric was a hollow waste of words. After all, Louis was their cutting edge. How could anyone who claimed to talk to God and hold court with angels be expected to coordinate and mobilize an effective group of genuine religious activists? I guessed they were just a circle of fools with minds up for grabs. A vanguard for the second coming? More like a psychiatric unit's day out.

A young woman handed me a small yellow towel. Mrs Robson was crying enough tears for all her family. Sean

King was asking me another inane question which I didn't hear.

Paul Julien had returned to the Carlsson Institute to make amends for his errors. In my own limited fashion, I had now done the same.

"You're still a bloody fraud!" yelled a man with a cropped head, pushing against a barrier at the front.

I rose unsteadily to my feet and looked down at him. "Are you blind?" I sneered. "Or just stupid?"

Perhaps he hadn't expected a reply. He looked fazed by my response, turning to those around him. When they failed to offer him encouragement, he shouted, "It's a con! You fucking cheat!"

I shook my head sadly and turned my back on him.

"Oh my God! Watch out!" screamed King, leaping away from me.

Something black sailed over my shoulder, just missing my ear. It clattered onto the floor. When I turned round, the heckler was vanishing beneath a barrage of blows from the security-stewards at the front of the stage. The missile turned out to be a large iron pin for fixing crowd barriers to the floor.

Panic was breeding in some sections of the audience. Over by the far corner of the stage, a furious group of protesters suddenly made themselves heard and seen. They started to chant. When Price's men tried to restrain them from pressing too forcefully against the barricade, a number of scuffles flared. They outnumbered and overpowered the security. Once they had successfully breached the ineffectual barrier, they clambered onto the stage and scurried towards me. They had anger blazing in their eyes and nonsensical diatribe frothing at their lips.

"Anti-Christ!" screamed a pale-skinned young girl near the front of the stage, whose demonic gaze reminded me of Linda Blair in *The Exorcist*. Under different circumstances, that comparison would have made me laugh.

Somebody tossed a small wooden crucifix at me. It flew over my left shoulder and clattered loudly as it hit the stage.

"Perverter of the innocent!"

"Heretic!"

"Satanic bastard!"

I peered down at the boiling, babbling faces. As usual, it seemed, the fanatics had it wrong. It wasn't me who was possessed. It was them. The Electric Church was filled with the magnified echoes of their hysterical cries. They sounded more diabolical than anything they were denouncing. Finally, it seemed, the Church of the Divine Science *had* made its move and it looked every bit as bizarre and fanatical as I could have expected. A team of losers who, for one moment, were made to feel worthy, unified by a cause, marching beneath a tatty banner.

The fact that both leader and doctrine commanded attention through pity or disgust, but not persuasion, didn't seem to make any difference. For once – and probably only once – they had something to live for. When it was over, they would meekly slide back into the slime from which they had briefly risen.

Those who had made the stage were intercepted by security. I saw Price dispatching an unlikely back-up infantry of production assistants, caterers, sound engineers and lighting technicians. Jackson appeared at my side and grabbed my arm.

"Come on. It's time to leave."

"Hold it a second!" protested Sean King. "I haven't finished . . ."

Jackson tore the microphone from his hand and lobbed it into the crowd. "Sure you have."

The brawl on the stage was beginning to spread like an epidemic. Two or three pugilists tumbled off the raised platform and disappeared into the turbulent crowd. The majority wanted nothing more than to steer clear of vio-

lence and leave the building, but they got involved nevertheless. Bottlenecks exploded around congested exits as
they tried to flee. Like tear-gas victims, they appeared
disorientated, striking out in every direction, clawing at
each other, trampling bodies underfoot, scratching at the
people in front of them and elbowing those who were
behind.

In the midst of all the ugliness stood Lorna Robson,
apparently oblivious to the surrounding carnage, as she
continued to wipe the blood off her skin. She dipped her
head one way and then the other, like a swimmer shaking
water from the ears. Mrs Robson still wore the blank
face of shock. Mr Robson gathered his stunned wife and
daughter, and started to push them towards the back of
the stage, hugging them tightly for protection.

Shirley Cooper knew what to do. Luke had been
returned to her and she wasn't about to let anyone take
him away again. She was heading for the same exit as I
was when a flabby man with a suede haircut blocked her
path. His soft belly hung over the top of his jeans. He
screamed something abusive at her, but before he could
do anything, she poked him in the eye with a finger that
was armed with a vicious, scarlet fingernail. As he
stumbled around in painful little circles, Shirley Cooper
pressed on towards safety, with Luke at her side.

We reached the partial sanctuary of the wings. I left
bloody footprints across the stage. My legs felt like they'd
just completed a twenty-mile gallop; weak and formless,
they found it hard to get accustomed to the walking step.
Gabriella appeared from the gloom of shadow. She
couldn't hide her concern and took hold of my arm.

"Come on!" cried Price. "We've got to hurry."

His shirt was stained with sweat. He led the way through
the labyrinth of narrow corridors behind the stage, moving
with surprising deftness for a man of his build. Bradfield
and Jackson were bringing up the rear, ensuring neither

Gabriella nor I slowed down. I felt dizzy and sick. My system was screaming for just a slither of respite. I forced my mind to focus on the bus. That was as far as I needed to reach. Once aboard . . .

"I hope to God the road's clear!" panted Price, as he ploughed through all oncomers, leaving space in his wake.

We stepped out of the building through a side-door. I saw the bus, parked at the edge of the road. Like all of Price's vehicles, it had dark windows. I could just see the driver, one hand on the wheel and a jittery foot hovering above the accelerator pedal. Gentle rain fell from the bleak sky. A vocal crowd had gathered in the Electric Church's car-park. They spilled onto the pavement and blocked the path of passers-by, who, in turn, stopped to have a look. I heard the bus driver priming the accelerator. The engine growled and then grumbled.

We surged forward. I was getting used to this by now; protests, insults and fists flying in every direction. We kept our heads down and pushed on relentlessly, fending off the incoming blows as best we could. Jackson and Bradfield dealt with the more aggressive elements with alarming ease.

Several sharp screams rose simultaneously from the crowd behind us. Price had just reached the bus. He had his right foot on the bottom step. We turned round. People started to scatter, radiating from a central point. From above, it must have looked like a human explosion, with a solitary individual at the core of the reaction.

Louis. In a matter of seconds, he was isolated. Nobody was near enough to make a move for him. He gripped the silver gun with both hands. I saw Jackson and Bradfield exchanging desperate glances. Even if they charged in unison, neither would cover half the distance to him before being cut down. They knew it and Louis knew it.

He stood absolutely still, with the handgun pointing directly at me. The rain ran down his cadaverous face, but he didn't blink. I was so close to the bus that I considered diving for the door. But once I started moving, he'd start firing. It was short range. I had no doubt he'd hit me. And if I was a moving target, he'd probably hit others. There were too many people standing too close to me.

I imagined the weather was different, but was everything else the same? We'd both stepped out of churches, to be surrounded by crowds. I pictured bright sun over Puno, whereas west London was bathed in rain. Had Lorenzo Sevilla's assassins stopped before shooting? Did he have time to examine their faces before they fired? I'd heard the screams and turned round, just in time to witness the crowd dispersing, leaving Louis stranded with his gun. Was that how it happened to Sevilla? Or perhaps his first sign was the glint of sunlight on gunmetal, as the killers darted through the congregation towards him.

This was the moment I was supposed to talk Louis out of it. In an eleventh-hour conversion, he was meant to be seduced by reason and blessed with compassion. Then he'd quietly surrender the silver handgun. I wondered if Sevilla had tried that. Maybe they blew him away before he could even try. I looked at Louis and couldn't think of a single, suitable word to say that would make any difference. He looked too far gone.

The breeze was blowing the rain into a slant. The street lights reflected garishly off wet skins. I heard car horns blaring in the Marylebone Road. Someone was yelling at the back of the crowd. The smell of diesel drifted across us. Louis never took his eyes off me.

I experienced the irrational calm of true fear and said to him, in an unemotional voice, "Are you going to do it?"

The rain streaked down his face, drops dribbling off the ledge of his brow. The hand holding the gun was steady. He said, "May God forgive you for your terrible sins."

I shook my head. "May God forgive *you*."

He smiled cruelly. "I thought you didn't believe in God."

I looked longingly at Gabriella and then back at him. "I don't believe in *your* God," I told him, now focusing on the black circle at the end of the silver barrel. "So whatever sins I may have committed, I can't be all bad."

Then Louis shot me. But one hit was not enough, so he just kept firing.

# Chapter Twenty-One

The power of each shot was astonishing. It was like being hit by one runaway freight train after another. They thundered into me in rapid succession. I raised my hands for protection and felt at least one bullet tear through both palms, popping the bones as it went. My body soaked up the crunching blows. I was slapped against the side of the bus and collapsed into a soggy pool of blood and rainwater. There was a moment of pure silence when the shooting finished.

An acrid, burning odour scented the damp air. Louis never even made an attempt to flee. He resigned himself to fate. Once he'd discharged the last bullet, he dropped the silver handgun to the ground and waited for the crowd to engulf him. Anonymous voices yelled for the police. Others cried out for an ambulance. A few just screamed hysterically. Gabriella and Price knelt beside me.

I was numb. My breathing began to falter. The greater the effort, the less air I seemed to be taking in. Each strangled gasp became shallower and quicker. Gabriella's face was just above mine. She was saying something but I couldn't understand what it was. I was shivering. I wanted to kiss her and tell her it was all right ... but I couldn't and it wasn't.

Someone said, "There's an ambulance on the way."

I heard Price reply, "We haven't got time to wait."

A random collection of hands scraped me off the concrete and carried me onto the bus. Pain started to seep through the veil of numbness, as they laid me down in the aisle.

"For God's sake, go!" Price ordered the driver. "Get us to a hospital!"

The door to the bus hissed as it closed, insulating us from the uproar outside. I heard the engine's pitch rise and felt the vibrations through the floor. We began to pull into the traffic on the Marylebone Road. Brian Bradfield removed his double-breasted jacket and draped it over me. Gabriella kneeled at my side and clutched my hand.

"Christian? Christian? Can you hear me?"

I nodded, weakly.

"You're going to be okay. We're on our way to the hospital."

A spasm gripped my chest, an invisible fist squeezing my heart to pulp. It was agony and my face reflected it. I tried to regulate my flickering life-systems, but it was a pointless effort.

I saw Lorenzo Sevilla smiling at me out of the colour snapshot. I'd been dismissive of his story at first, figuring it was another unreliable account from another century. Gabriella had been irritated by my cynicism. And then she'd tried her best to be reassuring when I discovered the link between Sevilla and the others. It had seemed completely illogical that I should necessarily become a member of their club.

My body was starting to feel as though it had been dismembered, not perforated. The numbing effect of the shock was fading and my wounds were really starting to crucify me. They began bleeding more heavily. I could feel liquid leaking from each injury but couldn't count the total.

"How . . . how many?" I asked.

Gabriella bit her lip and shook her head.

"Can't you . . . can't you . . . *do something*?" Price asked.

I knew what he meant. *Physician, heal thyself.* Or something like that. Maybe my ability to heal others had made me arrogant about my own fragile mortality. Even after the stabbing in Farm Street, I'd never really stopped to consider it. I'd needed stitches and medication, but in the general confusion of that moment and its aftermath, I'd somehow overlooked the significance of that. It seemed absurd that I was powerless to prevent my own life from slipping away when I could prevent it happening to other people.

"Please!" Gabriella begged me. "Don't ... don't ..."

She didn't want to say the word and I didn't want to hear it.

"It hurts!" I whispered, wincing as the bus cornered sharply and my twisted figure gauged the swing in pure pain. "Oh God, it hurts!"

There were a million crucial things I wanted to tell her in case I didn't get another chance, but when I opened my mouth to speak, nothing came out. I just gasped. I had tears in my eyes and could barely see her. Another spasm exploded in my lower back, sending electric charges down my legs. I tightened my grip on Gabriella but knew it was pathetically weak.

It seemed so wrong. All of us had something good to offer the world, but none of us were permitted to. Why not?

"Not long now," Gabriella assured me. "Just hold on, Christian."

"I ... I'm trying, but ... I ... *I can't!*"

I couldn't stabilize anything. It was all slipping away. Just as the pain became too vicious, it started to recede and the urge to submit to the inviting sleep took over. I knew I had to resist but the will to do it was disintegrating. The fatigue was overwhelming. The struggle was hideous and the alternative grew more enticing. Everything grew darker and dimmer. Fear of dying dissolved. It was getting easier. Why protest? The pain was gone. I couldn't feel anything any more. My eyelids were heavy. The fuzzy forms which moved above me were all talking nonsense and I wished they'd be quiet so I could rest. I wanted to tell Gabriella that I loved her.

It was as if she read my mind. She leaned forward, kissed my bloody lips and whispered into my ear, in a trembling voice, "I love you, too. Please don't leave me."

And then my fingers let go of her hand, unable to grip it any longer. I didn't even have the strength of a baby. My back was wet. I couldn't believe I still had more blood to lose.

The last words I heard were Gabriella's. "No! *Please!*"

My vision faltered. They were screaming silently at me. I couldn't hear a sound. My eyes rolled and I found myself looking up through the windows of the coach. Street-lamps and ragged tree tops raced past the rain-splattered glass. The lights from office blocks blurred. The clouds were purple and black. Sight was shutting down, leaving a few final fractured glimpses for me to cling to. Seats in the coach. Passing sign-post. Price's gold watch. Traffic lights. Double-decker bus. The light over the aisle. Her tear-stained face. Her dazzling emerald eyes.

Then it was over and darkness fell. In my mind, I saw Gabriella bleeding on the floor of an underground car park.

Some time after that, I died.

# Chapter Twenty-Two

I was dead when the coach arrived at the hospital. The heart was no longer beating. The last vital signal was blowing its final fuse. The rest were already gone; burned out and redundant. I was dead. But something brought me back.

Gabriella later told me how she watched the medical staff wheeling me away from her in the Admissions lobby, and how she thought she would never see me again. She stood still as my trolley receded down a corridor, resigned to what she'd overheard before the doors closed and I disappeared.

"Lost him," someone had cried.

The delivery was so flat, she later told me, so matter-of-fact that it seemed incontestable.

Meanwhile, the medical staff were racing time. They tried their best to kick start my dead heart before lack of blood flow meant that my oxygen-starved brain suffered irreversible damage. That moment came and passed and eventually they were forced to surrender. What happened next is still a mystery.

As the team dispersed, one nurse remained, in order to make preparations for my removal. According to her subsequent statement, she had her back to me when she heard a curious murmur, almost like a deep sigh. She felt a fragile breeze blow through her and when she turned round, I was breathing.

For two days I floated in the big sleep. It was on the third day that I drifted back towards the shores of light.

I remember being reluctant; it was comfortable where I was. A vast ocean of tranquillity and solitude. Gabriella was the last and first thing I saw. Her emerald eyes were the image I carried into the darkness and when I awoke they were still there.

I looked into them. Nothing. White walls and the smell of institutional disinfectant. Then the pain of my wounds began to creep up on me. They hurt. It wasn't an imagined pain. It must have shown in my face because that was when Gabriella smiled and kissed me. Then she cried and I knew I was alive. Her tears were on my face.

So this is how it really happened. You can forget all the rubbish you read in the papers and all the crap you heard on the radio, or saw on the TV. As for the healing at the Electric Church . . . those of you who were there can make up your own minds. The rest of you will have to take my word for it because they never screened the programme in the end. Alternatively, you could ask Louis for his opinion. To do that, you'll need to get special permission from the Home Secretary. Louis is currently a star patient at a maximum security psychiatric hospital. He displays no traces of regret and no signs of retracting his views, so I guess he won't be coming out. Ever. If anything good has come out of all this, it must be that.

When I was finally discharged from hospital, I still needed to convalesce. Gabriella and I came out here to America, as we originally intended. I spent the first two months in a Colorado clinic, enduring an extensive course of physiotherapy. Then we moved into a rented house up in the mountains. I still have to drive into town three times a week for further physiotherapy, but I don't mind. Things could be much worse.

I don't know where we'll end up yet – we haven't decided – but for the moment, I'm happy to be here with Gabriella. While we're in North America, I'd really like to trace Paul Julien, if it's possible. I want to speak to him. I *need* to speak to him. I don't know what to do about my healing. My self-preserving instinct tells me I should refrain from using it at all. I've witnessed its destructive powers too closely. On the other hand, it seems criminal to have such a power and never to utilize it. One thing's for certain: if I ever do use it again, I'll make sure I don't falsely raise the hopes of those I can't help.

Naturally, I've had plenty of time to consider my own life and how close I came to losing it. For a while, I thought of little else. To my way of thinking, I still find it ridiculous that I can heal someone as near to death as Luke Cooper, or indeed Gabriella, and yet I can't save myself.

The snow is still falling onto the tops of the Colorado mountains. It's been tumbling since I woke up a couple of hours ago. I love the way it looks when it's spilling out of heaven and the peaks are a brilliant white above the cut-off line for the pines. Gabriella is making coffee and the aroma is drifting out of the kitchen.

My life used to be so perfectly balanced, so organized and safe. There wasn't room for anything that I couldn't control, until I came across her in the underground car park. That was the moment the virus infected my perfect model and, from then on, the structure was doomed. It wasn't just the healing. It was *her*. I still occasionally think I might have controlled the ensuing chaos if I'd been able to ignore her, or keep my distance from her. Then I might have been able to return to what I considered normality. And nothing would have changed.

I carry scars now. There are the bullet wounds and the fading lines from the knife attack. And there are my stigmata scars. No one's really sure when they appeared. But they were there when I awoke on the third day.

I've got ugly shining patches on both sides of both hands. Similar marks adorn my feet. I've got a vile three-inch blemish on my side and a series of delicate lines across my forehead, just around the hairline and by the temples. Every time I'm in public, I feel intensely self-conscious. Gabriella says there's no need. The facial marks are small and since my feet and side are covered, it's just the hands that draw attention. Nevertheless, I hide them as much as possible.

The scars upset me. The first time I saw them reflected in a bathroom mirror, I cried. I'd never felt properly *stigmatized* before. When the healing was done and the blood was washed away, I used to feel human again. Normal. There was nothing to mark me out, nothing to say it wasn't so. But that's no longer the case; what I am and what I can do are now indivisible. My permanent wounds ensure that. I *am* different.

The scars of the stigmata have changed everything. For the first time, I really feel like a freak.

**CHAZ BRENCHLEY**

PARADISE

They call it Paradise. An inner city danger-zone, starved of resources, starved of hope. Run-down housing, run-down lives.

Then, a miracle. Literally a miracle: a dying boy made well, healed by the touch of a charismatic young man. And that's only the beginning. Richard brings light into the darkest places; his inspiration and leadership breathe new life into a sick community.

But where there are powers of light there are also powers of darkness. What starts as a revolution soon becomes a war. A war fought for the heart and soul of Paradise . . .

'PARADISE is the enemy of sleep; gripping, page-turning, filling the reader with an irresistible dread'
Val McDermid

'Hugely impressive and assured. From its touching and off-beat beginning, Chaz Brenchley's inner city epic of good and evil builds like a gathering storm'
Stephen Gallagher

**HODDER AND STOUGHTON PAPERBACKS**

**CHAZ BRENCHLEY**

MALL TIME

It was a place like no other, anywhere. It had everything:
department stores and speciality shops, a multi-screen
cinema, cafés and restaurants and Dreamland for the
kids. It was a warm, safe, wonderful world for you and
all your family.

And today was a very special day, a twenty-four hour
telethon spectacular. People were coming in their
thousands – down from Scotland, up from the Midlands,
in coaches from their clubs and planes from
Scandinavia. The mall rats, the born-to-shop and the
merely curious, everyone was coming to the big event.

But among them was one man who had his own vision
of the big event. Who had a balaclava and a camouflage
jacket, grenades in his pockets and an AK-47 in his
hands. Who was going to make today at the Meldon
Centre a day like no other anywhere . . .

HODDER AND STOUGHTON PAPERBACKS

**CHRISTOPHER PIKE**

THE LISTENERS

It started as a daring experiment in group-mind regression – back past the limits of historical memory and into the unknown realms of Deep Time itself.

But in those dark depths of the primal past there lurked an unsuspected nightmare – a nightmare waiting for just this chance to reach out and engulf the unwary souls of those who had intruded into its ages-old lair . . .

THE LISTENERS is another novel of high-tension, nerve-rending horror – his second for adults – from one of the world's bestselling authors of the fiction of fear.

HODDER AND STOUGHTON PAPERBACKS

# CHRIS CURRY

## THUNDER ROAD

Thunder Road, set deep in the heart of the Mojave Desert, leads to a haven for society's misfits.

Like the white-robed Apostles who are preparing themselves for the end of the world; like the Space Friends, a group of UFO enthusiasts; like the Peeler, an undetected serial killer who skins his unfortunate victims.

For a while these disparate characters live in an uneasy harmony. Until the church is vandalised. Until the ranchers begin to find their sheep mutilated and drenched in a strange blue fluid. Until an animal is mysteriously stoned to death. And people start to disappear without trace.

HODDER AND STOUGHTON PAPERBACKS